UNCONTROLLABLE

A NOVEL BY
SARA STAGGS

Black Rose Writing | Texas

ISBN: 978-1-68513-201-9
PUBLISHED BY BLACK ROSE WRITING
www.blackrosewriting.com

Printed in the United States of America
Suggested Retail Price (SRP) $22.95

Uncontrollable is printed in Book Antiqua

*As a planet-friendly publisher, Black Rose Writing does its best to eliminate unnecessary waste to reduce paper usage and energy costs, while never compromising the reading experience. As a result, the final word count vs. page count may not meet common expectations.

To Boz, who is my heart and home.

"The human brain has 100 billion neurons, each neuron is connected to ten thousand other neurons. Sitting on your shoulders is the most complicated object in the known universe."
  –Michio Kaku, Physicist

"The brain is a world consisting of a number of unexplored continents and great stretches of unknown territory."
  –Santiago Ramon y Cajal, Neuroscientist

"Your own brain ought to have the decency to be on your side!"
  –Sir Terry Pratchett, *Wintersmith*

UNCONTROLLABLE

APRIL 2006

PROLOGUE

Casey

This was it: the last day of the big show. I sat straight in my chair, next to my co-counsel, Arnon Swartz—my friend, my fellow third year—with whom I had spent so much time over the past six months preparing, studying, trying on different arguments, throwing away some ideas, developing others, to get here: The American Mock Trial Association National Championship.

We had spent the past two days taking turns questioning witnesses on direct and cross-examination, based on a case that the AMTA assigned months before. The four judges on the panel entered the room, and we all stood. I put equal weight on each high-heeled foot, rolled my shoulders back, and listened as my heart pounded in my chest, a sign of some nerves, but more of the energy of a fierce dog getting ready to fight.

"You may be seated," said Judge Woo, a woman with short jet-black hair that shone like smooth onyx under the courtroom lights.

"Are there any pre-trial issues that should be brought to our attention before we continue the trial?" Another judge—Judge Abernathy—asked.

I stood. "No, Your Honor."

A tall Black student from Harvard stood and agreed.

"Very well," said Judge Abernathy. He dropped his ice-blue colored eyes to the paper in front of him. "Mr. Dye, when we broke yesterday, it was your witness. Mrs. McQueen, please return to the witness stand."

A short woman in a flowered blouse and blue trousers walked past our tables and took a seat at the witness stand.

Arnon muttered under his breath. "Here we go."

I nodded and raised my pen, poised to take notes on the slightest weaknesses in her testimony, the smallest slip-ups that I could exploit during cross-examination. I paused as my head felt... something. *You've taken your meds. You got enough sleep. It's just stress. You can get through this.* I took a deep breath, trying to let out all the pressure, to forget about the national championship at stake and the potential individual glory. *Let's just get through this.*

"She didn't say that yesterday," Arnon whispered, pointing to a note on his pad.

I realized that I'd missed two questions and answers. *Thank God for Arnon.*

"Thanks for noticing," I said and refocused, shoving all thoughts of seizures and epilepsy away through the rest of the Harvard student's direct exam, and concentrated on taking notes as if my life depended on it. There could only be one winner here. And it would be Stanford.

"Thank you, Mrs. McQueen," the student concluded. "No more questions, Your Honors."

He walked back to his table without looking at me, which is more than I can say about the other teams we had beaten. *At least Harvard is going to lose with class.*

"Ms. O'Connell?" Judge Woo said. "You may cross-examine the witness."

I stood with a polite smile. "Thank you, Your Honor." Walking around the table towards the witness stand, I kept the same smile as I approached my prey. "Good morning, Mrs. McQueen. My name is Casey O'Connell, and I represent the defendant in this case, Chris

Bland. Now, you just testified that you live two houses away from Mr. Bland, is that correct?"

"Yes."

"Let's pull up a map on the screen over here, and we can look at the layout of the neighborhood. Mr. Swartz, Exhibit 101, please, on the screen."

The enormous screen in the courtroom to the right of the witness stand lit up and showed a satellite view of the neighborhood where Mrs. McConnell and our "client", Mr. Bland, lived.

"Thank you, Mr. Swartz. Mrs. McConnell, where is your house on this?" I drew out a laser pen from my pocket, no bigger than my index finger, and began dancing the red dot around the screen. I already knew the answer. Mrs. McConnell lived two houses away from Mr. Bland. She couldn't see his house from anywhere in her house. She couldn't see his backyard. As she was new to the neighborhood, she had never had much to do with him, and would barely recognize Chris Bland on the street if he passed by her in broad daylight, but suddenly, she was *sure* that he was the one responsible for a murder on November 25, 2004, because she'd heard screaming coming from the direction of his house, and she thought she saw someone who "fit his description" running away into the fog and the rain of South Boston.

I didn't think so. So, I lead her around and around, as I had practiced, letting her tie herself up in a knot of her own making without even realizing that she was doing it. The Harvard first chair objected over and over, and Judge Woo overruled his objections again and again, finally chastising him for holding up proceedings and advising him to consider his objections before he spoke.

Satisfied with my work and the bewildered look on Mrs. McQueen's face, I finally took my seat.

"That was awesome," Arnon whispered without moving his mouth.

"Thank you," I replied in a whisper.

The odd feeling in my brain returned. I sighed, annoyed, and rubbed my temples.

"You okay?" Arnon asked. He'd seen me have a seizure before.

"I'm fine."

"You want a break?"

Yes. No. My brain pulsed. I stupidly forgot my rescue meds in my backpack, which sat two rows back with the other members of the Stanford mock trial team. Literal medical salvation just ten feet away.

"No. You take over for a second." I stood, and crept back to the shiny row where my teammates sat, while the Harvard student tried to undo the damage on his redirect. "Where's my backpack?"

"Here," Emily, a tall, blonde first year, eagerly sent it over.

"Thanks," I said, immediately digging through the front pocket. Finding what I needed, I popped the two pills of Ativan in my mouth, and felt them dissolve under my tongue. In a minute, my brain would be quiet, and I could finish this trial.

Returning to counsel's table, I slid into my seat. "What'd I miss?"

"Nothing much. He's trying to re-establish that she could see the retreating figure and recognize him exactly as Mr. Bland. It's over for them."

As the blanket of Ativan covered my brain, tucking itself nicely in at the sides, I relaxed into my seat and took lazy notes on my legal pad, watching the Harvard student crash and burn.

•   •   •

"We did it! We did it!" The team jumped around our coach's small hotel room. Coach Steve laughed as Arnon waved the trophy in the air.

"We beat them! Stanford's number one! Stanford's number one!" Arnon yelled. The rest of the team joined in the chant. Soon, "Stanford's number one!" reverberated off the cream-colored walls as ten law school students expressed joy, some through tears, some with laughter, but all with a collective excitement.

"All right, all right," Coach Steve laughed, putting the trophy on the desk. "Calm down. How about we go celebrate outside of the hotel? I know New Orleans has a lot to offer. Let's grab dinner, and then have free time for everyone. Just be back at the hotel by midnight."

"How does it feel to be the W. Ward Reynoldson Award winner this year, Coach?" Arnon asked, a grin rising on his face.

Coach Steve shrugged, trying to be graceful about his win. "I'm very thankful for the award and the recognition."

We stared at Coach silently, waiting for him to drop this 'proper answer' act and join in the celebration. I crossed my arms and looked at Arnon, who raised his eyebrows.

Coach finally broke into a Cheshire Cat smile. "I mean, it's good."

The entire team started chanting, "Coach! Coach! Coach!"

"I wish we had a bucket of Gatorade or something," Emily shouted. "He deserves it."

"Oh, no, no, no," Coach said. "Let's get some Cajun food. And—if *anyone* is to be celebrated—let's have it be our champion All-American Attorney, Casey O'Connell!"

The team was upon me like a pack of wolves on a sheep. I fell back on the bed, laughing, the stress of a year of preparation leaving me like a cloud of mist. As I giggled at the smiling faces of my teammates, I felt that I had won more than just one trial today. I found Arnon in the crowd and fist-bumped him before I sat up.

"We did it, man," I said.

"And you heard what Judge Woo said about her, right?" Arnon yelled over the noise. "That she expects 'great things out of you, Ms. O'Connell', and—what was it? 'Your litigation career should be bright and successful.' Right, Casey?"

I shrugged. "Something like that," I said, for the first time in the entire process shy, a faint blush dusting my cheeks. Actually, Judge Woo's words had been, "You have intuitive skills as a litigator. Any firm would be lucky to have you, and I, for one, expect great things out of you, Ms. O'Connell. I expect that your litigation career will be long and successful. Don't you agree, judges?"

And they had all nodded.

I hadn't told any of the judges about my epilepsy. I didn't see the point. It's not like it was going to interfere with the competition or my career or anything. My future was bright—Judge Woo had said so. I couldn't wait until I had a second to call my boyfriend, Jonah. We were both graduating from Stanford in a few weeks—him from the M.B.A. program, me from law school—and we'd secured jobs in Portland, Oregon: his at a top advertising firm and mine at the prestigious defense firm, Cohn Steele & Lewis.

"Let's go!" I yelled, leading the others out of the hotel room and towards the elevators. "Cajun food!"

"Stanford's number one!" I heard someone shout. "Stanford's number—"

"Shhh," Arnon quickly silenced the shouting member. "Let's at least pretend to have manners. We can gloat in the streets."

The team stuffed into the elevator, almost glued together, one body at this moment of celebration. When we reached the lobby, we ran— forgetting all dignity—into the humid New Orleans night, and screamed our victory as we jumped up and down on the sidewalk.

SEPTEMBER 2016

CHAPTER 1

Casey

Sitting on the floor of the playroom, there was no way to get comfortable. I'd shifted from one hip to the other on the thinly carpeted area, my wrist holding most of my weight, and had finally chosen the left side, but because of restrictions in movement from the cut of my skirt, my left leg was now numb. With a grimace and a bit of effort, I slid back to my right side, avoiding the jumble of square and rectangular blocks in front of me: the children's extremely precarious wooden 'castle.' My discomfort added to my irritability, and I took a breath to temper my patience. Jonah, my dear, sweet husband, was late. I stole a glance at my watch and rolled my eyes.

"Here, Mommy," Sam said, passing me a smooth, curved piece, shaped like an arch. "You do one."

I smiled slightly, knowing that if I added this block to the already unstable wall, the structure would likely crumble, and I didn't want to deal with the aftermath: I just wanted to get to the office.

"You do it, Sammy," I said. "Where do you think it should go?" I stroked his soft brown curls and kissed the top where, five years ago, he had a soft spot instead of hair, and I was, as a new mother, terrified to touch him. Sam took his time coming into the world, waiting three days past my due date to make his appearance. He finally emerged after the doctors used an instrument resembling salad tongs to pull him out. Evidently, his head was in the 99th percentile of births. Still, when he finally agreed to join us, he looked perfect to me — even with the slight bruises on his rounded temples from where the salad tongs helped him along.

"Look how big the castle, Mommy!" Sadie squeaked in delight. Now almost three-years-old, her birth had been quick, as if she had somewhere to be and wanted to get there yesterday. She had rushed through the large path her brother left in my body, like a person riding a motorcycle down an empty six-lane highway, and arrived eager to start living and to do it her way.

"It's very nice," I said. Stretching out my legs, I switched my weight onto my sitz bones and leaned back on my aching wrists. My eyes flickered up to the entranceway and back to the children.

Where is he?

I heard the front door open, and pushed myself up from the carpet, adjusting my gray skirt suit and rubbing my left hip to massage out the pain.

"Daddy!" Sadie ran ahead, and I followed through the open-concept kitchen/living room/dining room: a modern inside that did not match the traditional Northwest craftsman outside of our home, but worked for our family.

Jonah bent over by the entranceway, untying his Nikes, back from his run. He glanced up, beaming, full of post-workout endorphins. With his thick, dark-blond hair streaked with sweat and his face flushed, he looked the pinnacle of health. I swallowed my jealousy at his ability to just throw on sneakers and raise his heart rate without a second thought. The last time I tried to run, I had a sudden seizure, ended up in the emergency room with a broken wrist and a cement burn down the left side of my face. The burn and wrist had healed. My bitterness had not.

Keep your heart rate down, my neurologist told me. *No more running.*

But that wasn't Jonah's fault, I reminded myself, glancing at my watch again, and then back at him. His movements were entirely too leisurely for my liking. *He's going to make me late.* My patience broke.

"What took you so long?" I snapped.

Jonah's grin faded, and he looked at his Fitbit. "Long? It was just an hour."

"Jonah, you know I wanted to get going early—"

"And, I'm back. What do you need, darling?" He released Sadie, stood up and held out his arms with a mock bow, the gesture made more effective and endearing with his British accent.

I took a deep breath, torn between wanting to stay angry and punish him, and wanting to laugh. The internal struggle frustrated me even more.

"I *need* you to take Sam and Sadie to daycare today. They're all dressed, diaper bag ready to go. I have to leave now for my meeting with Harold."

Jonah frowned at the mention of my boss, and moved past me into the kitchen. He turned on the electric kettle for his morning tea. I grabbed my keys and briefcase, and bent down to kiss Sadie on the cheek.

"Be good today and have fun," I said, smiling at her.

"I will, Mommy." She ran off to join her brother in the playroom. I heard a crash and knew it was time to make a quick exit.

"Case, we talked about this meeting last night," said Jonah, following me to the door. "You don't even know what it's about. It's so ridiculous."

With my hand on the doorknob, I turned to face him. "Jonah, it could be a million things, but I think it's going to be a *good* meeting."

"He's so unpredictable. What sort of man just summons his best associate to a meeting at the last minute with no indication of the topic? You've been so stressed this entire weekend. I'm really losing patience—"

"Jonah, I know that Harold's a crazy man, but other than him, I love my job. You *know* that. It's everything I wanted to do, always, and—"

"And that was fine when we were younger, no children, and could just focus on our careers," he replied. "But now things are different."

He gestured with his head to the open playroom door. "You know that you can't keep going at this pace, right?"

"No, I don't know that. Not right," I shot back. "I *can*. You'll see." I opened the front door, and he continued to follow me to the porch.

"Casey."

"*Jo-nah*," I said sarcastically. "I can do this. I can do it all."

"Not without having seizures, you can't. It's too much stress. How many seizures have you had in the past six weeks?"

"I dunno," I lied. I took a deep breath and looked up at the porch ceiling. The blue paint covering the wood had peeled a bit. *We need to fix that. Four.*

"Four," he answered. "Something has to give."

I sighed and pursed my lips. Shaking my head, anger rose like a bubble in my chest, then morphed into silent resignation.

"Jonah, you can't understand. My perfectly healthy husband, who doesn't have to walk around all day every day with a brain that might not cooperate, how can you—I don't *want* to give." Realizing I sounded like a child on the verge of throwing a tantrum, I blinked back tears and turned away, walking down the wooden porch steps and towards my car.

Jonah continued to follow me, and I stopped to face him before opening the car door. His eyes held that deep pleading expression that was so common as of late.

"I'm sorry, Jonah. I'm doing the best I can. I can't be everything to everyone and still get by."

"That's just it—I am not asking you to be everything to everyone," he said, his voice growing hard. "I am asking you to take care of yourself so that you can take care of our family. Before, it was just us, wasn't it? We could *be* selfish—career before everything if we wanted." He pointed to the house; through the open door, I could hear Sam and Sadie's voices singing somewhere in the background. "It's not just us anymore."

I felt my eyes narrow and my fingers tighten around my briefcase straps. "Jonah, I'm not the little woman who sits around and waits on her husband and children. We're a team, remember? And I went to school, I have a career — yes, sometimes it's stressful, but — "

"*Most* of the time it's stressful," Jonah interrupted, his voice stern yet emphatic. "I know we're a team, Case. I'm not asking you to sit around and wait on us. It's not just the work I'm talking about. It's Harold. He treats you like a slave. I know you see it, Case. It affects you, and it affects us. Maybe your brain could handle litigating full time, but somewhere else. Not for him."

"Daddy!" Sam's voice wafted through the air. "Your kettle's popped!"

"Look," I said, making a last attempt to salvage the morning, "eight years ago, Harold hired me — out of *all* the attorneys that wanted my job, he hired *me*. He's the best civil rights attorney in the state. Is he crazy, unpredictable? Yes. But now, I get to practice the kind of law I love, and if the price I have to pay is dealing with an undiagnosed bipolar psychopath daily, so be it."

Jonah shook his head slowly, his eyes grim and his jaw tense. "That is not the price you're paying, Case, and we both know it." He strode back into the house and slammed the door.

Alone, with no ready retort, I plopped into the driver's seat of my Subaru Outback and backed out of the driveway, furious with my husband for his lack of understanding, but also because I suspected that he was right.

•　　•　　•

The morning sunlight bounced off the glittering silver water of the Willamette River as I drove across the Hawthorne Bridge. In the maze of one-way streets of downtown Portland, I threaded through the city's colony of mismatched buildings: a random assortment of shapes and sizes, some gray and squat, a purple tower with a pointy top, a red brick rectangle with an American flag fluttering from the rooftop. I pulled into the parking garage of our office building, a tall glass edifice in the middle of downtown, and tried to calm myself. *It's just a meeting.*

Harold had that effect on me. I was doing well objectively: I'd won a trial two weeks ago after a week-long dog fight—though the stress had resulted in a weekend ER visit after a tonic-clonic seizure on Saturday morning. I'd made a police officer cry last month during a deposition when I grilled him about the use of force he employed on a Black man. Harold had to be pleased with his *protégé*, as he sometimes called me. I'd never heard him call any of the other attorneys in the firm that, but he could be fickle, starting the morning with incessant praise—*Oh, Casey, you're the best thing to happen to the firm, you're brilliant, what a writer, eloquent, the next Harold Charles Williams, Jr.*—and by the afternoon, he'd slam open the door to my office with a tirade of my mistakes: *How could you miss this? Have I taught you nothing?*

My first few years at the firm, those rants would bring me to tears in my office. Never in front of Harold, but as soon as he left, I'd be overcome with anguish, doubt in my abilities as a lawyer that I would then bring home to Jonah and release, sobbing in his arms in the kitchen.

"Leave," Jonah would say. "There are a million firms who would love to hire a Stanford law grad with top grades who started their career at one of the most prestigious firms in the United States before moving onto the Law Firm of that bastard Harold Williams. And I doubt there are many that treat their associates like complete shit all the time."

Harold had been different in the interview. We'd found common ground.

"What do you do in your free time?" Harold had asked.

"Assuming I have much, working at Cohn Steele," I'd joked. "I do like yoga."

"I enjoy it as well," Harold had replied, much to my surprise. "My wife and I love to do it together."

Looking at his wide frame, astonishment had rendered me speechless for a moment. I hadn't thought that this man had hobbies outside of the office. But then I'd smiled, and he called the next day, offering me the job.

It turned out that, after his divorce to this wife the following year (his second spouse—a fact conveniently left out), his love of yoga ended, and his true colors emerged. Hobbies evaporated, as he no longer had anyone to impress, and his rage and demands took their place.

But I stayed at Harold's firm because I loved civil rights litigation. I loved the clients, lived to see their faces light up, the smiles, eyes wide, moments of disbelief when a large settlement came in or when they won in court. That feeling that finally *something* went right for them, and I was a part of it.

I quickly moved up the ranks from associate to senior associate in less than three years, enduring Harold's moods better than most of my peers. Now, I'd built up the shell necessary to thrive at my job. I'd stopped bringing my emotions home, learned to roll my eyes at Harold's latest criticisms on my work. And now that I had experience, Harold complained less.

Still, the idea of a special meeting made my stomach twist into a knot I'd lived with for the past three days. He hadn't given any details—just left Friday afternoon with an order to come in first thing Monday morning, a few minutes before the office opened. I lacked the courage to ask what this meeting was about, and the possibilities hung around my psyche like a storm cloud all weekend.

A guilty twinge in my chest grew as I replayed the morning's argument with Jonah, absently touching my hairline. The stitches from the hospital visit a few weeks ago had healed, but a small scar remained pink and slightly puckered, a physical reminder of unwanted limitations. I had an appointment with a neurologist in a couple of weeks, and Harold had seemed understanding about my taking a few hours for medical reasons.

But I didn't trust him: with Harold, there was always a catch. Maybe this meeting would show me the catch. I parked the car and sat in the quiet for a moment, donning the mental armor I might need to get through whatever the morning held.

.   .   .

Inside the office, I knocked on Harold's shiny wooden door and waited.

"Come in," he said, in his infamous gruff voice.

Turning the brass knob, I entered the spacious office. Harold Charles Williams, Jr. sat behind an immense dark wooden desk littered with papers, his back to the floor-to-ceiling windows that overlooked the East part of downtown and the Willamette River. Mt. Hood, its snowy top against a blue sky stood tall in the distance, dotted with thin dark gray clouds that appeared to be approaching Portland. The bookshelves lining the walls held volumes of case law that hadn't been touched since the advent of legal research search engines—at least, not since I'd been here. Diplomas in opulent frames hung in the free space, along with an admission to the 9th Circuit, various awards gathered throughout his career, and a framed copy of a newspaper article from *The Oregonian*, interviewing him about a case from 2012. There were no photographs, nothing to indicate a personal life, which wasn't surprising, as I didn't believe he had one at the moment. The only personal thing I currently knew about him was that he was between wives after his third divorce. He lived to work—that was the beginning and end of it.

As I entered the room, his sharp eyes, dark and hawk-like, followed me to the brown leather chair in front of his desk. Even with graying hair that he'd started combing over a growing bald spot, he radiated power, confidence, and ego. This was the man responsible for bringing the Eugene police department to its knees in 2005, for exposing physical abuse within the Oregon prison system to the tune of $10 million in 2010, and for showing the State of Oregon again and again that police were not members of the military, bringing the question of what show of force is too much force to the forefront of the capitol. He was a legend among lawyers and legislators alike.

"Morning, Harold."

"Morning, Casey." He leaned back in his chair slightly and studied me. "So."

"So. What's up?" We spoke casually to each other; after eight years, all pretense of formality between us had vanished.

"Casey, you've been working here for what, six, seven years now?"

"Eight."

"Right. And over that time, I've seen a woman who has a good work ethic, is smart, learns quickly and has the impulse to win."

He paused and grinned at me, as if he wanted me to thank him for recognizing my hard work and potential. I sat silently, unsure where this lump of praise was going. I waited for the "but."

"There's a case that's just come to us—late Friday—and I'm assigning it to you."

"What kind of case?"

"Coincidently, it was in *The Oregonian* yesterday. A Sunday Op-Ed piece about the guard that sexually assaulted all those inmates at the women's prison near Salem? Did you see it?"

Of course I had. The piece was a poorly written overview of why we need to believe sexual assault reports in prisons and take them seriously. It had used as an example a criminal case tried last year that had been on every Oregon attorney's radar. A guard had been accused of raping several inmates at the state women's correctional facility. The criminal trial had been swift, and the guard now sat in prison for decades. Every attorney in Oregon knew it was only a matter of time before the civil case started, and that meant a lot of money. The question was which firm would get the case?

"The Kellan case, right?" I asked.

"Right." He pointed to his computer screen. "I have an email here from one inmate who reported the rapes. I don't know if she was the first, but she's out of prison now, and she contacted us about representing her and the other women. I'm going to forward it to you. Reach out to her. Set up a meeting. I'm giving you the lead on this case." He paused, but obviously with more to say. "Pick your team carefully."

I smiled inwardly, keeping a straight face. I knew that, although he loved the case because of the potential publicity and money, he lacked the skills to relate on a human level to sexually assaulted female inmates, which is what this case required. *And* he knew it was just the type of case I was dying to sink my teeth into. High-profile. A challenge. Something that could really show off my expertise.

"The media's going to go crazy for this one. It'll probably go national, so I don't think I need to tell you how important it is for our firm."

"Of course."

"And important for your career, obviously. It'll be especially challenging because the Department of Corrections is going to want to fight this case every step of the way. Is that going to be a problem?" His eyes drifted to the pink scar on my dark hairline.

"Not at all," I said, ignoring his glance.

"One more thing," he said, lacing his fingers together over his ample stomach. "If you work this case up right, I'll make you a partner when it's done."

The meaning of his words hung in the air. *Partner.* Exactly what I wanted the next step to be for my career, but the expectations were everything Jonah and I argued about. Longer hours. Extra work. More stress.

The gray clouds had thickened and rolled towards Portland, obscuring the view of Mt. Hood completely, but the anxiety I felt for the past three days melted away, replaced by a feeling of joy, like sunshine within my body. My ego inflated like a balloon, and a smile finally flickered across my face, unable to be kept inside. "I'll get on the case right now."

I left his office, silently repeating the words I'd been waiting for since I graduated law school: *Casey Scott, Partner.* Continuing down the white-carpeted hallway, I entered my office, a smaller version of Harold's. When I turned on the computer, the familiar hum of the machine waking up filled the room. Clouds now covered downtown and small drops of rain splattered on the glass, providing a trickle of background noise. Thinking about the argument I'd had with Jonah not an hour before, I paused before I pulled my phone from my briefcase. He'd want to know what the meeting that took up so much of my mental space over this past weekend was about. Pressing his name on my cell, I entered my password to the computer and saw my morning email count: fifty-five.

Jonah answered on the first ring. "Hi, Case." He sounded cold and distant, an icy aloofness in his tone. I felt guilty: my stubbornness caused this chill, at least in part.

"I'm sorry, Jonah," I said. "I'm sorry about this morning." As I waited for his acceptance of my apology, the line stayed silent. "Hello? You there?"

"I'm here." The remote tenor remained.

"Jonah, I'm *sorry*," I said again. I meant it. "I don't know what else to say."

I heard Jonah take a long breath. We both knew the words that I could say to make him happy, to heal our disagreement— *You're right, I'm slowing down, I told Harold, I'll work somewhere else* — but I couldn't make them come. Not now. Definitely not now.

"How did the meeting go?" he asked. The resentment remained in his voice, and I knew that the rest of the conversation wouldn't make it better.

I lowered my head and closed my eyes, dreading the next words. "Good. There's a new case. High-profile. He told me that if I do a good job with it, he'll make me a partner."

Silence again.

"Jonah?" I squeezed the bridge of my nose and waited.

"What did you say back?" he asked in a flat voice.

"What do you mean?" I wanted him to jump in and congratulate me, to assure me that this offer was a good idea. And I knew I waited in vain. "Harold assigned me the case and we'll just see how it goes. It's that inmate sexual assault case from the women's prison. Remember the criminal trial last year with the guard? The civil side could be massive. This is what I've been working towards my whole life. I couldn't say no." My voice rose, my mind excited, thinking about the possibilities.

"So you said yes."

"To the case? Of course. Jonah, this is huge—there was no saying no." This wasn't entirely true, and I knew it: technically, I could have tried to explain how unpredictable my brain had become and proposed Harold consider another associate. Still, my face flushed at Jonah's clipped tone. Was it too much to ask for him to celebrate this with me? To even *pretend* to be excited, just this once? "And, look, if he offers to make me partner, then we can set certain parameters— hours and stuff like that." Another lie, another false statement made just to sprinkle some hope into our lives, to buy some peace; a Band-aid on our strained marriage.

"Case," he said, his voice softening, "I don't want to hold you back, but there are certain realities that we have to face going ahead. You know that, don't you?"

Tears came to my eyes. Wiping them away on my sleeve, I lifted my head. The rain fell heavily now, large drops snaking down the window.

"I know," I whispered. "I know." I didn't want to face the facts as Jonah saw them. As I knew I should see them. "I don't want to talk about that right now. I just wanted to tell you."

"Okay. Congratulations, Case. Well done." I could hear through a slight thaw in his voice that he was proud of me. "You deserve to be recognized for all your work. It must feel good."

I rotated my chair towards my computer and stared at the red number in the white circle by the envelope sign at the bottom of the screen. Sixty.

"It does," I said. It *had*. But now I felt my ego deflate, popped by the needle of reality.

After we hung up, I turned back to my computer, imagining my new business cards: *Casey Scott, Partner.* I opened my email and perused the clutter that had appeared overnight. I smiled as I read the email Harold forwarded to me. This case could make my entire career, if my brain would let it.

CHAPTER 2

Jonah

After setting the children in Sam's bunk bed with some popcorn and a Looney Tunes episode on my laptop, I waited in the sitting room, pacing in front of the dark blue sofa. Casey and I had to talk before that reserved excitement in her voice this morning festered into something beyond her control.

When I met Casey fifteen years ago, she was standing on a street corner at Stanford in a yellow shirt that said "REGISTER TO VOTE" in big black print. She was the most beautiful woman I had ever seen, with freckles dotting her nose and cheeks and pitch-black hair in a ponytail. Clipboard in hand, she approached and asked if I was registered to vote. I told her I was not registered — true, as I was only in the U.S. from London on a student visa — but I would try if I could have her phone number. She stared at me with her mesmerizing light green eyes, seeming to consider the proposition, and not easily swayed, but I turned on the English charm that had landed so many girls during my educational career in the U.S., and she wrote her number on the back of my hand. I rang her that evening.

I never thought of Casey as someone who had epilepsy, whatever that meant, but that did not mean others would not. When I first told my parents about Casey's epilepsy, I was home for Christmas. While the three of us sat at the round kitchen table, thin gray light making its way to the white-tiled floor, I explained how Casey's brain worked. Their comments, so cruel and fueled by ignorance, shocked me.

"You mean she has *fits*?" my father asked, frowning. "How strange. Is it all the time?"

"No, Dad," I said, pushing around my fried eggs forcefully. "I've only seen her have two. And they're called seizures, not fits."

"Really? Shame, the poor girl," said my mother. She shook her head sadly and took a sip of tea before she continued. "And she's studying at Stanford or she just works there? I thought she was a student, but she can't be, can she?"

I tempered my frustration by reminding myself that they had likely never encountered a person with epilepsy and knew nothing about it except the general assumptions that people with epilepsy couldn't possibly be clever, fell to the ground and jerked around all the time, and that until I met Casey, I would have described seizures as 'fits' as well.

"I hate that word—fits," Casey said when she told me she had epilepsy after we had been dating for two weeks. "Fits. Two-year-olds have *fits*. I have *seizures*." The word sounded grand coming out of her mouth, something to be respected.

Even after my parents met Casey, even now—two beautiful, healthy grandchildren later, and the knowledge that Casey had a solid legal career—they still saw her as a girl with a broken brain who somehow functioned normally. On our last visit to England, two summers ago, I heard my mum talking with her friends in a low voice in the garden.

"Yes, Jonah's wife still has fits—I mean, seizures, we're supposed to call them—poor thing. She's quite clever, though, so you'd never know. Shame." Her gaggle of friends had nodded like bobblehead dolls.

They saw the opposite of what I saw: Casey's brain worked; she just had to be a little more careful than other people.

My phone buzzed as I paced back and forth, waiting for my wife to arrive. It was Tom, my mate at Grossman & Howe, the international ad firm where I worked. He graduated from Stanford a year behind me. I finagled him an interview at G&H, and taught him everything he needed to know. His text was three words: *Atchinson retiring confirmed.*

Three simple words that could change everything. Kevin Atchinson was the Director of Marketing at G&H's Portland home office, had been for over twenty-five years, and I was the head of his team, his direct report. For weeks, rumors ran wild about his potentially imminent retirement in December, but nothing had been confirmed. If he was leaving, that meant that there was a space at the top that needed to be filled, and, technically, I was the next in line.

Ten years of hard work flashed before my eyes—my life before children with long hours working up pitches for multinational corporations late at night. Every company wanted to have Grossman & Howe work on their ad campaigns: we were the best, recruited better minds than our competitors in every location we had an office - Portland, San Francisco, New York, LA, London, Paris, and Tokyo. I thought of those times that I had gone the extra mile taking an international client to a hip new Portland restaurant for dinner, only to see a senior position get snapped up by one of my peers. Finally, I was promoted to the head of the Portland marketing team, next in line for the Director of Marketing position. This time, it was my time. I could feel it.

But I could not get excited about this dream promotion right now. I shoved my phone back in my pocket as I heard Casey's car pull into the driveway. Tonight was about her.

When she opened the door, her eyes fell on my face apprehensively, and I knew she was wondering what I was going to say. I walked over and wrapped my arms around her waist. She nestled her face in my shoulder, her body relaxing into mine.

"I'm proud of you," I whispered into her hair. She smelled faintly like lemons, a scent left from her shampoo.

"I know," she whispered back.

She pulled away and set her briefcase on the floor, sliding it against the wall in the entryway.

"I talked to Holly on the way home." Her best mate since sixth grade, Holly lived ten minutes away with her husband, Rob, having moved here from Boston after Casey convinced her that we were serious about putting down roots in Portland. There were no secrets between the two—never had been since they met when they were twelve. "I told her about the new case and the possibility of making partner. She was happy about it."

Of course, Holly was happy about it. I doubt the conversation went past "Harold wants to make me a partner." Holly was as career-focused as Casey, except without the epilepsy or children.

Casey slipped off her heels and left them next to the door, then padded past the kitchen, pulling the shirttails out of her skirt.

"I told Mom too," she said, walking up the stairs to our room. "Where're the kids?"

"Watching TV on my laptop. I wanted some alone time with you," I replied, staying close behind her. "What did your mum say?"

She turned on the light in our bedroom, unzipped her skirt and pulled off her suit jacket. Pulling her skirt down and dropping the jacket, she left both on the floor as she walked towards the closet in her underwear and button-down. "Mom was happy, you know. But, same as you. 'Sounds like more stress. More work.'"

She pulled open the closet and took out a hanger. Walking over to the bed, she fell back on the mattress with a sigh, hanger in her right hand, her left hand by her side, and gazed at the ceiling, caught up in her thoughts.

I rested next to her and rubbed her hand.

"Case, you know that the way things are going, at the end of the day, you can't take the offer of partner, right?"

"I already took the case. I couldn't say no. It's my job." She dodged the question.

"Casey," I said, getting frustrated, "I didn't say the case." I did not think the case was a good idea either, but it would end eventually.

Partner was another link in the chain that kept her at Harold's firm, putting more stress on her. Stress her brain could not currently handle.

She closed her eyes. "*Ugh.* I don't know. I'm not thinking that far in the future. First, I have a case to win."

"Rubbish. I know you, Casey Scott—you can't lie to me. You *are* thinking about that partner position. But you know—I *know* you know—you can't do that to yourself. To *us.*" I sat up and my voice rose, fueled by frustration, anger, and fear. "You have to, at some point, face the reality here. You can't push like everyone else, Case! Not anymore! And being a partner at that bloody firm would have you pushing even *more* than everyone else!"

She opened her eyes and turned her face towards me, surprised and confused by my fierce tone. I never yelled. Sometimes Casey's voice rose, the passionate litigator coming out, but my wrath presented as icy, firm, British anger. Now, I found my heart pounding and tears in my eyes as I tried to get her to hear sense above the other noises in her head. What she was not saying, what she *would* not say, was that she *knew* she could not have what she wanted, and that made her furious. A tear slid down her freckled cheek.

"Case." I softened and took her hand to my lips. "I know you want this so much. But sometimes we can't have everything we want. Did you talk to Harold about easing up at work after this last ER visit?"

She shook her head slightly and touched her scar, her face now a mask of inexpression. This answer was unsurprising, as Harold's interest lay in the bottom line, the results for his firm, and not in his employees' health. For years, Casey had told him only the bare minimum about her seizures. *I need to leave early for a doctor's appointment.* Or, *I won't be in today, I'm not feeling well.*

"You and I talked about it a bit, Jonah. Argued, if I remember correctly. I never *agreed* to talk to Harold about anything."

Oh, living with a litigator.

"Alright." I squeezed her hand and wiped a tear from her face. "Let's put the partner issue on hold. Harold assigned you the inmate case just today, so we've got time." I wanted to avoid another circular argument that neither of us could win unless the other totally gave up what they wanted. "Let's see what the doctor says in a few weeks." After twelve years of marriage, I'd learned that part of my job as a Husband to a Person With Epilepsy was to keep her spirits up, to keep hope going. "Maybe there'll be something new to try." I laid down as my heart rate slowed.

"Maybe," she said in a hollow voice.

We stayed silent, holding hands, both staring at the textured, white ceiling.

"I love you," I said, squeezing her hand again to draw her out of her mind and back to the present.

"I love you," she replied, not moving her head or intense gaze from above.

Downstairs, we heard a crash and a screech.

She stiffened and sat up on her elbows.

"Where are the kids again?" she asked, as if suddenly remembering we lived with two small people who constantly relied on us.

"Watching Looney Tunes on the laptop in Sam's bunk."

"Huh."

I made a move to the door, but she grabbed my hand and tilted her head, listening for further sounds. All seemed quiet. A second later, we could hear Sam and Sadie chattering and laughing. Casey smiled and pulled me back to the bed.

"Let's just stay here for a moment. Can I tell you how the meeting went?" Her eyes sparkled, as if the story could lift her back to life. "You'll probably think it's sort of funny. It's classic Harold."

She turned on her side, propping her head up on her arm, her tears retreating as she retold the events of her day.

CHAPTER 3

Casey

It took me two full days to get through all the documents we had, put them in order, and compile a complete timeline of the Kellan case. The story wasn't pretty. Uglier than I'd remembered, actually. The women's state prison, Oregon Women's Correctional Facility, sat just outside Salem. I'd visited it a few times for other cases, and it was a colorless place, mostly beige, with a large outdoor area on which sat a garage that held a couple of John Deere riding lawn mowers and some golf carts for quick transport around the grounds. At the edge of the property stood a small run-down shed that no one visited. Almost no one.

George Hawkins was a guard who also ran the Shop program at the prison. In his early thirties, he had close-cut dark brown hair and a muscular physique that made him stand out among the other guards, most of them older with pot bellies. The Shop program was very popular for several reasons: it taught useful skills, it brought the women outside their dull indoor surroundings, and handsome Officer Hawkins paid special attention to his students — giving them cigarettes, compliments, and flirting with them. In Shop they received attention that they didn't get anywhere else while incarcerated. Attention that turned into grooming. Officer Hawkins was a master at seeing who responded the most to his efforts and making them feel extra special, extra liked, needed even. That way, when he invited them to tour the grounds in the golf cart with him, there were rarely questions by the other guards: this was just Hawkins taking his newest favorite out for a ride.

The ride, however, usually ended in the shed, and the stories from there were consistent and gruesome. After he raped the inmate, he would return her to the shop with threats of solitary confinement if she told anyone. He would tell her she shouldn't have been such a flirt, such a slut, that no one would believe her even if she told — who would believe a felon over a noble government employee?

For several years this worked, until one day Officer Hawkins picked the wrong woman. Kathy Kellan was twenty-one when she was sentenced to ten years in prison for mail fraud. At thirty, she applied for Shop, thinking that she would need a legal trade after her upcoming release, and wanting the fresh air the program provided. She responded to Officer Hawkins' attention like all the others, but she had a soul of steel that had been tested in the past, even before prison, and had hardened during her time behind bars.

After Officer Hawkins took her to the shed, she went to his superiors, Officer Gabe and Officer Stilton, and reported the rape. One of the most interesting facts was that she *wasn't* the first woman to report Officer Hawkins to Gabe and Stilton. There had been three before her—Georgia Leverene, La'Shanda Embry and Louisa Gutierrez—but the supervisors ignored their reports, and swept them under the rug. Kathy Kellan was the fiercest, insisting they look into her statement of abuse.

The supervisors noted her report, finally interviewed Officer Hawkins—who denied the rape—and closed the file. There was no investigation, they did not put Officer Hawkins on leave or suspension; however, they moved him from his position in Shop to checking in visitors at the entrance security point. Whispers began, women speculating about this shift, some angry at Kathy that their favorite guard had been moved, some relieved.

Kathy knew that this was not enough. Every day, she walked past the checkpoint and saw her rapist sitting at the security desk, watching the screen as visitors took off their belts and shoes and placed them on the conveyor belt. The day he looked over at her and winked as she passed in a line of inmates was the breaking point. Not sure how to get help, she'd sent letters to attorneys all over the state.

Smelling potential legal trouble, the Department of Corrections started an investigation, quickly put Officer Hawkins on leave and subsequently fired him. The supervisors were also put on leave, but soon allowed back at work. After a quick criminal trial with the government refusing a deal, a judge sentenced Officer Hawkins to twenty years.

The women were safe from Hawkins, but the four plaintiffs wanted more. That's where we came in: four women versus the Oregon Department of Corrections, the supervisors, and anyone who knew or should have known about these rapes. And with all the money potentially on the line, the D.O.C. was not going away without a fight.

Well, if they wanted a fight, they were going to get it.

I'd called Kathy as soon as I finished reading all the documents, and arranged a meeting at her house. Now, as I navigated the narrow streets toward her home in Gresham, I did my best not to think of Jonah and his insistence that I accept limitations instead of combating them. He's wanted to put the thought of making partner aside, but it made the idea burn even brighter in my mind.

"I can do it all," I said in the empty car. "You'll see, Jonah."

Kathy's house was a row-home off NE Glisan Street. An abandoned train track ran a few feet from the backyard, separated by a chain-link fence. A boarded-up convenience store stood empty on the corner with an 'AVAILABLE' sign tacked to the door across from a strip club that promised 'GIRLS & THE BEST STEAK IN PDX'.

I parked in front of her house, hurried up the cracking cement walkway, past overgrown, dead grass, and climbed the crumbling front steps. A woman's voice responded, "Yeah! Coming!" to my knocking, and the sound of a deadbolt being pushed back preceded a face peeking out from behind the chain-locked front door. As she took in my navy slacks and white-collared shirt, she unlocked the chain and opened the inside door, leaving a dirty screen between us.

Kathy Kellan regarded me with wariness, arms folded over her front, hip cocked like a sassy teenager. Though I'd never met her, I'd seen her photograph. She was only thirty-two, though the bleached-blonde curls with about an inch of dark root made her look older. Her brown eyes held the same defiance they'd held in the mugshot photo I'd seen, taken a decade earlier. Her skin still bore the memory of youth — tiny strawberry freckles over the bridge of her nose — but the dark circles under her eyes and lines around her lips told a different story.

"You the lawyer I spoke to?" she asked.

"Yes, hi. It's nice to meet you," I said, smiling in an attempt to win her trust. "I'm Casey Scott." I held out a business card.

She opened the screen door and glanced at the card. Under a light gray T-shirt with a faded picture of a raccoon, she wore oversized blue-jeans that drooped over her bare feet so that only her toenails peeked out, covered in chipped dark red polish.

"Well, come on in," she said, turning away from the screen door. I stepped inside.

The place smelled like cigarettes and, faintly, cat urine. Trying not to gag, I smiled again instead. "Could we sit somewhere?" I asked. "We might talk for a while."

She nodded and led me down a short hall to the open kitchen and living room, separated only by a mint green linoleum counter. Orange-and-brown flowered wallpaper covered the walls. Dark, dinged fruitwood cabinets sat under and above the yellow kitchen counters. A small off-white fridge hummed in the corner, creating an unceasing background noise, and the layers of grease and burned electric coils showed the age of the stove.

I sat at a round table in a rickety wooden chair that tipped back and forth, and tried to pull a yellow legal pad out of my bag without falling over.

"Just so you know, I didn't want this," Kathy mumbled, setting a pack of menthols and an ashtray full of old butts in front of her. She pulled up one knee and rested her chin on it. "I just wanted it to go away. I heard the only way I could really stick it to them was to go for the money."

"I understand."

"For the girls still in there, you know. They deserve better."

I nodded. "Of course. I agree. How have things been for you since your release? Has your transition been all right?"

She shrugged.

"Are you working?"

"Yeah. I work the night shift at a warehouse downtown. It's fine." She stared at me, unblinking, but with a deer-like vulnerability, as if she could and would flee at any moment. "This place is my brother's. He and my mom's the only ones in my family who still talk to me." She looked like she might say more, but then she tapped a cigarette out of the pack, brought it to her lips, and lit it with a blue Bic lighter.

"Kathy, I want the people who did this to pay as much as you do. I want to make it better for the other girls too," I said. She took a drag of her cigarette and let her shoulders drop a bit. I was getting there. "I have most of the details of the case, so I'm not going to ask you to rehash everything, but I want to confirm a few things with you."

A fluffy gray cat poked its head in the doorway. "Shoo, Muffin," she said to it, waving a hand. Undeterred, it looked curiously up at me and then jumped onto the counter, settling on the windowsill over the scratched metal sink.

I reviewed the notes I'd taken, trying to decide where to start. Then came the pressure on the left side of my head, that familiar feeling of a wave that started from the back of my brain and moved towards the front, a warning that a seizure might be on the way, an aura. As always, I had my rescue medications in my bag—one milligram of

Ativan to quell the aura or a five milliliter vial of liquid midazolam to shoot up my nose with a foam applicator if things really went south. Just what I needed today: to squirt some midazolam up my nose in front of a new client. *Hi, I can handle your case. Mind if I just take some of this controlled substance to quiet my brain? Yes, it goes up my nostril.*

Pushing on my left temple, I kept staring at the paper. *Please, not today. Not now.* The wave of electrical activity inside my brain drifted forward again, undaunted.

"You okay?" Kathy asked me.

I cleared my throat. "Yes. Just a little headache. Could I have a glass of water?"

She stood up and took a glass from the cabinet. "Just water? Or something stronger?" She winked. Although it was barely noon, I wasn't sure if she was joking.

"Water's good," I said. I slid my hand into the side of my briefcase and grabbed the Ativan, popping the tiny white pill under my tongue just before she turned around and came back to the table.

She set the glass down. "I have some aspirin, if you want it?"

"No, this is great." I took a sip of tepid, metallic-tasting water. The pressure subsided, and I breathed a sigh of relief. I was just over fourteen days from the seizure that sent me to the hospital. On my brain's current schedule, I was due for another one in the next two or three days, and the stress of this case and everything riding on it wouldn't help keep my neurons quiet.

The auras stopped as the Ativan spread its reliable cover over my brain, keeping my nervous system alert but mellow. I got through the questioning without much trouble. As we spent more time together, Kathy's posture relaxed: she put her leg down, and leaned forward.

"Thanks for taking this case," she said as she walked me to the door. "And for coming here to see me, Ms. Scott. I don't have a car, so I use my brother's pickup when he comes home from work."

"Oh, I understand. And please, just call me Casey."

She smiled for the first time. "Alright. Casey."

On the drive home, I replayed the meeting in my head. Whenever I met a new client and connected with them, it made the case a lot more personal than on paper. I always wanted to win, but now I *really* wanted to win this case, not just for myself, but for Kathy and the other women involved. Harold was right to assign this case to me: he could never have made the connection I just did.

When I pulled up to my house, I saw the brightly lit inside through the full-length front windows. Sadie ran past the windows wearing only a diaper, chased by Sam in spotted pants and a superman cape. Sadie's short blonde hair resembled her father's in color, but lay stick-straight like mine; Sam had the thick curly hair of his father's side and my dark coloring. I turned off the car and enjoyed the scene unfolding inside. Sadie laughed and Sam yelled something at her as he ran. He caught his little sister in the living room and wrapped her in a bear hug.

I entered the house to the joyful shrieks of "Mommy!" and a smell of spaghetti sauce in the air. Jonah came over and kissed me on the cheek.

"Have a good day?" he asked, pulling garlic bread out of the oven with green mitts. Dropping the tray on top of the stove, he looked over at me, waiting for my reply.

"Yeah, it was good," I said, sliding onto a bar stool on the opposite side of the kitchen counter. "I met Kathy. The meeting went well. So, overall, a good day."

"Overall? Did you have an aura?"

I paused for a second, suddenly at a crossroads. Then I shook my head. "No, no, nothing like that." I could see his shoulders relax at this lie. "Just the facts of this case, you know. So sad."

Sadie crawled into my lap, snuggling up to me like a puppy. "So sad, Mommy?" she asked. "You so sad?" She searched my face for signs of sadness — tears, a down-turned mouth, wet eyelashes. I smiled at her and squeezed her soft body.

"Not me, Sadie. Especially with this dinner your daddy's cooking." Looking up at Jonah, I was glad that I had lied. As he stood in repose on the other side of the counter, wearing a gray t-shirt under a brown and white checkered apron with "No Artificial Anything" printed on the front, peace seemed to fill the house and settle on the bodies and minds of everyone in it.

OCTOBER 2016

CHAPTER 4

Casey

With a deep, calming breath, I entered the Portland federal courthouse. I always found the building itself so soothing. My heels made a satisfying click on the marble floors as I strode across the lobby, a trickling, elegant waterfall to my right. The yawning staircase next to the waterfall led to various conference rooms, and to the left of the stairs stood a bank of elevators. Judge Rosta's courtroom was on the fourteenth floor, and I boarded the elevator alone, thinking about what Harold told me years ago before my first federal court hearing:

"Just be prepared. And don't overtalk. And try to get the last word, if you can. But don't overtalk."

I hadn't slept well last night, thinking about the hearing and reviewing my arguments in my mind over and over. I checked the clock every few minutes until finally giving into a fitful rest at 3:45 a.m.

It wasn't just that I really believed in this case. I *had* to win it: though they wouldn't be in the courtroom today, Kathy and the other women were depending on me. The stress on this hearing went beyond the usual butterflies, and that extra pressure combined with a lack of sleep, well, I knew what that meant. I had no illusions that the Ativan I took this morning could save me today, but maybe it could get me through the hearing.

Please, please. Just give me a few hours, I begged my brain, hoping that it would listen.

The elevator opened, and I stepped onto a thick, white carpet. The heels that clicked downstairs became mute, and the entire floor seemed serious and silent. On my right side, a wall of windows opened onto an expansive view of downtown Portland: the State courthouse visible past a small grassy square in front of this behemoth of a building. To my left, three sets of shiny double wooden doors spaced out evenly for the three courtrooms on the floor.

I walked into the third courtroom. Wooden benches sat against the back wall for spectators with five rows of seats in front, for those who wanted to be closer to the action. Standing in the entrance of the empty courtroom, I breathed in the smell of polished wood and heavy leather, which in my mind was the scent of the judicial system, and savored the rich silence. Being earlier than my opponent, I had the liberty of choosing my side and setting up my notes in peace: a few minutes to myself before the war began.

The low dividing gate that separated the spectators from the attorneys and their clients swung open as I passed through, and I slid my briefcase onto the table to the left: a mammoth dark wooden creation that comfortably sat three people and allowed for documents to be spread out several feet. No longer did I bring the entire paper file I had on a case for a hearing; instead, I pulled out one page of notes and set it on top of the thin folder specific for today.

The courtroom door slammed open, and I looked over my shoulder with a start. Rolling my eyes, I turned back to my notes as opposing counsel, Doug Randall, marched in. Short and plump, his thin blonde hair retreated into a widow's peak that he hadn't had last year when I saw him on another case.

He slipped his briefcase down on the other table and held out his hand. "Casey," he said. "Good to see you."

"Same." His grip was light and loose, his palm moist. I pulled my hand away quickly. Then, I felt it—the pressure, the aura—now stronger than at Kathy's; the warning my brain gave before the main event.

Shit. Not now. Not now.

Lowering myself into the large, leather chair at my table, I breathed slowly and deeply, in and out, grasping at any little trick to relax my brain. My hand wandered towards the rescue med pocket of my briefcase and then stopped. *If you take your midazolam, the hearing is done. You'd be so loopy, you'd have to reschedule. The Ativan might hold long enough.* I sighed, decided to take the gamble, and concentrated on breathing again.

"You can't possibly think you can win this hearing," Doug said, opening his briefcase and taking out his file.

I stared at my notes while the energy in my brain pulsed and abated, pulsed and abated. The aura gained strength. I reached for the midazolam again, but stopped short of curling my hand around the vial. Instead, I brought my palm back to the table and interlocked my fingers, squeezing them tight as if my life depended on the pressure between each digit. *Breathe in, breathe out, breathe in…*

Doug seemed to take my unresponsiveness as disagreement. "Well, we'll see."

We rose when Judge Rosta entered and took his seat behind the bench.

"Good morning, counsel," he said courteously. I'd never appeared in front of him before, but knew that he was the first Latino judge on the federal bench in Oregon and he'd been a successful defense litigator.

"Good morning, Your Honor," we responded together, like obedient students addressing a strict teacher.

I focused on one spot on the shiny wooden table, trying to stop the inevitable.

Stop, stop! I shouted to my brain. *Please.* I knew it was futile. Brains responded to science, not to begging. Only my neurons decided which way my day was going to go.

"This is the hearing on the defendant's motion to dismiss the case of Kellan versus the Oregon Department of Corrections," Judge Rosta intoned. "Counsel, please state your name for the record."

I shoved myself to my feet. "Casey Scott for the plaintiffs, Your Honor," I said, the words tumbling out of my mouth as one. I sat as quickly as possible.

Doug stood, unreasonably confident I judged through my haze. "Doug Randall for the defendants."

Please, hurry, Judge. I don't know how much longer I can hold on. My aura now felt like waves crashing against a dam on the left side of my brain, a force of energy that moved from the back of my head up to the front, over and over and over. I didn't know how long the dam could hold. Sometimes it held, but many times it broke.

"Mr. Randall," Judge Rosta was saying, "it's your motion. You may begin."

Doug stood and began to speak, but I couldn't understand what he was saying, now lost in the pounding of waves against my brain, and praying to anyone or anything listening to stop what I knew was coming.

Hold, brain, please. I pleaded with my brain, again and again. Just let this be a powerful aura without tipping over the edge. *Hold, hold, hold.* I briefly thought about standing and asking for a continuance, to reschedule the hearing, but my brain had taken over, gone rogue, and I couldn't trust myself to speak, if I even could, much less to explain my request.

No matter how many times my brain failed me, I never learned. I never wanted to learn.

•   •   •

I opened my eyes and saw paramedics leaning over me. They started talking when they saw I was conscious.

Why are paramedics here? I wondered. Thoughts came haltingly, as if caught in a bog, only able to get through in pieces. Then I recognized the thudding in my head.

"Casey," a paramedic with short gray hair said, "do you know where you are?"

I moved my head from side to side, and took in a big room with shiny hardwood floors, large tables, and a tall judge's bench with an American and an Oregon flag hanging limp on either side. *Courtroom.* I held up one finger as I dragged myself to a seated position and rested against the low wooden divider.

Wait, wait. I hoped the paramedic could read minds. *Courtroom.*

"Courtroom," I said thickly, my tongue just starting to re-connect to my brain.

I gazed at a man with short dark hair in a white-collared shirt and loosened tie sitting on the ground next to me, and tried to place him. *I know him. How do I know him?* The answer came through my hazy thoughts, and, horrified, my heart clenched as if grabbed by someone's hard fingers: *Judge Rosta. Oh, God. Oh, no.* He looked much smaller on level ground without his robe, and his face held a paternal-like concern, which made him seem kinder, less intimidating.

Another man, plump and blond, sat in a chair, his suit jacket off, staring at his phone. He flashed me an insincere smile, more like a sneer, that I tried to return, but couldn't yet. My face wouldn't cooperate. *Who is he?* I tried to remember him, but the effort was beyond my current ability.

I turned back to Judge Rosta.

"Are you okay, Casey?" he asked, rubbing my shoulder.

In answer, I struggled to get up. *Fine. I have to leave now,* I tried to say, but couldn't put the sentence together.

"Stay down!" The paramedic with gray hair yelled, pressing his hands on my shoulders.

Judge Rosta shook his head at the paramedic, giving an order without speaking.

The paramedic released my shoulders and sat back. "Just be careful," he said, shooting the judge a sideways glance.

"I'm fine," I said, my tongue still feeling thick in an attempt to enunciate. "I'm fine."

Trying to remember why I was in a courtroom, pieces of the day floated together like a fuzzy puzzle of one color that I had to assemble before moving forward in life. *The hearing.* Rubbing my eyes, I willed the pain in my head to stop. Nausea crept into my stomach as I slowly remembered the significance of this morning. *Fuck you, brain.*

"I'm fine," I repeated. "Let's go on with the hearing."

The blond man looked up from his phone and smiled brightly. "If she wants to go on," he gestured to me, "I'm ready —" He stopped talking as Judge Rosta glared at him.

Ah. Randall.

"I can still do it," I said. "Just need a second to... get myself together." I tried to stand up again and failed. My legs were always the last to work. "If someone can just help me up, then I can go to the, to the... the bathroom. Just need a moment to... to... reset." I pulled on the paramedic's arm, but still couldn't stand, and slouched down in defeat. *You win, brain.*

"No, no," Judge Rosta said, gathering his robe over his arm. "We'll reschedule." He rubbed my shoulder again, seeming unfazed by the fact that I had just had a tonic- clonic seizure in his courtroom. "Is there someone we can call to help you get home?"

Oh, yes. I felt my heart clench again. *And he won't be pleased about this call.*

"Jonah, my husband. He works at —." I closed my eyes and tried to remember the name of the company where Jonah had been employed for over ten years. "Grossman & Howe. The ad firm. His number's in my... my... phone." I nodded to my briefcase where my phone was on silent and then tipped my head back against the divider. Exhaustion from the seizure set in.

After I could sit in a chair, I assured the paramedics that I would be just fine without them. They packed up reluctantly, leaving a yellow piece of paper detailing information about seizures and when I should go to the ER, only agreeing to leave because Judge Rosta promised to sit with me until Jonah arrived. Staring at the paper and the file folder on the table in front of me, I slowly realized that I should take them with me and clumsily stuffed them in my briefcase.

Doug shoved his folder in his briefcase, all pretense of civility gone. "Feel better," he called over his shoulder as he left the courtroom. The doors whipped closed behind him and I was left alone with the judge. We sat next to each other, still and silent.

Jonah arrived and took in the situation, giving me a half-smile tempered with concern in his eyes. "Thank you, Judge, I've got it now," he said, and helped me out of the courtroom.

I sagged against him, my legs still not able to hold my full weight, every part of my body aching, my head pounding.

"Bad night of sleep?" he asked, as we walked towards the elevators.

"I'm sorry," I said. I couldn't think of anything else to say. I *was* sorry: sorry for not sleeping, sorry for interrupting his day, sorry for having epilepsy. Sorry for him and for myself.

"I'm sorry for *you*, Case." He kissed the top of my head and put his arm around my waist in the elevator. Leaning against the shiny gold rails, I rested my head on his shoulder, my brain beating against my skull. I felt the tears come, as always, and hid my face from the guards and others in the atrium as we left the building.

Safe in Jonah's car, I curled up in the passenger seat and cried. He patted my knee, but stayed silent, eyes on the road. He knew there were no words to stop my self-pity, nothing he could say to rush the inevitable repair of my aching body and splitting headache. And I knew two things: first, that I needed to sleep in a dark room for the rest of the day, and second, that Harold would be livid when he heard about this.

•   •   •

"You had a *seizure* in *court?*" Harold sat back in his desk chair, incredulous, when I told him the next day. "A seizure?"

"Yes," I said, my body stiffening with fury at having to suffer this indignity. "Harold, you knew I had epilepsy when I started working here." Of course, that had been eight years ago. I remembered his words to me clearly: "That won't interfere with your ability to do your job, will it?"

My answer, back then, had been the truth: *No. Of course not.*

But things had changed.

"Well, you've never had a seizure in court before."

"To be honest, things haven't been improving in the epilepsy department," I said.

I didn't think I'd have to say it out loud: he must have noticed the bruises I'd tried to cover with make-up from falling, the various stitches from ER visits this past year, the increasing frequency of the times that I'd worked from home while I recovered from a seizure. But maybe he *was* that oblivious. I'd never had a seizure at work, mostly due to luck, but partly because of my dedication in avoiding alcohol and getting enough sleep during the weekdays. I realized years ago that as long as I did my job well, Harold wouldn't care what chronic condition I had. And I did my job very well.

"What happened?" he asked. He rubbed his chin, looking like a man contemplating his next move in a chess game. I'd seen this gesture many times, usually when he was trying to decide how to get more money from the other side or how to fire an assistant without getting sued.

"I just had a seizure, Harold. I didn't get enough sleep." He tried to interrupt, but I spoke over him. "I'm handling it. So far, my epilepsy hasn't been a problem, has it?"

Harold looked at me with narrowed eyes, as if sizing up the strength of an opponent. "So far," he said slowly, "it hasn't been a problem…" He didn't dare finish the sentence. We both knew the Americans with Disabilities Act, and—although I didn't consider myself disabled—I would in court if Harold fired me for having epilepsy. For a man who loved publicity, Harold didn't want *that* case going to *The Oregonian*, much less getting all across the medical community and leaking into any national press.

"I have an appointment with a neurologist tomorrow," I said, glaring at Harold.

He looked down at his desk and shuffled some papers, seeming embarrassed by the word. "Fine."

"Oh, I wasn't asking for your permission," I said, and stormed out of his office.

CHAPTER 5

Jonah

Two days after Casey's seizure in court, we walked through the doors of the red brick hospital in North Portland under the fading afternoon light, ready to repeat Casey's story to a Dr. Duncan—her new neurologist after her old one retired a few months earlier. Yet another person to teach her lengthy medical history, spanning the entire thirty-six years of her life.

We held hands through the main lobby and into the tiny elevator. I tried to be cheerful, not just because I wanted to keep Casey's spirits up, but because I wanted—I *needed*—to believe this new doctor could help. But, after fifteen years of being together, I knew the statistics. I knew that once a person failed to achieve seizure control after trying two anti-epileptic drugs, chances of seizure freedom plummeted. Casey had failed seven.

A nurse in purple scrubs escorted us into a bland examination room, no different from the dozens we had visited in the past: tan-colored walls, a computer on a small gray desk with a padded black swivel chair for the doctor, two uncomfortable plastic chairs against a wall of windows for the patient and their plus one, and a long padded examination table covered in thin white paper. Variations of the same design with different muted colors in rooms in hospitals all over the city. Casey picked a chair, took off her gray coat, and folded it over her lap. I did the same, and she took my hand.

A minute later, the door opened. A man in his mid-fifties with short black hair and a close-cut beard walked in.

"I'm Dr. Duncan," he said, addressing no one in particular as he took a seat on the swivel chair and turned to the computer on the desk.

"I'm Casey Scott," she said, caught off guard by his blunt manner. She smiled a tight smile that did not reach her eyes. "And this is my husband, Jonah."

Dr. Duncan wheeled his chair away from the computer, looking at Casey for the first time. "Right," he said. "I've reviewed your charts and I'm very concerned. Your chart says that you're having frequent tonic-clonic seizures uncontrolled by medication." He spoke quickly in a monotone.

"That's right," Casey said warily.

Dr. Duncan studied the computer screen. "And you've been through several medications, it seems: Tegretol, Carbatrol, Neurontin, Topamax, Lamictal, Keppra, and Vimpat."

"That's right."

"Well, Casey, if this pattern continues, SUDEP is a real possibility," he said, turning back to face her. "And probably before you're forty. Maybe forty-five." His voice was matter-of-fact, as if he had just told her it was going to rain next week or recited the answer to a math equation, and yet the hastily thrown acronym dropped like a bombshell between us. I glanced at Casey: she was staring at a poster of the brain on the wall opposite us, her face rigid.

SUDEP. Sudden Unexplained Death in Epilepsy. I had heard the term before, and vaguely understood it was when someone with epilepsy died and no other cause of death could be found. But, although I considered it a very sad event, I never considered it applicable to *our* situation. In my world with Casey, seizures did not kill people; they especially did not kill Casey. I looked around helplessly, as if there might be a poster on the wall to explain what this nitwit had just said. One poster silently ordered, "Get a flu shot!" Another showed a picture of the brain, its parts labeled. Nothing that announced "Hello! Your wife could die from SUDEP!"

Casey's seizures were uncontrolled, that was true, and she had hurt herself during some of them, but I had never thought that she would *die* because of epilepsy. Wasn't just having it punishment enough? This was not how this meeting was supposed to go; we had gone off-script quickly. I had imagined this appointment, looked forward to it, built it up in my mind all week. At this appointment, Casey would agree to slow down at work, Dr. Duncan would be a kindly person who could convince her with science that more work— and a promotion to boot—was not currently in the cards considering how often she was having seizures. He would then find another medication, which would make her seizures less frequent, and we would leave, discussing a brighter future, and complimenting the doctor's knowledge and brilliant bedside manner.

That dream shattered into a million pieces as soon as this fat bastard burst into the room.

"Casey?" Dr. Duncan's voice brought me back. "Did you hear me? I said that if you don't get these seizures under control, you will likely die in the next few years."

"I heard you," she said, and squeezed my hand reflexively, her voice rising. "*We* heard you. And so what? What are *you* going to do about it? Because it's not fair to come in, tell me I could die if I don't get these seizures under control and then not have a plan!" At the end, her voice trembled with rage.

Dr. Duncan's expression changed from empty to startled and perplexed as his eyebrows lifted, his eyes widened, and his mouth moved into a confused frown, like an upside-down croissant. "Have you considered surgery?" he asked.

Casey scoffed and looked at me for relief from this conversation.

I stepped in smoothly. "Dr. Duncan, she had very detailed imaging done at Oregon General Hospital in 2014, and the epilepsy department at OGH looked at it and said that Casey was not a candidate for surgery."

Casey crossed her arms and fixed a vitriolic stare on Dr. Duncan. "I thought you looked at my records before this meeting."

"I did," said Dr. Duncan. He sat back in his chair and his face lost its clinical look, taking on what I could only assume was an attempt to seem compassionate, which had to be an unfamiliar feeling for him, as his facial muscles did not take to the expression naturally. "I don't think that they had enough information to make that decision. I'd like to refer you to a Level 4 epilepsy center—I'm thinking St. Lutheran's Hospital in Cleveland, Ohio. They're one of the best in the country. They'll do a proper pre-surgical workup: a stay in the epilepsy monitoring unit, an MRI, CT scan, everything. Then you'll know for sure. But just keeping the status quo, well..."

Not enough information to make that decision. Anger gave way to another feeling I could not immediately place. *Hope.* When the OGH doctors came back with their decision, Casey had cried, and I had tried unsuccessfully to put on a brave face. But now this prick of an M.D. thought that surgery might be an option? It was as if a door we thought closed forever suddenly reopened.

"Ohio? How long would I need to be there?" Casey asked. She crossed her arms and frowned.

"Yes, Cleveland, Ohio. For testing." Dr. Duncan swiveled back to the computer and began typing. "The workup would probably take a couple of weeks. A stay in the EMU and the imaging should take about fourteen days."

"Two weeks in *Ohio*?" She turned to me and shook her head. "Impossible. I can't do it. What about you? Your work? The kids—"

"I can handle it for a couple of weeks. I can work on my schedule. We can call your mum in. We'd figure it out." I tried to rid my mind of the thought of a life without Casey. "You have to go."

Casey shook her head again, her brow furrowed. "I can't go. I mean, what? Just pick up and leave to go wherever the hell Cleveland is—leave work and—oh, fuck." Casey looked at me, eyes wide, almost panic-stricken. "What am I going to do about Harold?"

Adrenaline suddenly coursed through my veins, hot and dangerous. His was the last name I wanted to hear at this moment.

"Casey, did you hear Dr. Duncan at all? *SUDEP*, Casey? You're worried about leaving for two weeks? What if it was *forever*? Harold can replace you. I can't." My voice shook slightly, and I took both of her hands. "You have to go," I said again.

Watching Casey's face, I saw it change from closed and stubborn to a more softened expression, and I knew she understood that there was no amount of professional satisfaction worth dying for. In ten minutes, the game had completely transformed. She knew what she had to do.

Casey turned to Dr. Duncan, who was still on the computer, fingers flashing over the keys.

"Send in the referral," she ordered. "Today."

•   •   •

The day after Dr. Duncan's disastrous meeting, I thought of a different day, long ago, when Casey and I laid on a picnic blanket under a tall oak tree, enjoying the Palo Alto spring weather. With Casey's head on my chest, we discussed our future careers.

"Litigation for me," Casey said, and I felt her smile. "Litigation's in my blood."

"In your *blood*?" I laughed, watching the bottle green leaves sway in the breeze on the branches above us. "Your father's a cardiologist and your mother's a professor."

She stretched her neck back to meet my eyes. "Yes, but you'll see. I've always loved to argue. One day, I'll be the best litigator in some state, wherever we land. Maybe even the nation. You'll see."

"Wherever *we* land?" I said with a small, teasing smile.

"Oh, Jonah, you know we'll land together." She interlaced her fingers with mine, and we laid together in silence, each lost in our own dreams of professional success and love.

Now those dreams seemed naïve, shattered by epilepsy. But Casey marched on, and, like a general going to war, she lined up soldiers to support her in her campaign—at home and abroad.

Casey's mum, Ellen, agreed to come stay in Portland. We explained the situation to her, and she offered almost before we finished the story.

"Anything you need, I'll do," Ellen said emphatically. She lived in Boston, but since she retired last year from teaching social justice at Boston University, there was an energy radiating from her to be needed. Casey's dad died from cancer when she was a second year in law school: it had struck hard and progressed quickly. From the time he found out to the time he died, not even a semester passed. After he died, Ellen attempted to strengthen her connection with her only child, her only child's spouse, and her two grandchildren: visiting several times a year, calling her daughter almost daily, making her family her priority in life. "I'm here for you as long as you need me."

"I guess I'll ask Holly to go to Cleveland with me," Casey said as we sat next to each other on the sofa, drinking tea after the children were asleep. She wrinkled her nose and frowned, as if she smelled something foul. I knew it was hard for her to ask for help with her seizures, as if asking was admitting defeat, showing the world the chink in her armor — although Holly already knew the chink and had taken care of Casey throughout the years in various capacities, from holding a garbage can for Casey to vomit into when an attempted medication change went toxic to getting the children from daycare when Casey had a seizure on her scheduled pick-up day to just sitting in our bedroom with the lights off, offering support and comfort while Casey cried in pain and depression after a severe seizure.

Casey pulled her knees up to her chest and cringed as she pressed Holly's number.

"Of course I'll go!" I heard Holly scream through the phone after Casey explained the situation. Casey held the phone away from her ear and put Holly on speaker. "Let me know the dates. You know I can work from anywhere. Just give me my laptop and some Wi-Fi, and I'm in."

"Don't you want to talk to Rob?" Casey asked.

"No. He'll be fine. Am I on speaker? With Jonah?"

"Yes."

"Jonah, Rob will be just fine taking care of the cat and playing video games while eating gummies without me to nag him. But, J, maybe just reach out every once in a while."

"I will," I promised.

"It's just two weeks," Casey said hurriedly.

"Whatever it is will be just fine," Holly said. "Don't worry, Case. It's not good for your brain."

Casey's eyes filled with tears. I put my arm around her and pulled her towards me.

"I've always wanted to go to Cleveland," Holly said.

"Really?" Casey replied.

"No. But now I get to say that I did."

We all started laughing. Looking over at Casey, I knew this was what she needed — to laugh, to have the reality of the situation pushed out of her mind, even if it was for just a minute. Maybe with Holly there, St. Lutheran's would be an easier experience. Maybe Holly could keep Casey laughing.

.   .   .

The Monday after Dr. Duncan's appointment, I entered the buzzing atmosphere of G&H, now more frenzied than ever. Rumors flew around the office about what was *really* happening with Kevin Atchinson: he had cancer; he had a fight with the founders — Jonathan Howe or Jacob Grossman — and was being fired, but for company morale was claiming retirement; he was moving to Bora Bora. Whatever the reason, the one constant — and the only thing tentatively confirmed — was that he was leaving. He had been a mentor to me, and I loved the man as much as one can love a colleague or a superior, but now, if the rumors about his retirement were true, I would soon be Director of Marketing for the Portland office, and that was a whole other level of professionalism in the advertising world. All we needed was the official announcement from HR about his departure, and the naming of his successor. Throughout the day, I smiled as I envisioned my colleagues clapping me on the back, congratulating me on my well-earned promotion.

Packing up at five o'clock, I slid a folder and my work laptop into my messenger bag. I would have to work after the children were asleep tonight, but it could not be helped. That's what happened when you had to leave the office before 5:30, at least at Grossman and Howe. Yes, I had learned to work efficiently, but there was still a huge amount to be done at the end of some days. Today was one of those days.

I waved to my team as I walked down the hall towards the glass staircase that curved to the main entrance, which was decorated with log-paneled walls and a black marble floor. The message, G&H's brand in every office around the world, was basically "We're laid back, but we get it done." Of that, half was true—we got it done.

Driving to the daycare, I wondered why I had not told Casey about the opening yet. I had not even told her that Kevin was leaving. We had been so caught up in the Cleveland trip—recruiting help at home, finding someone to go with Casey to the hospital, stalking every doctor at the St. Lutheran's epilepsy center online—that we had not talked about my job much, or at all, really. At home it was all phone calls, scheduling, children, and Cleveland, Cleveland, Cleveland, Harold, Harold, and Harold. But I knew that if the roles were reversed, if I had epilepsy and Casey did not, she would not even mention Harold. And if the roles were reversed, *I* would have to say no to the promotion. That was really why I kept Kevin's retirement a secret: I could not handle the hurt and angry look in Casey's eyes while she tried to hide her resentment that my career could progress while hers could not.

Pulled back to the present, I parked in front of the children's daycare, a long one-level cement building with large windows plastered with pumpkins made by toddlers and kindergarteners—a reminder that Halloween was just around the corner. Walking to the front door, I pressed the code to get in. I gathered Sadie first, and she flew down the hall to get Sam from his calmer classroom. We all held hands as we walked out the door, both children chattering at the same time about their days spent coloring, cutting, learning ABCs, and how a girl in Sam's class named Molly fell down at recess and scraped her knee and had to go to the front office and came back with a Band-aid.

Their high, staccato voices faded into white noise as I began imagining my new office, how I would rearrange my team, and the bump in my pay. Especially the money.

"What are you smiling at, Daddy?" Sam asked as we drove home..

"I'm just happy," I said, glancing at him in the rearview mirror. "Just a happy daddy."

CHAPTER 6

Casey

"Defendant's Motion to Dismiss denied," Judge Rosta said and banged his gavel.

Those sweet words reverberated in my mind, and the image of Doug Randall's puffy, shocked face stayed with me as I walked out of the courthouse with a wide smile after the rescheduled hearing. I immediately texted Harold the news, and cooperating with his response, I turned towards the bar between the two courthouses to await his arrival.

We sat in a red leather booth in the back of a bar frequented during lunch and happy hours by lawyers, judges, clerks, and the occasional tourist. The win was enough to put a smile on Harold's temperamental face. He raised his glass of bourbon, neat, to his lips and took a long draught; I swirled my Pellegrino with lime.

"Cheers," he said, lifting his glass again.

"Cheers."

"You've done a good job, Casey."

"Thanks." Taking a sip of my drink, I recognized that it was time to tell him about Cleveland. I knew I appeared confident on the outside even though inside I felt the fight-or-flight impulse move towards flight. "Harold, I've been meaning to talk to you about something."

He put down his glass, looking immediately suspicious, eyes narrowed and chin raised. I straightened my posture and pushed on.

"I have to go to Cleveland, Ohio, for about two weeks next month," I said, squaring my shoulders, and ready for the pushback I knew would come. "The neurologist I saw a few weeks ago recommended that I go to an epilepsy center there and have some testing done to see if I'm a candidate for surgery. Brain surgery. Scheduling called and they have a bed available in the epilepsy monitoring unit in early November."

His suspicious look morphed into a frown, his thick eyebrows coming together. "What's an epilepsy center?" He took another sip of bourbon, staring at me, unblinking, over the cut glass.

"It's a specialized unit for epilepsy patients. They run special testing, have epileptologists instead of just neurologists, things like that."

He was still frowning, but suddenly I didn't care. Jonah said that Harold could replace me; Jonah didn't know. Harold didn't want to lose me. I'd already said yes to the dates and bought the plane tickets. I just hadn't informed my boss. But I was going either way; this wasn't a negotiation.

"It'll only be two weeks, Harold," I said. "And if I *am* a candidate for surgery, and if it helps—and it likely will—I'll be able to handle more work and continue working towards what I want, which is to be a partner."

Behind us, a group of suits burst out laughing at some joke; to the side, a waitress leaned over the wood-paneled bar and put in her order to the harried, white-aproned bartender. I waited for Harold to speak.

"And while you're gone, who will be the point-person on the Kellan case?"

"Kristin." She was a junior associate, on the new side, but a female, which was why I chose her. "The rest of the team can help her out if she needs something. I'll make sure they're well-versed in everything before I leave. And if they need me, I'll only be a phone call away."

He leaned back on the worn red leather and drained the rest of his bourbon. "I do need you, Casey. You're the most valuable associate I have. Go and get better."

As always, he spoke as if I was asking permission rather than transferring information that was already cemented on the calendar, an ordeal I would endure with or without his support. I didn't correct him, and I didn't thank him, either.

Leaning back, I felt adrenaline leave my body, replaced with relief. I hoped that Harold's accepting attitude would last, but I'd dealt with his fickle emotions for eight years, which was long enough to know that continued support was probably wishful thinking.

CHAPTER 7

Jonah

I heard the door to Sam's room close with an "I love you, Mommy. Goodnight." Casey took soft steps through the hallway and into the sitting room, avoiding the hardwood boards that squeaked until she stepped onto the rug — safe. She collapsed onto the sofa and moved closer to me.

"Room for me here?" she asked playfully.

I put my arm around her, and she rested her head on my shoulder.

"What did you find?" she asked.

We received the name of the doctor in charge of her case when the packet from St. Lutheran's came in the mail today: Dr. Fadi Alem. Casey immediately started searching on her phone for anything and everything connected to him — any information about the man who would soon be in charge of her brain. Then, Sam and Sadie burst out of their rooms wanting snacks. She looked up at me and shrugged, with her "We can do this later" smile.

Now it was later. Dr. Alem's picture from the St. Lutheran's website showed a man with short black hair, graying at the temples, a broad smile, and cheery brown eyes. We watched the video attached to his bio over and over. He sat at a table in his white physician's coat, crisp collared shirt and dark blue tie, a wall of windows behind him. He smiled as he spoke, nodding every once in a while.

"Since I was a child, I have been always fascinated with how the physician will talk to the patient for five, ten minutes, examine the patient, touch them, look at them, and then he'll say 'Ah! I know what's going on!' He will prescribe the medication, and the next day or the next week, the patient is doing well." Dr. Alem had an accent that I could not place and spoke formally, like someone who learned English from textbooks instead of at home.

Casey paused the video and shook her head. "Is this guy for real?"

"Shhh." I touched her arm. "Let's see what else he says." I pressed play to start it again.

"We have different types of patients at St. Lutheran's. We have the newly diagnosed patient who shows up with his or her family, completely scared. The second type of patients, are those patients who had seizures for a long time. They've been treated by multiple, very capable colleagues of ours."

"Well, I guess that's me," Casey said, pausing the video again.

"Maybe," I said, and started it.

The camera zoomed in, showing Dr. Alem from the chest up. "The third type of patients are referred to us by colleagues who deal with epilepsy patients—neurologists, neurosurgeons, in some situations, epilepsy specialists—and for a very single purpose, which is to find out if these patients are surgical candidates. We continue to use the latest surgical techniques, where the surgeon carefully identifies and resects or removes the section of the brain that is the pacemaker for seizures—"

Casey paused the video. "That's enough."

"No." I was impatient now. "Let's just finish it."

She rolled her eyes and started the video.

"But nowadays - even without opening the brain—we can put small probes inside the brain and, using laser technology, eliminate the area the seizures may come from." Suddenly there was an obvious edit in the video as the camera angle changed to show Dr. Alem head on, and his voice rose in excitement. "I'm very optimistic that in the next ten, twelve, fifteen years, we're going to continue to bring to our patients and their families much better technology for the diagnosis and treatment of epilepsy." The screen faded to black.

"Well, that was hopeful," I said to Casey, trying to sound cheery.

"He wanted to be a doctor because he saw other doctors give pills to patients that cured them in a week?" she responded, disapproval and sarcasm dripping from her words. She gave me a dark look and shook her head.

"Give him a chance," I said. "Please. This hospital looks wonderful."

"Uh huh," Casey said, having already turned back to Dr. Alem's main page to study his CV. "He attended medical school in Lebanon."

"That's the accent, then."

"And he speaks English, French, and Arabic."

"Clever man."

Casey shrugged, now furiously attempting to search versions of 'Fadi Alem St. Lutheran's', 'Fadi Alem Cleveland', 'Fadi Alem epilepsy.'

I wondered what sort of man this doctor would really be, besides just clever. Kind? Curt? In his video, he sounded patient, friendly, and confident. But, after working in advertising for over ten years, I knew first-hand that videos were rarely accurate. They hid the problems and exaggerated the good qualities. I did it for my clients every day. But Casey did not need to hear that.

"Well, he sounds wonderful. Very capable, don't you think?" I said, giving her thigh a squeeze.

"Yeah." She touched her head, and I tensed. Habit. Every time she touched her temples, I stiffened, waiting to see what would happen next.

"You okay?" I asked.

"Just a small aura. I'm tired. It's been a big day with telling Harold about Cleveland and the rescheduled hearing. And I'm leaving this new associate — well, newer associate — Kristin, as the point person on the case. I told the women to call her and she could call me with any questions. I just picked her because she's a female and none of those guys at the firm could really, I mean *really,* relate to these women, what they've been through." She shut the laptop and rubbed her temples with her right forefinger and thumb. "I need to go to sleep. No more screens." Tipping her head back on the sofa, she closed her eyes.

"Jonah, I don't want you to take this the wrong way," she said, eyes still closed. "And you have to promise not to use it against me." She opened her eyes, lifted her head, and looked intensely at me, a mixture of vulnerability and determination.

"I promise."

Closing her eyes again, her head fell back. As we sat enveloped in silence, I studied her face. She looked at peace, the stress of life gone for a few moments.

"I don't know that working for Harold is good for my health," she said. "I mean, we'll see what happens in Cleveland and how I'm feeling when I get back, but..." She trailed off and I stayed silent, not believing what I was hearing. "Maybe it's too much. He's changed. I've changed. My brain has..." She left the words unsaid. "I mean, I'm not leaving before this Kellan case is resolved. But after. Maybe after. We'll see." Finally opening her eyes and sliding a look at me, I could see she was attempting to read my thoughts, wondering if I would keep my promise.

I tried not to smile and kissed the top of her head. "I understand."

"Maybe I'm just tired. It's been a long day." She rose from the sofa and tipped my face up, her eyes serious, but her mouth smiling. "I love you. I'll be waiting upstairs if you want to, you know." Her smile turned mischievous and her eyes went from serious to holding a naughty sparkle.

I wanted to 'You Know', but she needed sleep. "Go to sleep," I said. "Schedule it for tomorrow?"

"Deal."

As she left the room and I heard her walk up the stairs, I almost opened the laptop to search 'Part time litigator' or 'Civil rights firms Oregon', but stopped myself because I did not want ammunition the next time we argued about Harold or work. And there would be a next time at some point.

Litigation is in my blood, she said over ten years ago. That had proven true, but we never considered the cost of her passion. Leaving the laptop on the sofa, I followed my wife to our bedroom.

NOVEMBER 2016

CHAPTER 8

Jonah

I stood at my desk, brainstorming the right words for the pitch this afternoon. A large bright green sneaker with a dark sole and that telltale checkmark—the swoosh—lay next to me, the object of the account. I picked it up and examined it: weight, height, length, design. *'Who would buy this and why?'* were the questions G&H paid me to answer. I always enjoyed having the product with me while I thought about exactly how to present it. Creative already decided the tag line, and we worked to put the slides together. My job was to just perfect the words and delivery—to convince the executives that our ideas would sell the most shoes for them.

An email popped up from the head of HR with a simple subject: *Kevin Atchinson.* My heart skipped a beat as I opened it. Jonathan and Jacob let rumors fly for over four weeks instead of satisfying the throng with truth, but it looked like HR was finally ready to put an end to all the chatter.

Dear Grossman & Howe employees,

Kevin Atchinson will retire this December after 27 years as Director of Marketing in our Portland office. We will miss him terribly and wish him the best of luck. We will honor him at our annual holiday party on December

16th, and we look forward to gathering together to acknowledge his devotion and dedication to G&H.

We will begin searching for his replacement, starting tomorrow. As you all know, we prefer to promote internally, and will reach out to suitable candidates at G&H. Interviews will begin on Monday.

We wish Kevin the best of luck in his future and thank him for his dedicated service in growing Grossman & Howe to the powerhouse it is today.

Sincerely,

Lynn Foster
Head of Human Resources

Interviews, plural. I stared at the word until my eyes burned. As the lead on Kevin's team, I was the natural person to fill his spot. Why was Lynn saying they would reach out to candidates, again plural? Perhaps it was just a formality, something HR had to say before talking to me to be sure that I would take the promotion. That must be it.

Then I remembered a lesson learned long ago. At thirteen, I was back from school for the holidays, and my dad, my grandfather, and I relaxed in my grandfather's sitting room, surrounded by dark wood-paneled walls, built-in bookshelves groaning with books, heavy maroon curtains pulled back, and a fire crackling in the fireplace. My grandfather, who worked with my dad in real estate, was telling a story of a deal that had fallen through earlier that day. A deal they had been sure was done. Grandfather even brought the papers to the lunch meeting.

"We finished lunch," Grandfather said, "and had moved on to business, discussing the sale and the final agreed-upon price. I pulled the papers from my briefcase and was just about to hand them to him when he had a heart attack at the table and died right there."

My dad shook his head, not in disbelief, but in frustration. "What did you do?"

"What *could* I do?" Grandfather responded sharply. "I called the waitstaff over. The restaurant manager rung an ambulance, but it was too late." He sighed, annoyed. "Now we have to start negotiations over with the son." He turned to me, his deep brown eyes peering from behind thick glasses. "Let this be a lesson to you, Jonah. There's many a slip between cup and lip."

I never forgot that lesson. It seemed possible that the deal I thought done was not considered final at G&H by any means.

I gritted my teeth. Few people at work knew what happened in my family life. The rest of the team could stay at the office until eight every night, while I had to leave at 4:30 on some days to pick up the children from daycare—5:30 latest. No one else left in the middle of the day to rescue their spouse from court after she had had a seizure. Some people on my team were married, but most were not, and none had children. They were completely unencumbered millennials, perfectly happy for G&H to be their work and social life. I did not have that luxury. At least, not anymore.

Now, with Casey leaving for two weeks, I would be needed at home even more. However old-fashioned, Jacob and Jonathan valued face time at the office: they equated being in the building with professional dedication. Although I had learned to do twice the work of my team in half the time, I could not be at my desk or in a boardroom after-hours, except for emergencies. With this promotion, I would show them that just as much work could be done at home as here—perhaps even more without the social distractions and the "water cooler" chat.

I realized that I was clenching the shoe I needed to present in three hours, and released my grip, turning back to the slides, now determined to land this account, to show all those single, childless people on my team, as well as Jonathan and Jacob, how a real man, a father, a husband, someone with outside responsibility could do it. The promotion was going to be mine. No slip.

•   •   •

"Diversity becomes more and more important every day," I said from the head of the conference table to the Nike execs, repeating the script I created. "Nike is a leader in social justice, a brand that stands not only for outstanding athletics, but speaks to the underdog. Top athletes from immigrant families telling their stories keeps the brand relevant and forward-thinking. We're not only selling a shoe—we're selling hope.: 'I Rose.' 'I Rose.' 'I Rose.' says each A-list athlete. And the end of the commercial: the Nike Swoosh."

The Nike execs, Jim Klein and Alisa Barlowe, smiled.

"If there's anything you don't like, of course, we can change it," said Dwayne Richards, rising from his chair at the back of the table and making his way up to the screen. He was thirty-five and cocky beyond his years. Yes, he did some good work, landed some good clients, but he never knew when to shut up.

Jim and Alisa frowned.

"Thank you, Dwayne," I said, blocking him from the front of the room. "I think that goes without saying." *Sit down or I'm going to be really, really pissed off.*

Alisa shifted in her seat, examining the packet we placed before her fifteen minutes ago, when I began to speak. "I liked it all," she said. "Is there something *you* don't like, Jonah?"

"I think it's a relevant campaign, considering the current political climate, and I think it would land very well with your audience and buyers," I replied. I shot a quick 'Don't say a word' look at Dwayne, who returned my gaze with what could only be called an icy hatred.

Jim smiled again. "Great. Well, I loved the pitch, and I think Mark is going to really like it too. Good work, everyone."

The team stood as I shook hands with Jim and Alisa. I knew they had to check with their CEO before saying a definite yes, but they had been our clients for so long I also knew what their optimism meant: the pitch had been a success.

"I'll email you the go-ahead later today," Alisa said as I walked her out. "Who was the other guy who spoke?"

"Dwayne Richards," I said, trying to keep a smile on my face and not betray my true feelings. "He's on my team."

"Huh." She pursed her lips as she continued to walk down the stairs. "Well, anyway, I'll be in touch with you later today."

"Wonderful."

As soon as they were out of the building, I ran up the stairs two at a time and went in search of Dwayne. He stood in the conference room talking to some other team members, who appeared to be trying to escape. Within our team, we understood no one could stand Dwayne.

"Dwayne," I said sharply. "My office. *Now.*"

He looked at me disdainfully and then shrugged, following me out of the room to my office.

As he closed the door, I rounded on him. "Dwayne, you almost blew the bloody pitch! What were you *thinking*? N*ever* make the client doubt themselves. They know if they like something or not. Do you understand me?"

Dwayne shrugged again. "I was just giving them options."

I took a deep breath, struggling to remain a somewhat professional leader while furious that this tirade did not even seem to make a dent in Dwayne's thick millennial skull. "Dwayne, they will *ask* us to show them more if they are not satisfied. *That's why* we always have a back-up pitch, Dwayne. Did you ever think of that?"

Dwayne stayed stone-faced. "Anything else?" he asked. His voice sounded dry and bored.

"Yes. In these meetings, Dwayne, do not speak unless either the clients ask you for your opinion or I ask you to speak. Do. You. Understand?" I spoke the last words as if talking to a small child. "Say 'yes' or 'no'."

"Yes," he said, fury in his eyes. I did not care.

"Good." I glanced at my watch. 5 p.m. Sighing, I packed up my bag.

"Where're you going?" Dwayne asked.

"I have to pick up my children from daycare," I said. "You can go now."

"Oh, that's right. You go *home* while the rest of us work late."

"I work *at home* after my children are asleep, Dwayne, as you very well know," I snapped, turning off the lights in my office. "You can reach me after 7:30 if you need anything."

"Uh huh." He turned to leave.

"Have a family, then come talk to me about how you're going to spend your time," I said, pushing past him and waving to the rest of the team, who were still in the conference room. "You know where to find me if you need me, right?" I said to the group, leaning into the room, and enjoying pouring salt in Dwayne's wound as he sulked behind me.

They all smiled and waved goodbye. I left the building, taking a deep breath of the cold, crisp late afternoon air as I walked to my car.

CHAPTER 9

Casey

Sitting at the dining room table, I finished my work for the rest of the week and closed my laptop. The Kellan case could rest for fourteen days. I'd explained to the women that I'd be gone for two weeks—"personal reasons" I'd said—and referred them to Kristin if there were questions. "But nothing is going to be happening for a bit," I assured them. "We're right on track."

I slid the laptop into its padded brown protector, zipped it up, and left it on the table while I walked into the kitchen for a glass of water. Jonah and my mom had taken the kids to the Oregon Museum of Science and Industry two hours ago so that I could finish packing. Jonah hated going to OMSI, and this showed in yet another way how important the Cleveland trip was for both of us.

"It's only two weeks," Jonah and I repeated to each other, as if by saying that the fourteen days would go faster or be easier. We whispered it to each other in bed, bare arms around naked waists after sex. We texted it to each other with smiley-faced emojis when the topic came up or one of us found another article on Dr. Alem. We'd forced smiles when we told Sam and Sadie, as we sat in the living room. Jonah gave each child a cup of hot chocolate with marshmallows to improve their starting mood.

"Two weeks with just Daddy and Nana!" I said. "I'm going to get better in Cleveland, and when I come back, maybe my brain won't be so naughty." I made a silly face and Sadie laughed.

Sam snuggled closer to me on the couch.

"Who's going to tuck me in?" he said, staring at the steaming mug in his hands.

"I will," Jonah said. "I can do it."

Sam looked up at me. "Daddy doesn't do it right," he said, as if we were the only two in the room.

It was such a little thing to me, but to Sam it was an essential part of his bedtime routine. When I tucked him in, Sam told me all the secrets that he had held back during the day. Sitting on the floor next to his bed, stroking his hair, with only the glow of the nightlight behind me, I listened each night as my son unloaded his soul directly to my heart.

"I'll teach Daddy how," I said, and kissed Sam lightly on the head. "It'll be fine." They were too young to realize the unsaid truth: *Because we don't have a choice, Sammy. It has to be fine.*

As I finished pouring my glass of water and waited for the Subaru to pull up, a heavy feeling of despair and depression covered me like a dark cloud. *Go away.* I shrugged my shoulders violently, as if doing so would change the deep feelings inside me: the emotions I tried to ignore every time my brain failed me. The cloud moved, hovering, ready to come back and make my body its permanent home.

I sauntered through the dining area towards the hallway leading to the kids' rooms, the long wooden table on my left, the kitchen with its white counters and tall stools on my right. Turning around, I studied the living room near the front of the house, with its long blue sectional and leather chairs that Jonah and I bought right off the showroom floor. The rectangular Pottery Barn coffee table stood in the center of the area. The most expensive thing in that part of the house was the rug Jonah and I proudly purchased from a locally famous rug merchant on NW 23rd Street after my first big settlement with Harold. When we bought the house, we were twenty-seven, newly engaged, and it seemed so big. What were two people going to do with two floors, four bedrooms, all this space, we wondered? But, bit by bit, we filled it: books, couches, children. Now it seemed like a house that adults lived in. It was a home.

And I'm going to leave and go to a city halfway across the country for what? The thought crashed through my mind. *To see if these doctors can keep me from dying?* The practical challenges of what I was going to do, what I had to do, took my breath away.

I heard a car pull into the driveway and doors slam, followed by Jonah and my mom's voices in discussion. Watching through one of the front windows, I smiled in pity as the two adults opened the back doors of the car and released each child from their restrictive seats. Deep voices intertwined with the higher registers, and I laughed, surveying the scene as Jonah and my mom tried to control the chaos.

"I want to see Mommy!" I heard Sam say. He ran up the porch steps and rang the doorbell over and over. When I opened the door, both children thrust themselves at me, and I toppled backwards from their combined weight and speed.

They started yelling about a dinosaur exhibit at OMSI.

"Big dinosaur!" Sadie shouted, showing me the size with her arms.

"It was really neat," Sam said, making himself comfortable on my lap. "There was a T-Rex and a stega-stego-stegsaurus!"

Jonah walked into the house with my mother trailing behind. Both looked tired from a morning essentially spent trying not to lose either child while listening to an endless monologue from each one.

"We had quite a morning," Jonah said, his voice thin and worn.

"It sounds amazing," I said to the kids, giving each a kiss on the cheek while holding them both tight. I looked up at my mom and Jonah. "Thank you."

"Pleasure," Mom said, smiling. She looked the least damaged— never a blonde hair out of place.

I raised my eyebrows.

"They do have a lot of energy in the morning," she admitted, blushing.

Jonah looked more serious and turned to fiddle with the straps on the diaper bag. He wanted something. I patted the kids on the back and released them. "I need to talk to Daddy now. Go play with Nana for a minute."

"Come on, everyone," my mom said. "Let's read a book." She shepherded them toward Sam's room, the children arguing over which book to choose.

I stood up, dusted off my jeans, and smoothed out my white t-shirt. "Thanks for this morning," I said, kissing Jonah on the lips. "I'm all packed and my work's done, so Harold can't complain. Well, he can, but..."

Jonah stared at me, but said nothing.

"What is it?" Taking his hand, I led him to the couch.

He sat and seemed to consider his next words. "I'm concerned about you going to Cleveland," he said finally. "I wish—I—I want to go with you. I'm worried about what's going to happen in the epilepsy monitoring unit. I know the hospital is good, but what if you have a seizure and they don't get to you in time or you hurt yourself or—I mean, any number of things could happen, couldn't they?"

I had the same fears, but left them unspoken, instead tucking them away and ignoring them. There they remained, deep into my soul, with the box locked.

"I'll be fine. It'll all be fine. I promise," I said, trying to be upbeat, but the words rung hollow. "If you think about it, St. Lutheran's EMU is the safest place to have a seizure. They have all the rescue meds right on hand—Ativan and whatever else—and nurses and doctors everywhere, I bet. Don't worry about me. Just concentrate on holding the fort here." I tipped his chin up, so that he looked directly into my eyes. "Thank you for doing this. It'll be better for all of us in the end."

He cupped my face in his hands and his eyes moved from my forehead to chin and back again, as if he was trying to memorize my features. Finally, he let go, took a deep breath, and stood. "Probably time to leave just now. Luggage upstairs, then?"

"Yeah."

"I'll get it." He blinked rapidly as he walked away from the couch. From behind, I saw him wipe his eyes quickly with his flannel sleeve.

I stayed seated in the living room. Closing my eyes, I listened to the lift and fall of my mom's voice reading to Sam and Sadie, and the rhythm of Jonah's steps going up the stairs. And I knew I had to have hope. *I have to do this.*

I stood as I heard Jonah bringing the luggage down and walked towards Sam's room to tell our children that it was time to go to the airport and say goodbye to Mommy for a little while.

CHAPTER 10

Jonah

After dropping Casey at the airport, Ellen, Sam, Sadie, and I parked in the waiting area and watched the planes take off and land.

"Which plane Mommy's?" Sadie asked.

"None of these. Her place doesn't leave for a few hours," I said.

"That one?" She pointed to a small yellow plane that was likely flying to Seattle or Medford, not halfway across the country.

"Maybe that one."

Casey had been gone for mere minutes, and already life felt wrong.

"Let's go home," I said sourly, checking my work email from my phone. Even on a Saturday, it was a habit hard to break. My breath caught when I saw an email from the head of HR, sent just a few minutes ago, with the simple subject: *Interview Invitation.* I opened the email eagerly.

Dear Jonah,

We are delighted to extend an invitation to interview for Director of Marketing at Grossman & Howe. Your interview is scheduled for Monday at 8:30 a.m. in the Tilikum Room. Please confirm that this time works for you.

Sincerely,

Lynn Foster
Director of Human Resources
Grossman & Howe

Fury mixed with confusion rose in me again. Was this a joke? I had to interview for a promotion that I should just *have*?

I typed quickly. *Lynn, That time works. Thank you, Jonah.*

"Daddy?" Sam's voice dragged me back to reality.

"Yes. Off we go!" I forced a smile at him through the rearview mirror, trying to push away the anger I felt from the email.

Perhaps the children sensed something was off as, from the moment I put the car in gear to pull out of the airport lot, things quickly dissolved into utter mayhem. Sadie began crying almost immediately, insisting that she join her mother on the plane to Cleveland. Sam's attempts to calm her only escalated her tantrum. Ellen tried to bribe her with the promise of a cookie when we got home, but Sadie continued to scream.

"Sadie, be quiet!" I finally broke. "Enough!" My raised voice silenced everyone in the car with Sadie retreating into sob-related hiccups, and Sam leaning from his car seat to pat her leg. The guilt of my outburst stayed with me throughout the car ride. Even Ellen seemed to be cautious when conversation began again at the house.

That evening, neither child would go to sleep: Sadie cried for her mother, and Sam sat up in his bed, patiently waiting for something or someone to tuck him in properly. Me, I supposed. Ellen helped as she could, but her ways were strange to the children: they were not Casey's ways.

I walked into Sadie's room to soothe the loudest child first. Ellen crouched next to her bed, trying to sing one of the show tunes that Sadie supposedly loved to hear.

"Sadie, you need to stop crying, alright?" I said, kneeling next to her. "Mummy is going to come home. Just not today."

"How many days?" Sadie sniffed.

"Fourteen." In the darkness of the room, lit only by the small pink seashell nightlight and dim light coming from the hallway, I could see Sadie's lip tremble. "But when you wake up tomorrow, it'll only be thirteen," I said quickly. "And then twelve, and then how many?"

Her lip stopped trembling as she thought through the problem. "Eight?"

"Close. Eleven."

Sadie wiped her eyes with her stuffed bear and took a deep breath, relaxing into her mattress and pillow. She seemed to have cried herself out of energy.

"I'm going to see Sam," Ellen said. "Goodnight, Sadie darling." She kissed her granddaughter on the forehead and left.

"What song would you like me to sing to you?" I asked. I hoped Sadie would choose one that I knew; otherwise, I would need to make an off-routine suggestion, which could have repercussions.

"Young Cowboy," she said. "It's one of Mommy's favorites."

"It is, isn't it?" I could hear Casey's voice in my head as I began to sing. "There is a young cowboy. He lives on the range..."

Sadie closed her eyes, and as I sang her to sleep, I thought about the interview.

It is just a formality. No one in my department has given as much to that firm as I have. Jonathan and Jacob have to see that. I hoped so because I had little time to prepare before Monday. Then again, I sold people on ideas every day. If Jonathan and Jacob needed convincing, I had been training for this interview for over a decade.

I closed the door softly behind me as I left Sadie's room. Ellen sat on the sofa, exactly where her daughter had been the night before.

"Tea?" I asked, turning on the kettle.

She shook her head. "I'm going to go to sleep. I'm not as young as I used to be. 'Night, Jonah." She patted me on the back as she passed the counter. "We can do this."

I listened to her steps fade up the stairway, and the door to the guest room close. The house felt vast and empty. As I stared at the kettle, watching the red numbers on the stand creep up towards boiling, and the steam blow through the spout, I felt an ache in my chest. The other part of my heart was almost 3,000 miles away.

CHAPTER 11

Casey

I woke early, and spent most of the morning curled up in the large, plush chair by the floor-to-ceiling window in our hotel room, pouring over the copious packet from St Lutheran's epilepsy center. The packet included a map of the campus, instructions on how to find the right office, a form for new patients to fill out that covered everything from birth date to what medications I took to whether I had ever attempted suicide. Holly sat at the desk across the room, her fingers clicking away on the keys of her laptop, her curly, short red hair falling on either side of her face.

As the date of my departure had drawn closer, Harold switched gears, insinuating that only his magnanimity allowed me to go to Cleveland. He'd dropped little hints such as "You know, we're going to be unusually busy when you get back," and less subtle, more offensive phrases like "So, when you come back, you won't be jerking around in court anymore?", after which he immediately mumbled something akin to "Sorry" when he saw the anger on my face. Then, while leaning in my office doorway, he'd asked whether I could work from the hospital. I glanced at the piles of papers on my desk that I organized for Kristin and the few other associates that I trusted not to mess up the Kellan case and my other work.

"No," I'd replied, imagining myself setting up shop and litigating from a hospital bed. "I said I'd be available if Kristin or another associate had a question—but that's it. If things get messy—well, they just won't, Harold."

He'd huffed and left.

Sitting in the hotel room and reading the documents from St. Lutheran's, I knew "no" had been the right answer. I sighed and pulled at my lip nervously.

Holly stopped typing and looked up from her laptop. "You okay?"

"Yeah," I lied.

Holly raised her eyebrows and waited for me to tell the truth.

"Well, no. Not okay. This whole epilepsy monitoring unit stay sounds like a nightmare."

She smiled reassuringly. "You're going to be fine."

"Did you know they might take me off my meds? And I'm not supposed to sleep a lot? All with electrodes stuck all over my head for a twenty-four-hour EEG, monitoring every single brain wave? Do you know what electrodes are?"

Holly shook her head.

"Well, last time I checked, they were little metal circles glued on all over your scalp. Not very conducive to rest, which I guess I'm not supposed to get anyway. And there'll be a video on me all the time?" I crossed my arms and glared at her, as if EMU protocol was her fault.

She swiveled the chair towards me. "What else?"

"I don't know," I said, looking back down at the sheet. "They just want me to have as many seizures as possible. I mean, reading between the lines, that's what I'm getting."

"Well, that makes sense, right?"

"I guess," I said. "I mean, they need to find out where the seizures are coming from, so they can take that part out. It'd be pretty irresponsible of the surgeon otherwise. Just to take some piece of my brain out." I tried to make a joke, to lighten my mood. Holly gave me an encouraging small chuckle.

Turning to the window, the outside looked dismal. I watched the swirling snow fall relentlessly from the light gray clouds above; the wind refused to let the flakes move straight through the air, instead pushing them around in harsh circles before allowing them to land far from where they began.

"What if the surgeon makes a mistake and takes too much?" I wanted to curl up into a ball, to disappear into this chair, anything to avoid this EMU stay.

"Let's just get through this first step—seeing if you're a candidate for surgery," said Holly. "We don't have any information about your specific case, if you think about it." Her words brought me back, out of the fear and into reason.

"That's true." Suddenly, I wanted to start whatever lay ahead. "Let's go," I said, standing up. "I can't sit in this room anymore wondering 'What If's.'" Stuffing the paperwork into my gray backpack, I pulled Holly up from her chair. "Come on."

We slipped on our puffy coats, mine black, Holly's a bright pink that clashed with her hair, and left the hotel.

With our heads bowed against the biting wind that blew sharp, small ice particles the morning weatherman had mislabeled as snow, we marched for two blocks to the hospital, where we stumbled into the building through a heavy wooden door on the side. Holly shook the snow and ice off her jacket and removed her hood, adjusting her short hair back into place. I took my hands out of the pockets of my coat, wiped off my jeans, and stomped my feet to rid my blue Converse sneakers of snow.

We stood in a long, dimly lit hallway, where large portraits of various white men lined the walls, each labeled with a copper plate below.

"Albert Gropher, President of St. Lutheran's, 1909-1922," Holly read as the portrait of Albert, gray-haired and frowning, loomed on our left. "Looks like a nice guy."

I couldn't bring myself to laugh at her joke. Taking in the almost deserted hallway, I scooted closer to her. We walked down the hall to a bank of elevators on our right. When we arrived at the elevators, we saw that this dim, quiet hallway connected by a small passage on the left to another area of the hospital. Moving through the passage side-by-side, Holly and I entered an expansive hall that I quickly realized connected to the main entrance of St. Lutheran's Hospital.

In front of us, an enormous wall of windows gave onto a huge circular driveway curving around a large, low cement fountain. The muted outside light drifted softly in, and to my right, down the hallway, I saw half of a round atrium. On the other side of the driveway stood an opposite wall of windows and a mirror-image hallway. The building rose high, innumerable stories tall. An escalator descended behind us, labeled "To Underground Walkway." Looking outside at the swirling ice, I understood the allure — and necessity — of that feature.

Doctors and nurses walked by purposefully, dress shoes and heels clicking across the floor, with badges attached to their white jackets or colored scrubs that pronounced "I CARE" and "PATIENT FIRST." Throughout the hall and at every door, men and women in red jackets stood sentry with lanyards announcing, "ASK ME." Wheelchairs pushed by uniformed attendants shuttled patients through the building; people in street clothes looking bewildered with papers in their hands moved slowly towards the atrium, as they attempted to navigate whatever challenges lay ahead. In the distance, a piano played, almost drowned out by the din of different conversations that surrounded us.

I stepped even closer to Holly with a child-like urge to hold her hand or have her put her arm around my shoulders. For a moment, I wished she were Jonah. As the daughter of a doctor, I always thought myself used to hospitals, comfortable in any medical setting, but this giant space, with its noise, constant movement, and sterile smell, overwhelmed me.

St. Lutheran's main campus spanned several city blocks. Pulling the map from my backpack, I focused on studying the squares and labels, trying to orient myself. According to the map, we stood in the main building: it housed the cafeterias, gift shops, and connected through a labyrinth of halls to various other buildings, like a giant rectangular spider. Across a courtyard stood two separate buildings with their own sets of labs and specialty offices. It would be easy to get lost, even with written directions and a map. I compared the address of the epilepsy center to the paper in my hand.

"L42. L is the building," I said, looking around for signs. "Ah— there—" I pointed to the passageway we just crossed.

Holly gestured to the sentries with their red jackets and "ASK ME" badges. "Can't we just ask someone?"

"No, I got it," I said shortly. "Forty two…" My brain could still handle a lot of things, and, unreasonable as I knew it was, I intended to prove it with this minor task. I studied the map again. "Four is the floor and two is the desk."

"Fourth floor, desk two," Holly repeated. "Do you want to go up? We still have forty minutes until the appointment."

"Sure." Something inside me wanted to make sure that the address of the center was still the same, needed to be reassured that everything was where it should be in this strange new world.

The elevator came, and we squeezed in behind a gray-haired man in a wheelchair. When the door opened to the fourth floor, a sign that announced "St. Lutheran's Epilepsy Center" hung on the wall in front of us. As I stared at it, my body tensed: the reason for this trip became real. I had almost forgotten the stakes and the endgame.

"You okay?" Holly asked. I nodded silently, and we moved out of the elevator into the waiting room.

A greenish-gray carpet covered the large room. People sat among the wooden chairs and padded benches set out in a "U" shape, some murmuring quietly with their loved ones, most staring at their phones. Outdated magazines—*People, Neurology Today, Home & Garden*— fanned out on the end tables, and two televisions displayed a muted talk show with closed captions.

"Do you want to stay here?" Holly whispered. "We could go explore and then come back in twenty or so."

"Where do you want to go?"

"I don't know. I've never been here before either. Bet there are shops or something." She took my arm, turned me around, and pressed the elevator down button. "Come on."

As we wandered around the first floor of the main hospital building, we discovered that there were several gift shops, a Starbucks, and found a cafeteria with room after room of different food choices—Chinese food, a salad bar, a hamburger station, Greek food, a pizza nook. Some stations were more popular than others, with long lines of people chatting, laughing, and looking at menus high on the walls.

"Hungry?" Holly asked.

I shook my head.

"Have you eaten today?"

I shook my head again.

She sighed. "Don't you want to get something—"

"Let's go back to the gift shops," I said, desperately wanting to leave the noise and lines, again overwhelmed in what should have been a reasonable environment, again wishing that Jonah stood beside me, and, with a glance at Holly, again feeling guilty for that wish. I rushed out of the cafeteria and strode down the long hallway into the gift shop closest to the atrium.

"Think I should buy some of these?" I asked, fingering the adult coloring books on a rotating shelf.

"Sure. What else do you have?"

The packing list for the EMU had included recommendations of cards and other games. I wasn't sure why. Suddenly, a coloring book of ocean life seemed a necessity; it could be soothing. I bought four coloring books, a pack of over-priced markers, and stuffed them in my backpack.

"Let's go back to the center," I said, glancing at my watch. We had been wandering around for almost half an hour, and the appointment was in seventeen minutes. "Hurry."

Holly and I retraced our steps to the epilepsy center, and found two seats together in the waiting room. As I lowered myself into the chair, I looked around, subtly taking in the crowd. A few of the people were wheelchair-bound, obviously needed help with their daily care. One woman jerked spontaneously from time to time. Each time, her caretaker turned to her and asked if she was okay, to which an unintelligible "Argh" emerged in response. It must have meant something to the caretaker because, like a mother who understands that her one-year-old means "book" and not "bottle" when he says "ba," the caretaker simply nodded, and went back to reading his magazine. I wondered whether she had always been that way or if she slowly deteriorated over the years, finally relying on the charity and patience of others for her survival. The latter option terrified me. A vision of my future self, ten, fifteen years from now — if I survived that long — wheelchair-bound, communicating in a language that only Jonah and perhaps Sam and Sadie understood, my legal career long gone, my downfall swift and complete, invaded my mind. I worked to rid myself of the image.

Of course, there were the other sort of patients in the waiting room: the patients who looked as if they could conduct themselves normally. These people always reminded me that epilepsy could be an invisible condition: no one looking at them could tell that they had any sort of health issues. It also reminded me that epilepsy could affect anyone — regardless of age, gender, race, ethnicity. Seizures didn't care. These patients unnerved me as well for reasons that I couldn't ever say out loud, not even to Jonah: they were too much like me and they were still here, seeking treatment, needing help, probably not seizure-free. Like me.

I looked at my watch. 11:30. 8:30 in Portland.

Sam and Sadie are at daycare. I wonder what they're doing. Jonah is at the office.

I imagined him standing in his collared shirt and jeans or slacks behind his desk, and realized I knew nothing about what was going on at G&H. Lately, we'd been so focused on my trip, on me, that we hardly ever spoke about his work. I assumed everything was okay, status quo. He'd tell me otherwise; we always shared our work issues.

But, I'd been so busy setting up for this trip, dealing with the Kellan case and Harold, that asking Jonah for details past "How was your day?" wasn't part of the conversation.

It's fine. If anything was really going on at work, he'd tell me. He always told me.

Mom is probably at the house. She'd take care of dinner, food, groceries, which would make things much easier for the whole family. I wondered if she and Jonah had worked out a schedule for picking up the kids yet.

And Harold. What would Harold be doing? Truthfully, I didn't care. This was a place where he didn't belong—not even the thought of him.

Picking up an outdated copy of *People* magazine that promised an in-depth interview with a famous singer detailing his Halloween plans, I flipped through it, my mind tumbling around scenarios of what my future could look like with or without seizures, until a nurse called my name.

•   •   •

As we waited in the examination room, I paced around, touching things, trying to place my nerves somewhere outside my body, anywhere—the metal cupboards filled with nothing, the examination table, the pull-apart plastic model of a brain. I peeked out the large window.

"Just a view of another building," I said to Holly, as if she couldn't see for herself.

She stopped tapping on her phone and put it in her purse. "Are you okay?" she asked.

"Yes," I said as I sat and jiggled my leg.

"Dr. Alem looks and sounds very smart."

"Yeah. Online, definitely."

Stilling my leg, I tapped my foot on the linoleum floor. There was a knock at the door as it opened.

A broad-shouldered man with dark hair graying around the temples and dark brown eyes entered the room, smiling.

"Casey?" he said. "I'm Dr. Alem."

I stood up, and we shook hands. His handshake was firm, reassuring: the handshake of a person confident in his intellect and his area of expertise. He was taller than I expected, but otherwise he looked and sounded the same as in the videos Jonah and I had watched incessantly the weeks before I left for Cleveland. I felt that I already knew him.

"Nice to meet you," I said. "This is my friend Holly."

He greeted her with a warmth that relaxed me even more.

"Let's sit." Dr. Alem gestured to the chairs. "There is so much to talk about." He spoke as if we were old friends catching up, and I almost laughed. Taking the chair at the computer, he pulled up a blank screen. "You've been referred to us for a pre-surgical workup." He left the sentence open, halfway between a statement and a question.

"Yes," I said.

"I have some notes," he said without looking at his screen, "but I'd like to hear your seizure history from you."

"That's going to take a while." After a deep breath, I began to speak. The narrative spilled out of me like a rehearsed monologue in a play: I'd given this speech so many times, I could recite it in my sleep.

"I was diagnosed with epilepsy at eighteen-months-old. I think I had my first seizure before, but it was during a fever, so the doctors thought it was just a febrile seizure, you know."

"Yes, many children have those. Not uncommon," Dr. Alem said. He turned to the computer to take notes as I spoke.

"Right. But then I had another, and this time without a fever, so they said 'Well, let's do an EEG,' and they did one. Mom says that it was a nightmare. I kept trying to pull the electrodes off my head—imagine a toddler in the 1980s who's supposed to sit still with a bunch of flat plastic or metal discs glued to her head—and because Mom had to keep me up all night to get my brain agitated, I was so grumpy." I smiled, remembering Mom telling the story again and again.

"Anyway, so then the EEG was abnormal, and that was that. I started medication — Tegretol."

"Tegretol. That was a good call, especially for a child."

"Uh huh." I'd never thought about how my first neurologist decided on a medication, and Dr. Alem's comment threw me off my monologue for a second. "So, um, yeah, so the seizures were pretty well-controlled while I was growing up. I played sports, got my driver's license, played piano. Just a pretty normal childhood. But then, when I went to college, they came back. I had no idea what was happening when I had the first one — one second I was talking with my roommate about going to the dining hall for lunch, the next thing I knew there was a paramedic over me asking me my name and who the president was. And I couldn't answer him."

"So, tonic-clonic seizures?" Dr. Alem looked up from the computer. "You'd lose consciousness? Fall to the ground?"

I nodded. "Yeah. So, we changed meds — Carbatrol — "

"Which is basically the same medication as Tegretol," Dr. Alem said. He shook his head and sighed. "It works the same on the brain."

"Oh. I didn't know that. I mean, at eighteen I just took what they gave me and — "

"And did it work?"

"Uh, no."

"Right. Please, go on."

"So, then I learned about 'triggers,' how some things could change my brain chemistry enough so that the next day I might have a seizure. You know, staying up late, stress." I paused, embarrassed about the next part. "Sometimes drinking too much."

Dr. Alem smiled as he finished typing the sentence. "Just being a college student," he said. "I have two. I understand."

I blushed and glanced at Holly. She smiled and gave me a thumbs-up. Taking a deep breath, I continued. "But, the thing is, Dr. Alem, that even if I did go out, or get stressed, or went to sleep late, I wouldn't always have a seizure the next day. It was like Russian Roulette. Then, I figured out that if I didn't have a seizure by eleven the next morning,

I wasn't going to have one. And another thing was that they didn't even *usually* come. There wasn't really a pattern to it—or one that I tried to notice."

Dr. Alem nodded, now taking notes quickly.

"Anyway, so I went through several other medications, but none of them worked and the one that did had too many side effects— nausea, pins and needles that kept me up at night, stuff like that. By law school, I finally ended up on a combo of Lamictal and Keppra, and I've been on that ever since."

"But here it says that you are having tonic-clonic seizures every ten to fourteen days," Dr. Alem said. He turned towards me, his eyes dark and concerned. "So, what happened between being in law school until now?"

This was always where the monologue got a little tricky, where I had to pretend that I was talking about someone else. I'd mastered it. I took a breath and imagined that I was standing next to the person on the chair, looking down as she spoke, and that she was talking about a stranger, the poor thing. The only people I'd told about this trick were Holly and Jonah.

"I don't think that's healthy," Holly had said. "You should probably go talk to someone."

"You know," Jonah said, "I've heard of British soldiers who came back from World War II using that as a coping mechanism for PTSD."

"Well, then I'm using it too," I said stubbornly. "That's how I get through these meetings recalling these awful things."

And here we were, at the part where I separated myself.

"After law school, I got a job at a big law firm, then moved to where I work now. Then, in my early thirties, I noticed I was having seizures when I did things that wouldn't have provoked a seizure before. One or two drinks at karaoke, going to bed an hour late, and I'd have a tonic-clonic seizure the next day. So, I asked my neurologist at the time what was going on.

"'All those seizures you had in your twenties strengthened the neural pathways and made them more responsive to each other, so you have more seizures with less of a trigger,' he said. I asked him what that meant in actual English.

"'Your behavior in your twenties over years and years lowered your seizure threshold. Basically, you were training you brain to have seizures.'

"'Why didn't anyone tell me this before?' I asked him.

"'I don't know, but that's what happened,' he said."

I paused for a breath and noticed that the room was still.

"I mean, I didn't *know*, Dr. Alem," I said, wanting reassurance that I was still a good person, and trying to defend any damage I inflicted. "Maybe if I'd *known* things would have been different, but... but maybe I'd be here anyway." I stopped talking, and the person beside me slipped into my body against my will. "Now, I'm having at least two tonic-clonic seizures a month. I walk around with a tightness in my chest, like my sternum is being pulled by a rubber band that's never released, and a doctor just told me I could die in a couple of years if things keep going this way. I mean, I've got two young kids..."

Dr. Alem stopped typing and handed me a box of tissues for the tears I hadn't realized were in my eyes. "You've been through a lot," he said.

"Yes." I took the proffered tissue. *Soon would be a time for tears, but this was not it.* I'd always been determined not to cry in meetings with my neurologists. I didn't want to be the patient who blubbered and needed tissues and time to gather herself. I wanted the doctors to know that I was the tough one and that nothing they could say would bring me down, and I had a fear that if I cried, they wouldn't include me in the full conversation, that I would be left out of the club of neurology, not knowing what I needed to know. This meeting tested that resolve. Looking at my jeans, I blinked away tears and took a breath to steady myself.

"Do you think you can help me?"

"Good question," Dr. Alem replied. His smooth, even tone was soothing, cementing my confidence in a man I'd officially just met but whose voice I'd heard for weeks. "Let's just say we hope so. We have a very comprehensive pre-surgical workup planned for you."

As he reached for the plastic brain, I glanced at Holly, who pulled out her phone to take notes.

"First," he said, "we start with the imaging: MRI, CT scan. We've looked at your past images and don't see any structural defects in your brain, which is a good thing on one hand—you don't have any lesions, tumors, things like that, but, then we are left with the question 'Why is this person having seizures? Where do they come from?' We've scheduled a stay in our EMU for you, where you'll be hooked up to an EEG—the outer electrodes on your scalp—we'll record you having seizures and then analyze the data to see if they are coming from one discrete area, a few areas, or if the whole brain is firing at once."

The process sounded very streamlined in theory, very slick. *We do this all the time,* Dr. Alem seemed to say. *Trust me. You won't feel a thing.*

He held up the model of the brain. "If, as I suspect in your case, the seizures are starting in one or two discrete areas, then we have to decide if we can remove those areas without causing you to lose speech, motor skills, or causing any sort of cognitive deficit."

I almost laughed at the last term, which I'd heard so many times from so many neurologists. I learned years ago that 'cognitive deficit' was doctor-speak for losing some intelligence or—worst-case scenario—any ability to reason or remember that one might have left after years of seizures or anti-epileptic drugs.

"Definitely can't have any 'cognitive deficit.' My job depends on my cognitive ability."

"Yes. I see that you're an attorney?" Dr. Alem asked.

"Right. So, I need all the brain power you can leave." I wondered if I would give up some of my IQ to be rid of seizures forever. Seizure freedom for less intelligence? I wasn't sure. I hoped I never had to choose. "How do you determine which areas do what?"

"We've learned over the years which areas of the brain control which functions to a certain degree," Dr. Alem said. "But we recognize each person is different, and we need to find out exactly what would happen if we removed a specific part of the brain. So we have technology that lets us do what is called *intra*cranial monitoring and brain mapping. This would be a second step in the pre-surgical workup process. We put the electrodes actually *in* the brain itself and then stimulate each electrode and see what happens. But we'll see if we have to go there after the initial EEG monitoring."

I felt horrified and fascinated. After several EEGs over the last thirty years, I'd seen the size of the electrodes. The flat half-inch-wide discs were smaller now than three decades ago, but I couldn't imagine them *in* my brain. Wouldn't the discs move, slide around? How would you place a flat disc *in* a brain? Before I could ask questions, Holly jumped in.

"Wait," she said. She had stopped typing and glanced over at me, her skin paler than usual. "Electrodes *directly* in the brain? How do you do that?"

"Do you have to cut my brain open? The electrodes are flat discs, aren't they?" My heart started pounding against my chest, and I had a distinct urge to run from this room, back to the hotel, and book the next flight back to Portland.

Dr. Alem must have sensed our growing panic. "Let me explain," he said, and held up the plastic brain. "This intercranial monitoring, it's called SEEG. The surgeon places up to fifteen small electrodes — they look like little straight pins, not the flat discs used on the outside of the scalp — directly in the brain through holes drilled through the skull." He gestured to the brain model, pointing to different areas.

Holly covered her mouth too late, as an audible gasp escaped.

"Drilled holes? In my skull?" I said. The words came out disjointed, as if I couldn't bring myself to form complete sentences.

"Yes. We position the electrodes in targeted areas that we determine are involved in seizure activity based on the initial EEG observation," Dr. Alem said. "Then, during the brain mapping, we stimulate each electrode to see the result. It gives us a better picture of which areas are specifically responsible for speech, reading, motor skills, or if one particular electrode causes a seizure."

SARA STAGGS

"Uh huh," I said, still processing this new information. Some needle pokes, seizures to analyze, gluing a few electrodes here and there on my scalp—all that I had expected and mentally prepared for. But electrodes *in* my brain were a whole other realm of testing that I hadn't even known existed. "Well, guess I have time to get used to the idea of holes being drilled into my skull. And here's hoping, right?"

Dr. Alem set the brain model back on the table. "We're looking for the pacemaker, Casey. Usually, there is one point in the brain that starts all the seizures. If that part is in an operable area, then we can remove it and there is a good possibility that the patient will be seizure free."

Seizure free. Though I couldn't even imagine what that life would look like, Dr. Alem was entirely serious. I'd forgotten what it was like to live without fear of having a seizure. Without having to go down the trigger list: *Have I had enough sleep? Did I drink too many beers? Is this workout making my heart rate too high? Am I too stressed from work? From Harold?*

Seizure freedom. That term was surprisingly apt. Epilepsy kept you in an invisible cage: the more frequent the seizures, the smaller the cage. Seizures took away your ability to exercise, the desire to socialize, to advance in your career. *Seizure freedom.* The words made me hopeful and depressed at the same time. It was as if Dr. Alem stood outside my invisible cage and told me he might, just *might*, have the keys to open the door.

Holly broke the silence. "So, if she's a surgical candidate, you could cure her? Like, no more seizures? Can you imagine, Case?" Her brown eyes sparkled with hope and optimism.

"Potentially," Dr. Alem cut in quickly. "We have quite a bit of testing to go before we get there, but, yes, potentially." He turned back to me. "First, we have a bed for you in the EMU tomorrow evening, so you should come to L42 at 4 p.m. You should have received a packet a few weeks ago with information about what to bring with you. Something to keep yourself occupied—books, a laptop, maybe some games. You won't be having seizures all the time, but you will be in bed most of the time."

I hadn't considered that I wouldn't be having seizures all the time, but suddenly that seemed obvious. I thought of the games I packed and was glad for the impulse coloring-book buy.

"Do you have any questions?" Dr. Alem asked. He leaned back in his chair and looked at both of us.

I was sure that any questions I might have would be answered through experience. "One day of freedom left," I said with a sly smile. "How should we spend it?"

Dr. Alem raised his eyebrows and broke into a wide grin that showed my question surprised him. I felt myself regaining control of the situation: the woman who didn't cry was back. He wrote the names of several restaurants on the back of his business card and assured us that these were the best in town. "And we're only a mile or so from the museum district, if that interests you," he suggested.

I left feeling hopeful that at least the next twenty-four hours would be a diversion from the coming lockdown. As we exited the elevators into the dreary wood-paneled hallway and prepared to go outside into the biting wind and hard snow, I smiled under my puffy hood.

"I think he'll be able to help me," I said as we reached the end of the hallway.

Holly squeezed my arm with her mitten-covered hand. "I think so too."

Opening the heavy wooden door against the elements outside, we trekked back to the hotel in silence, our mood brighter than when we began, our hope protecting us from the icy blasts of wind and stinging snow.

CHAPTER 12

Jonah

"Yes, I know. I am so sorry. Casey is out of town, and we just couldn't get the children to daycare on time —" As I spoke, the oven timer went off downstairs; robotic beeping filled my ear drums even through the closed door to our upstairs' bedroom. "Just a moment, Jonathan."

I pressed mute, yanked open the door, and yelled down the stairwell, "Ellen! Can you get that, please?"

"Sorry!" The beeping stopped.

Closing the door again, I took a breath, and unmuted the call.

"Okay, I'm back," I said to Jonathan Howe.

"You know what — not a problem. We're happy to reschedule," Jonathan said. He had always been a decent guy, amiable, easy to get along with. Maybe too easy. He told people what they wanted to hear, and left the hard news — layoffs, slashed bonuses — to Jacob Grossman. Grossman was the businessman at G&H, the man no one wanted to cross. "Everything okay at home?"

"Yes, yes, fine, thank you," I lied, pacing the bedroom floor. My bedroom had been the only place I could find peace from the chaos of preparing dinner, so, like a sullen teenager, I retreated upstairs when the expected call came.

"Do you have an *au pére*?" Jonathan asked. "You should get one. *So* worth it, Diane and I found."

"Yes, we've looked into that option. It's just a bit expensive compared to daycare." I tried to hurry the call while remaining professional. "So, I look forward to the interview tomorrow afternoon."

"Good, good," Jonathan spoke, his tone relaxed and unhurried, as if he had spent all day tooling around a golf course and was now sitting for a drink at some club. Envy filled my chest, like lava waiting to burst from a volcano. "I'll see you tomorrow at four."

"Wonderful. See you then."

I threw the phone on the bed, where it landed with an unsatisfying thump. Opening the door and running downstairs, I heard clanging and movement in the kitchen, now mingled with the shrill cries of the kids: Sam yelled from his room for Ellen, and Sadie wailed from the chaos.

"Daddy, Daddy!" Sadie screamed from her booster seat at the kitchen counter, and pointed at the oven. "Oven beeped!" She pulled a peanut-butter cracker from the plastic plate in front of her and shoved it into her mouth. Crumbs fell out and onto the floor.

"I know." I moved past Ellen to check on the sweet potatoes wrapped in foil. Soft. Good. One thing ready.

"Nana!" Sam shouted again.

"I'll go get him," Ellen said, leaving to see to her grandson's needs.

"I want Mommy!" Sadie shrieked and threw the rest of the crackers on the ground.

I took a deep breath and forced a smile. *Find sympathy. She doesn't understand.*

"I know, Sadie," I said, bending over to pick up the crackers, now in pieces on the floor. "Mummy will be back soon."

I tossed the remaining snacks in the rubbish bin and sighed. I had canceled my interview this morning with Jonathan and Jacob because neither child cooperated nor listened to either me or Ellen, so I finally lost patience, and stuffed a wailing Sadie in the car, still in her pajamas. Sam grumpily followed suit in a t-shirt and pajama bottoms, after also refusing to get completely dressed. By the time we left for daycare, it did not matter who drove them: I couldn't make it to G&H on time for the 8:30 interview.

I called the office from the car after I dropped off the children and arrived at work at nine.

It occurred to me, more than once since Casey left two days ago, that running a household was a delicate dance that we had mastered, and Ellen was still trying to learn. Hopefully, she would learn quickly, and I could not be impatient with her. My mother-in-law was doing us a favor, after all. And it would only be fourteen days.

As I tried to unwrap the sweet potatoes, burning my fingertips in the process, Ellen walked into the kitchen with an armful of folded laundry, and Sam trailing behind.

"Where would you like me to put this?" she asked.

"I told Nana that I heard the dryer make the big noise," Sam said proudly.

My mind reeled as I stared at the clothes. I knew Ellen was trying to pick up the household chores that Casey usually took, but she folded the children's clothes differently than Casey did—over horizontally instead of up vertically—and hung one of my work shirts without buttoning the top button, which stretched the collar. I breathed deeply to avoid screaming at everyone in the room, which I knew would accomplish nothing, and swallowed my frustration as Sadie continued to yell.

"Just put it on the sofa," I replied over Sadie's cries. "I'll get to it just now."

I turned back to my daughter, who was sweating and red-faced with her little rage, her tiny fingers pulled into fists by her side.

"Where Mommy!"

Sam walked over to her booster seat. "Mommy's still in Cleveland."

This set Sadie off into a greater frenzy. She swiped her arm across the countertop, sending the remaining food spiraling to the floor, her high-pitched voice filling the room with shrieks, as if she was in physical pain.

I glared at Sam and walked over to release Sadie from her booster. Burying her face into my shoulder and arms, she sobbed.

"Sadie," I said, stroking her hair. "Mummy will be back so soon."

"How soon?" Sam asked. He looked hopeful, as if he expected the answer to have changed during the day.

"About twelve more days now," I said. Ellen walked into the kitchen, laundry-free. "Isn't that right, Nana?"

"Exactly," Ellen said. She glanced over at the crock pot where shredded chicken and vegetables had braised for eight hours. The sweet potatoes didn't really matter: we just made them for Sadie, the picky eater. She could live on peanut butter crackers for a night. "And dinner will be ready in just a few minutes. Who's hungry? Go wash your hands."

Both children raised their hands at the mention of dinner. Sadie stopped crying and wiped her nose on my shirt. She slid down my torso and legs, and followed Sam, who was already running the water in their bathroom to half-wash his hands. I decided not to inspect too thoroughly. That was Casey's job.

Casey promised she would join us for dinner on FaceTime, so I set a symbolic place at the dining room table for her, complete with a laptop, charged and ready. We texted throughout the day, but I wanted to hear more about her meeting with Dr. Alem. Texts were fine for coordinating FaceTime chats, but not for details from extensive meetings with epileptologists. After reviewing Holly's notes, I had some questions.

The computer made the short, low beeping noise associated with an incoming FaceTime call. *Thank God.* Casey's face appeared on the screen. She was sitting in a bed, against a padded headboard with pillows fluffed around her, and waved from under the white comforter.

"How're you doing?" she asked.

Before I could answer, Sam and Sadie burst into the room, both screaming. "Mommy! Mommy!"

Ellen walked over with a serving bowl of the chicken-vegetable mixture and a large spoon. "You made it!" she said.

"Wouldn't miss it," Casey said, grinning.

"So, how was Dr. Alem?" I asked.

Casey pursed her lips. "It was… interesting. They have this test they can do." She talked about something called SEEG. "And they can position electrodes directly in your brain —"

"Mommy, today I painted a tree," Sam interrupted.

Casey stopped talking and smiled indulgently. "Let's talk about SEEG later," she said. "Tell me about your tree, Sammy."

The conversation turned to Sam's tree, Sadie's new classmate, both children speaking directly to the computer, as if Casey were actually at the table. Finally, after they covered all their news and ate enough dinner, Ellen told them to go play in their rooms, and they skipped off, away from the table. Casey resumed her description of SEEG.

"This new technology is crazy. They put the electrodes *in* your brain." She inhaled deeply, whether from fear or awe at the science or something else, I could only guess. "But we'll see if we even get there. We have to do just regular EEG first."

"How do they get them in there?" Ellen said. She took a bite of her chicken and wiped her mouth with her napkin.

Casey explained a procedure that included holes drilled into her skull. I did my best to hide my horror from Casey as I imagined it.

"The crazy thing is, I'm actually hoping for this SEEG thing," she said slowly. "It means they think they can do something, you know? Or at least they think there's a chance. If my entire brain is going off at once, what can they do? Remove the whole thing?" She laughed harshly, but I could hear the fear behind the joke.

"Let's hope that it works out, then," I said, not quite sure what I meant. "What do we have now? Twelve more days, isn't it?"

"That's right," Ellen said. "We're getting there."

"We're getting there," Casey agreed.

The conversation lagged.

"We miss you," I offered. I wanted to say anything to keep her here, to keep her face in front of me.

Her smile faded, and I knew I had said the wrong thing. "I know," she said. "I'm sorry, guys." Her eyes clouded over, and she shifted her gaze to her lap. "I'll be home soon," she said, sounding less sure than she had before. "Soon as I can," she qualified.

Dinner passed with small talk about the weather in Cleveland, Casey's strange lack of communication from Harold, and some family member updates from Ellen.

"Everything at the office is fine," I said with a convincing smile, when asked. "Busy, but good." I still had not mentioned the interview or Kevin leaving. We did not need another layer of stress as a family, but I felt ill inside. This was the first time I had kept a work update—especially one this important—from Casey. I was not lying, though; I tried to sell myself on this justification. Not really. Just an omission for her own good, wasn't it? I knew that my litigator wife could tear that reasoning apart in a second. But I still could not bring it up. *Maybe later.*

We called Sam and Sadie back to the room. They said goodbye with reminders from Casey to behave and to listen to Daddy and Nana. As I clicked off the FaceTime, Casey's face froze for a second with her lips together, brow creased. I could feel the concern through the screen.

She is worried. I am worried too. I closed the laptop with a snap, and Ellen began clearing the table. We worked together to get the children to bed. Tonight went smoothly, and only after I kissed Sam goodnight did I go upstairs and allow myself to get lost in the pictures on my phone, staring at Casey's face in each image as I scrolled through our memories.

CHAPTER 13

Casey

Holly watched me get settled in the hospital bed that would be my temporary home and took a picture.

"Send it to Mom and Jonah," I said. I slid around on the mattress, pushing the buttons to move the bed up and down, and touching the padded sides: such a novelty right now.

"Sent it," said Holly, bringing her phone over for me to see the shot.

The picture showed me sitting up in the bed, shoulders back, beaming. The early evening light falling through the large window opposite my bed lit my face, while white bandages wrapped around my scalp to keep the electrodes glued into place. Circular heart rate monitors sticking to my chest peeped through the V-neck in my dark blue pajama top, and the stark white of the bandages contrasted with the wood-paneled walls behind me and the blue padding on the sides of the bed.

A young man with short brown hair in blue nurse's scrubs walked in.

"I'm Joe, and I'm here to place your IV." His voice held a light tremor and his hands moved quickly, as if trying to hide his nerves.

I held out my left arm and felt my heart rate rise as I watched him quickly pull out the IV kit and place it next to my leg. "Try this side," I told him.

Joe nodded and swallowed, his Adam's apple bouncing up and down like a small rubber ball in his throat. My eyes caught the subtle movement, the nervous tic, and I stared at my arm. His fingers rubbed along the various veins while he tried to decide where to place the needle.

"I think this one'll do," he said, his voice rising at the end of the sentence in uncertainty.

Holly stiffened as she finally picked up on his tension. "Have you been a nurse long?" she asked, her voice light but taut.

"It's my first week, actually," Joe said. "Little poke." He inserted the needle into the back of my left hand with shaky fingers.

I kept my eyes on him, grinding my jaw and breathing deeply through my nose to avoid screaming in pain as he moved the needle around in different directions like a compass trying to find North.

"Gosh, your veins are so tricky," he said as he stabbed indiscriminately under my skin. "I just can't seem to get one—"

"Stop!" I yelled. "Take it out."

Joe seemed frightened by the force of my voice and slid the needle out quickly, placing a piece of square gauze over the puncture. "I can try the other side—"

"Go get someone else."

Joe stood staring at me, as if unsure of what he had heard.

"Go!"

He slunk out of the room with the air of a chastened student. A few minutes later, a woman with long straight hair and a lace head covering appeared, and introduced herself as Glenda. She quickly inserted an IV into my left hand, flushed it with saline, and left with a smile and a promise to come if I needed anything.

I sat back in the bed, rubbing the small plastic tube now poking out of my hand. "Well, that was an adventure," I said to Holly, who lifted her eyebrows.

"Understatement," she replied. Pulling a sturdy padded chair from the corner of the room, she parked it next to my bed, and sat. She examined my IV without touching it. A light purple bruise emerged where Joe's needle had been. "Are you okay?"

"If that's the worst that happens, I'll be just fine." My smile faltered as the reality of the situation hit me: this was just the beginning, the first needle poke, the first challenge. This wouldn't be the worst by a long shot.

Holly reached over and touched my IV-free hand. Her palm was smooth, her skin soft, and her touch comforting, as if she could protect me, shelter me from what could be coming. I thought back to high school, to middle school, when Holly stood tall and confident under her then-long red mane, leading the way through the confusion of puberty, somehow knowing how to deal with boys' attention. We'd been carefree, full of laughter, and big dreams. She'd stood by my side as my seizures worsened, and I'd stood by her side when her dreams of starting a family fell away, regardless of all the science and money she and Rob had invested in every avenue. When they finally decided that enough heartbreak was enough, I was there for her. She held my hand through each setback, and I held hers. And here she was — over twenty years from the day we met — still by my side, still holding my hand.

"Let's talk about the evenings," I said. "I don't want you to stay overnight, so you'll need to bring the wine in somehow before you go."

"Are you sure that's a good idea?" she asked, scrunching up her nose with a nervous look in her eyes.

"A hangover is one of my biggest triggers," I said, shocked that she would even question our plan. "I want to get in and out as quickly as possible."

She shifted in her seat, her decades-old tell that she was uncomfortable with the subject of the conversation.

"You need to bring it in somehow, so that the video doesn't see it," I said.

Holly sighed, resigned to the plan, and reached into her leather tote bag, where she pulled out a large purple metallic water bottle. "I already thought of it." She stretched back in her seat to see that the door was closed, then placed the bottle on my plastic table with a substantial *thunk*. "I'll fill this with wine and bring it in when I come. I figure I'll get some lunch somewhere, and I can bring it back then. It's already filled for tonight. The finest gas station Chardonnay."

I grinned. It was as if we were teenagers again, trying to sneak alcohol bought with fake IDs into parties and school events. "Perfect. And let's keep with white wine," I said. "I don't care what kind, but red will leave a stain."

"I'd only do this for you, you know."

I reached out and squeezed her forearm. "I know. And I love you for it."

Her pale skin seemed almost pearl-like under the waning sunlight, as she replied, "You better."

CHAPTER 14

Jonah

Standing in my office, I gazed at the Pearl District, watching the shadows grow under the fading light, thinking about the interview while absently observing hipsters saunter down the cobblestone streets between refurbished warehouses, and fit people run in Nike or Adidas gear—one of those companies still our client thanks to the work of my team, and despite Dwayne. I thought about any potential roadblocks that I might encounter in this meeting, and silently reviewed the reasons that I was the man for the job: I was a good leader, I worked hard; the clients liked me, everyone on my team liked me, except for Dwayne, but he was just a snotty kid, walking around the halls in trendy jackets and tailored jeans, scoffing at his co-worker's ideas, and bringing an attitude to meetings that annoyed the whole team.

I was also next in line, so this entire interview process was nonsense; however, I would not say that. I was the man everyone expected to fill the position.

"I don't know why they're even doing interviews," Thomas texted when the email came from HR last week. "Everyone knows you're the guy. It's gotta be just an HR formality thing."

But I did not get the feeling that it was an 'HR formality thing.' I had seen some of my team members get called in for interviews. None of them I saw as actual competition, except Dwayne. For all his faults, on paper, he was almost perfect for the job. Single with no kids, he worked insane hours and had landed several medium-sized accounts with his pitches, and one rather large client. As much as I disdained him, he could be innovative. He had been at the firm almost as long as I had, and I knew Jonathan liked him. I left for the interview and forced thoughts of Dwayne out of my mind. This pitch was about me.

As I walked down the hall, I saw that almost every conference room was filled. Grossman & Howe couldn't just have numbers for their rooms: The G&H firm vibe was "local" and "cool", so in Portland all their conference rooms were named after bridges in the city: Tilikum, Sellwood, Hawthorne, St. Johns. The list went on and on.

Opening the door to the Sellwood Room, I put on my client smile — not too big, sincere, yet professional. Jonathan and Jacob sat across the table from the door. Jonathan, tan as always, his brown hair just showing streaks of gray, wore a fitted t-shirt and dark green jacket. He loved running and kept a slim physique. Jacob was almost the ying to Jonathan's yang — burly, with his hair completely silver. He wore a collared shirt with a loosened tie. Legend was that they never argued about anything to do with G&H: proof that opposites could indeed attract.

"Jonah," Jonathan said, smiling. He gestured to a chair. "Please, sit. I'm sure you're wondering why we're even going through an interview process, with you being the lead on the Portland marketing team, and working directly under Kevin."

"I have to say, I am a bit surprised," I admitted, still smiling.

"You're an asset to the firm," Jacob said, staring at me straight-faced. This seemed promising, as Jacob was known to be stingy with praise.

But how much of an asset was I? Clearly not enough of one to be given the job without making me dangle from a hook. When I spoke to Jonathan yesterday, I hoped he would reassure me that this interview process was just a technicality, that the promotion was mine, and the interviews were just a distraction. He had not done so.

"It's just that we have so much talent here," Jonathan said. "We want to find the best fit for the job."

"I completely agree," I said. "And I believe that fit is me. I've been leading the marketing team under Kevin for over two years now, worked with our top creatives and marketing execs in all the G&H offices to land and keep major accounts. The people here like me, my team likes me, and I get the job done."

Jonathan and Jacob glanced at each other. They seemed to communicate without words.

"We agree with all those achievements," said Jacob. "Our concern is your time dedication to G&H."

"Sorry?" I must have misheard him. "Jacob, I'd think that you would know after over ten years, after everything I've achieved, that I'm dedicated to this company."

Jacob shifted in his seat and licked his lips, unused to pushback. "We see your commitment, Jonah. And your skills are not the issue, not at all."

Jonathan nodded. "Our concern is time at the office."

"Right," Jacob said, crossing his arms and leaning back in the plush leather chair. "So, the issue is that we need a Director who can be here without question, keep morale going. A Director who understands that G&H is a top priority in his or her life. Someone willing to give up time on weekends, evenings. Someone who can be present for the team and really make it work."

"I have a wife and family," I said. "Kevin does as well, doesn't he? And I work from home on evenings. My team understands that."

"Yes, well, most of them do," Jonathan said. "And the thing is that Kevin was *here*. It's true that you'd naturally be his successor. We just worry about your commitment to putting G&H first, whether you would be willing to make the sacrifices required at the Director level."

"Do any of the other candidates have children?" I asked.

Jonathan hesitated before answering, and glanced at Jacob, who nodded slightly, seeming to give him the go-ahead to answer.

"No," Jonathan admitted. "Some are in serious relationships, a couple are married, but you're the only one with children."

"But Kevin has a family," Jacob said. "And a long-standing marriage. It's possible to do both. You just have to be willing to put in the time." He paused. "The time at G&H, I mean."

Kevin's wife was a stay-at-home-mum, I almost pointed out. *Not a litigator. No coordinating of schedules, no rushing home from offices to make dinners. You don't quite get the difference.* For a second, I wished that Casey would just stay at home, but that was not who she was. Thinking briefly of that day under the oak tree years ago, I knew that was not who I married.

The room went quiet while I considered what they were actually saying: *Pick. Home or G&H. Time with your wife and children or a promotion.* Ironically, G&H prided itself on recruiting based on boasting a priority of work/life balance. But now the truth: You can have both, but not really.

My frustration overcame my intuitively nuanced side. "I think we all know the right thing to do here, don't we? I am the right person for this position. Even though I have a family, I get *all* the work done, and more."

"Well, your team does…" Jacob began.

"A good leader delegates," I replied shortly. "I have trained up a well-oiled team that works well together."

"And that team includes several candidates who can spend the extra time at G&H," said Jonathan, no longer amicable. "What is the right thing on what level? For the company?"

"Morally. Honorably," I said in disbelief. "Choosing the best person for the job."

"To be honest, Jonah, we're not worried as much about honor as we are about the bottom line and keeping clients happy," Jacob said. "This isn't England."

There was a hard silence in the room. Then, I found my client smile again. "Of course the bottom line is important," I said. "And we always want to keep clients happy. If I *was* to promise to be at the office late, to come in on weekends, to do what Kevin does, would you offer me the position?"

They looked at each other, again communicating without words.

"Yes," Jonathan said, the smile returning to his face. "Are you open to that?"

"Let me think about it," I said. "That's fair, isn't it? I'm older than anyone else I've seen you interview, and I'm the only one with children. So, let me think about it."

They glanced at each other again, and Jacob nodded to Jonathan.

"That's the thing," Jonathan said, his smile fading, and his eyes somber as he shook his head. "You shouldn't have to think about it."

"Thanks for your time, Jonah," Jacob said, standing and holding out his hand. "Like I said, you're a real asset to G&H. We'll let you know about final interviews."

I left the room in shock, dropping my smile as soon as I turned away.

After checking on my team and letting them know I was leaving, I walked to my office and replayed the interview in my brain—especially that last line from Jonathan: "You shouldn't have to think about it."

I strolled over to the long window in my office, taking in the view of downtown over the short buildings in the Pearl. Casey's office stood a quarter mile away, although her window was on the other side. The gray sky continued into the distance, masking what should be the evening sun. Dark clouds threatened to rain.

Staring out the window, I realized that I could walk back to the Sellwood Room, tell Jonathan and Jacob that I spoke with my wife and she was completely supportive of this promotion, and all the conditions that went with it. But I had not even told her about the promotion prospect yet, and, just as Casey's promotion to partner would mean more stress on our family, my promotion would mean I would be there less for her and the children. On the other hand, I would make a lot more money. A *lot* more. It might not be fair for me to demand Casey cut down on work while I did the opposite, but I was doing it with *us* in mind. Our family. Her health. With this promotion, we could afford a nanny, maybe a live-in, and Casey would not have to work. She could just rest.

I picked up a photo of the two of us, taken at the beach last year. She'd had a seizure the day before the picture, but it was minor and she recovered quickly. The four of us spent a day at the coast, and it was exceptionally windy. In the picture, Casey's dark hair whipped around her head and she was laughing, monoliths poking out of the cobalt ocean behind us.

Casey had been gone four days; she had been in the EMU since this afternoon. Maybe she had already had a seizure. I did not know how EMUs actually worked. Holly's texted photo showed Casey smiling in a hospital bed with stark white bandages circling her head. It made me uncomfortable to see her like that, living a completely different life half a continent away.

I glanced at my watch. Past eight in Cleveland. Ellen had picked up the kids, made dinner, and knew I would be home late. I texted Casey.

Good time to talk?

I waited for a response, watching the three dots like a teenager with a crush.

Yes.

She picked up on the first ring, sounding tired and depressed. "Hi, babe."

"Long day?" I asked.

"Sort of," she said. "Lots of caffeine and stuff. And now visiting hours are over, so I'm lonely. I feel like shit."

"I'm sorry, darling. Any seizures?" I asked hopefully.

"No." Her voice held a note of frustration and melancholy. "Just some really powerful auras. I don't know why they can't just count those and get me out of here."

She was off her normal dose of medication, which meant it was hard to make coherent sentences. Holly reported that Dr. Alem said being off the medication Casey had taken for over ten years would affect her mood and her ability to concentrate. But it was also supposed to bring seizures faster.

"It'll happen, Case. I bet tonight or tomorrow morning," I said.

"I hope so."

I wanted to touch her, to rub her back, and hold her hand. I would have stayed overnight at the hospital, no matter how uncomfortable it was, and helped her through her lowest times. I knew that Casey sent Holly back to the hotel to get a proper rest, so that she could return bright-eyed and fully awake each day. I could only do my job through the phone.

"You can do it, Case. I know you can."

"Everyone I talk to says that, but you don't know. The nurses don't know. The doctors aren't doing what I'm doing. Mom doesn't understand, Holly doesn't get it, you don't get it. You're not here! No one else is me!" With every word, her voice raised with the unfairness of the situation. She let out a sob, making me feel even more helpless.

"Oh, Case," I said. "It's not going to be forever, you know. You'll be home soon."

"I know."

"Well, things are alright over here," I said, pushing the conversation away from her, trying to provide a distraction by being bright and positive. "We're in a rhythm by now. Your mum takes Sam and Sadie to daycare, picks them up, and makes dinner. She's been so helpful, you know."

"That's good," Casey said listlessly.

I almost told her about the interview, but I just could not do it, and this was not the time. Even if she was rested and on her full dose of medication, she would be furious that I was considering a bigger position without consulting her—rightly so, I decided, especially after what Jonathan and Jacob had made so clear: G&H before all else. I had not taken the promotion, anyway. Technically, it had not been offered, so really, what was there to talk about? I still felt sick inside.

I stared at her office building again and started tearing up. *Come home*, I wanted to say. *I need you. I need your advice to keep me grounded.*

"Where are you?" Casey asked. "It's so quiet."

"I'm in my office, looking at your building." I smiled, and hoped that in that small hospital bed on the other side of the country, she was smiling too.

"Go home," she said. "I have to work on getting drunk."

"Good luck, babe."

"I love you," she said before ending the call.

"I love you," I whispered. My heartstrings pulled in my chest, an emotional pain as strong as a tsunami. I turned off the desk lamp in my office and watched the beams of city light bounce off the picture of the two of us, highlighting the one thing in the room that showed only us together, a couple, a team. As I walked out of the building, I wrapped my jacket tighter across my body, trying to ignore any part of my ego that attempted to convince me that more time at G&H would be good for my marriage.

CHAPTER 15

Casey

"Harold called," I told Holly as soon as she walked into my hospital room. "Can you believe that?"

"Yes. Because he's a psycho." She sat on the padded chair and leaned her large bag against the side. Then she stood and began cleaning off the plastic table in front of me: slipping the large metallic purple water bottle into her bag, throwing away the stacked Styrofoam cups that had been filled with bitter coffee from the nurses' station. "So, no seizure, huh?"

"What?"

"I just thought you'd probably lead with that." She pressed the assistance button.

"Can I help you?" came a nasal voice from the tan, plastic rectangle, resembling a 1980s TV remote, next to my leg.

"Yeah. Can we get some fresh ice water in here, please?" Holly asked, frowning at the old, tepid water in my hospital-issued plastic jug.

"Sure." A click and then silence.

"I'm sure they'll be right on that," I said. "Customer service isn't the priority here. I'm betting you'll see a nurse in about ten, fifteen minutes. *Maybe*."

Holly sighed and settled back in the chair. "So, what did Harold want?"

"Ugh. He wanted information about a case that he could have asked *any attorney in the office* to find. I can barely hold a conversation, and he wanted me to find a document for him that Kristin could easily have found." My words came out slower than usual and stilted. After tapering down my medication to almost nothing, the effort to make a cohesive sentence was a Herculean task. "Then he asked if I'd still be back next week." I rubbed my eyes; I was so tired. Depriving myself of sleep on purpose had become a dreaded nightly habit, but it seemed almost expected here.

"That last part was probably the reason for the call," Holly said. "What'd you say?"

"Well, I'm almost fully off my meds now, so I'm a little cranky and not really all there. I reminded him that I'm in the hospital and couldn't make things go any faster than they were going, so I said that I didn't know. That things were going slower over here than I thought they would." My voice shook, as I thought about how disappointing the days were without a seizure, and how long the nights had become.

We both knew that the way things were going, the two-week deadline was probably shot. We had yet to talk about it, but we both knew.

"We didn't leave on good terms," I said, clearing my throat. "He was annoyed. I was pissed. I mean, there's nothing more I can do to speed this up. I'm trying, Holly. I'm really trying." A heaviness in my chest felt like a rock holding down my heart.

"I know you're trying, Case," Holly said, rubbing my arm.

Jonah called later in the morning, and I repeated the story to him. "Anyway, let's talk about something else," I said, sniffling.

Just then, his call-waiting beeped.

"Case," he said, his voice taking on an edge of stress, "I have to go. The daycare is calling."

"What?" I said, trying to work through this thick brain fog and feel alert.

"I just have to take this—"

"Call me back."

Ten minutes later, Jonah called to report that Mom was on her way to pick up a vomiting Sadie from daycare.

"Shit, I hope it's not a norovirus. That's super contagious," I said. "Keep the kids separate, just in case."

"Alright."

My thick, slow mind tried to concentrate, to work in disaster relief mode, and I attempted to rearrange the afternoon as if I was in Portland. My thoughts came out in bits and pieces, punctuated with a lot of "Just a sec—let me try to think" while I closed my eyes and rubbed my temples. Finally, a plan from my hospital bed: Jonah would need to pick Sam up at daycare, which meant Sam staying late, which meant Jonah needed to call the daycare and let them know. At home, Mom would take care of Sadie. But how would that go? When Sadie was sick, she just wanted me. I had always been there.

This would be so much easier if I were home.

"So that's it," I said, finally at the limit of my ability to think linear thoughts. "Keep me updated."

There wasn't time for long comforting words—phone calls needed to happen, and children needed comforting.

"I love you, Case," Jonah said before beginning our plan. "Go have a seizure."

•   •   •

The wind blew hard against the large window across from my hospital bed, snow swirling in violent circles against the pitch-black sky. Besides the howl of the wind and the slap of the ice on the window, the only sound in the room was the pulsing of my orange leg compressors: the slow fill of air to squeeze my calves, and the hiss of release as they deflated. The cycle repeated until it became such a part of the environment that I almost didn't notice it.

The fluorescent overhead light lit the room harshly, aided by the lamps that flickered occasionally on the ridge above my head. More empty Styrofoam coffee cups, a half-full purple metallic water bottle, and a laptop with *The Bachelor* on pause covered the movable plastic table in front of me. I glanced at the time on my phone. Ten p.m. Another few hours, and then I would let myself sleep until seven.

A coloring book lay open on my lap. Picking a red marker from the box wedged next to my leg, I made abstract designs on the corners of the open page, too confused, drunk, and tired to try coloring in the lines.

I felt nauseous, which was not surprising since I had choked down cup after cup of coffee, trying to keep myself awake long enough to ensure a seizure in the morning. I drank the coffee black: the liquid was bitter and strong. I'd recently started on the wine, which was, as always, cheap and sweet. I couldn't finish the whole container, but had gradually been able to drink more and more as the nights went on. After the second night, I'd concluded that there was nothing more depressing than drinking shitty wine alone in a hospital bed with the goal of making yourself hungover.

This was day four, night five. I'd managed one seizure in conditions that at home, in normal life, would have meted out at least two a day. It was the lack of stress, I decided, keeping me from having as many seizures as I should have. The EMU was like a sick mini-vacation: there were no deadlines, no constantly furious boss, no chores to take care of, no one pleading for my attention, none of the stress that followed me through my daily life. Here, I could watch television and movies all day on less medication, trying to make myself sick with the help of Holly and the doctors and nurses, to perhaps make me well in the end. What was missing were all the issues that came with real life. Instead, I was confined to a bed with padded sides, staring out a long window, worrying only about myself.

The nights were the worst. True, the days could be bad, disappointing if I didn't have a seizure or boring, as my lack of normal medication made it almost impossible to concentrate, to hold a conversation of any length, to read or even play one of the several board games I had so naïvely packed. But at least I had company during the day, a bit of distraction. Holly was always there with me, and Dr. Alem came in the afternoon and evenings. I had phone calls, emails, FaceTime, texts from people outside the EMU, although since yesterday the only calls I had the energy to pick up were Jonah's or my mother's, giving updates on Sadie that I returned with updates about my lack of progress here.

I'd decided there was no point in checking in at the office. My email was automatically set to an "out of office" response, and I'd briefed enough lawyers in the firm to handle my cases for a while. I'd assumed that Harold understood this after our last call ended on terse terms. My assumption proved wrong.

He'd called again this morning, as I finished coloring another masterpiece, and Holly worked next to me on her laptop. When Harold's name appeared on the display, I rolled my eyes. Holly told me to answer it.

"Harold."

His words hit me like gunfire. "Your little associate is fucking up the entire Kellan case!" he shouted.

"She has a name, Harold, and it's Kristin. What's going on?"

"Doug Randall called with a simple question, and she gave the wrong answer. She came into my office practically trembling when she realized what she'd done."

I felt pulses in my brain, stronger than the last time he called. I noticed Holly watching the monitor that showed my heart rate, oxygen level, and brain waves.

"What was the question?" I asked.

"I don't know. Some simple discovery question, and now we're going to get hit with more discovery requests from the State — all I know is that she fucked up."

Of course he hadn't listened to her fully. I remembered my first few years at the firm, and the terror I felt about telling Harold about any mistake; the poor woman probably thought she'd get fired on the spot. Trying to think of a solution was like thinking through mud: ideas were slow and messy.

"Okay." I shut my eyes, and rubbed the bridge of my nose, fighting to keep my thoughts on track. "Tell everyone that all questions about the Kellan case should be directed to me through the front desk. I'm out of the office—obviously—as my email says, so have Violet put all calls about the Kellan case to my voicemail or tell the person to email me, and I'll deal with it all when I get back." My brain pulsed and pulsed, my auras getting stronger.

"When are you going to be back?" he barked.

"I've already told you, I don't *fucking* know, Harold!" I snapped. "I'll contact you when I get out of the EMU."

Harold was silent on the other side of the phone. This was the first time I'd ever cursed at him. It felt good. He hung up.

Holly sat, staring at the vitals screen with a bemused smile on her face. "He needs to go on medication," she said, returning her gaze to me.

"Jesus, he's such a child," I said to no one in particular. "I wonder if I could just take the case with me."

Holly shrugged and patted my hand. She knew what I was saying.

"This is a conversation for another time," I said. The pulses in my brain stopped, my heart rate slowed, and I no longer shook from anger. *Leave the firm.* It wasn't the first time I'd thought of it in the past year. I'd danced around the idea with Jonah before I left for Cleveland. But I wasn't in a place to make that decision now. I tucked the idea away, to be revisited another day, when I had my full mind back, had thought about it more, considered the repercussions, and could weigh pros and cons.

Now, alone at 10 p.m., time hardly seemed to move. I leaned against the thin pillow, so useless in its one job of being able to provide physical comfort, and stubbornly tried to find a resting spot. The electrodes—flat metal circles stuck with hard glue onto my scalp all over my head—made it almost impossible to get comfortable, much less get a decent rest. Of course, here that was a good thing.

Maybe just a little nap and then I'd stay up until two. I pressed a button on the side of my bed to turn off the overhead lights, and another button to move the top half of the bed horizontal. It reclined with a whir until reaching the stopping point. The wires attached to my electrodes shifted, and I scratched at the bandages wrapped around my head. With no shower in four days, my scalp was oily and itchy, and the little sink baths allowed daily were not much good at keeping me clean. At least I could change my shirt every day and my pajama pants every other day since Holly took my clothes back to the hotel and used the laundry room there.

The world seemed to spin when I closed my eyes, and I waited to see if I would vomit. Loneliness crept into my chest, making its home there like a hibernating bear. A tear rolled down my cheek and sunk into the thin hospital bed sheet as I drifted off into a fitful sleep.

CHAPTER 16

Jonah

Sam and I held hands as we walked up the stairs to our porch, and he squeezed my fingers, our secret sign for "I love you." His cheeks flushed pink from the cold, and his eyes shone bright from the wind we had faced on our Saturday morning walk.

"Let's get inside," I said, jiggling the key in our old lock. The door finally gave, and we hurried in, shaking off the freeze from outside. "And let's be a little quiet. Sadie might be sleeping still."

In a distant part of the house, we heard a soft low voice — Ellen's — and a high-pitched sob. Sadie's. I peeked around the corner of Sadie's doorway, keeping Sam purposefully away, and took in the sight of my daughter in her new toddler bed, hunched over a white plastic bowl, her small body heaving with a force I would not have thought possible. Ellen rubbed her back, holding the bowl, and wiping Sadie's mouth with a paper towel.

"It's okay, Sadie," she murmured, carefully pulling back my daughter's hair. "You're going to be just fine."

Sadie looked up at Ellen. Her chapped lips and flushed face were the picture of despair as tears ran rivulets down her cheeks. "Mommy," she whispered desperately, all the longing put into that one word. "Please. *Mommy.*"

I walked into her dimly lit room, and crouched down by her bed. She slid her head onto her pillow, her eyes partly open.

"Mommy," she said. "Please…"

"Soon, darling," I promised.

Ellen rose with the full, plastic bowl, and pushed an empty one against my thigh. I heard the plop of thin, gelatinous liquid fall into the toilet, followed by a flush and the running of the sink in the children's bathroom. Sadie's eyelashes lay heavy on her cheeks, her breathing shallow.

When Ellen returned, the bowl smelled of Clorox, and she placed it next to the bed.

"You shouldn't stay long around here," she whispered. "I think we're almost through the worst part. The doctor says just to keep her hydrated. She's taking little sips of Pedialyte, but I don't know how much she's keeping down. If she doesn't stop throwing up by tonight, we might have to take her in, get her some fluids." Her eyes studied her granddaughter's red face.

"You mean to the ER?"

"I mean somewhere. I don't know. Dehydration can be really dangerous." Ellen stroked Sadie's forehead.

What would Casey do? That was the question. Casey would be in Ellen's place if she were here. She would take control and launch into "doctor-mode" as I called it. I looked at Ellen, who continued to stroke Sadie's forehead. Casey's eyes were the same shape and color; genes passed down to Sam. Casey's jawline was the mirror of her mother's as well, and many of their mannerisms were the same. Ellen was almost an older version of Casey, almost—as if someone had painted a picture of my wife thirty years in the future, but changed some details: the mouth, the ears, the hairline, and made her blonde instead of dark.

"Let's just see, shall we?" I said.

"Daddy?" Sam peeked around the door frame. "Can I come in?"

"No, Sammy, I'm coming out. Nana has it under control now. Right, Nana?" I raised my eyebrows to signal what she should answer.

"I do. Make sure to wash your hands before you touch anything, Jonah," she said firmly. "And I've just Cloroxed the doorknobs and every surface in the bathroom, so they should be clean."

I stared at my daughter, now deep asleep and breathing more evenly, then rose to scrub my hands in the bathroom. Sam followed me close but silent, his eyes glued to my face.

I dried my hands, trying to touch as little as possible. "Let's go to your room," I said to Sam. He nodded and led the way.

I closed the door behind us, and we sat on the floor in front of his bunk bed, leaning against the wooden frame. I pulled him onto my lap. "How're you doing, Sammy? Alright?"

"Okay, I guess. I miss Mommy. And Sadie's sick." I waited for more. "And Mommy's not here to help."

A beat passed, and he did not continue.

"That's true." I gave him a squeeze around his belly. "I know Mummy wishes she was here. And I know she misses you, too."

Sam sniffed and rubbed his nose. He was crying. *He has not cried at all since Casey has been gone. Or, he has not cried that I have seen.* Guilt washed over me as I realized that I had taken my five-year-old son for granted: accepting and expecting his good behavior while his sister was sick and his mother gone.

"Sammy, it's going to be okay." I turned him to face me. "Mummy will be back so soon." I wiped his tears, now falling from his chin.

He stared at the ground, shaking his head. "Not really. Not today, she won't. Goodnights aren't the same." He looked at me, blushing. "I don't want to hurt your feelings, Daddy..."

A lump grew in my throat, and sadness joined the guilt washing over my body: he was only telling the truth. I did not have the soft touch that Casey employed so easily; she had learned it as a child, whereas, I had learned that a brief kiss and a closed door meant bedtime. As a result, since Casey left, Sam's bedtime had become a cursory kiss, the tucking in of blankets around his small body, and a quick "I love you" before closing the door to his room to help Ellen with Sadie's retching and fever. I had taken Sam's stoicism, his calm outer shell, to mean he felt fine, unbothered by this lack of attention. But now, I took a closer look.

"You're not hurting my feelings." I hugged him tighter. "I miss Mummy too, and I know it's different at home without her here."

His body relaxed in my arms.

"I have an idea," I said. Sam's eyes widened, his look hopeful. "Let's ring Mummy, shall we? Check in with her." 9 a.m. in Portland, noon in Cleveland. "She's probably having lunch right now." *At least it's lunchtime.* Holly told me that Casey just picked at her food the past few days, saying that she felt too sick for a meal. "Want to try it?"

Sam nodded vigorously, and I pulled out my phone, pressing Casey's number.

"Here we go," I said.

One ring. Two rings. Three rings. Sam frowned, staring at the phone with longing in his eyes. I could almost hear his thoughts. *Please pick up, Mummy.*

"Hi," Holly said. Loud voices echoed in the background, intermingled with a constant fire-alarm-like wailing sound.

"It's me and Sam," I said, loudly. "Can we talk to Casey?"

"Uh, she can't talk right now," Holly said.

I felt Sam stiffen in my lap. "It's okay," I whispered to him. "Why not, Holly?"

"Well — good news — bad news if she wasn't in the EMU, but good news here. She just had a second seizure." Holly sounded distracted. "Like, *just* now. All the nurses are in here. Dr. Alem was stopping by when it started, so he got to see it. It was pretty big — "

"Fantastic," I said, cutting her off before she could go into detail with Sam listening. "That *is* good news." I smiled at Sam, who sat with his brow creased and his mouth tightly closed, back to his stoic self. "It's good news, Sammy," I repeated. "We've been waiting for this. It means Mummy is closer to coming home now." The fire-alarm sound stopped, but numerous voices remained in the background.

"Just a sec," Holly said. I could hear her muffled voice on the other side of the phone intermingled with the voice of a person that I recognized from the videos Casey and I so diligently watched. "You still there? Putting you on speaker."

"This is Dr. Alem," the familiar voice said. Sam sat up straighter in my lap. He had been around enough doctors in various ERs to know that we expected him to sit straight and still when one was around.

"He can't see you, Sammy," I whispered to him. "Just relax." He collapsed into my chest, nuzzling his head under my chin.

Dr. Alem explained that the recording of this second seizure gave them enough information to discuss Casey's case at the department meeting Monday morning. "She can go back on her medication now," he said. "We'll know what the next options will be Monday and can talk more then. Until then, rest," he said, presumably to Casey. Holly and I thanked him.

"It was quite a seizure," Holly said quietly, taking us off speaker phone. "And you won't believe what the final trigger was. *Harold* called her this morning. That's the *third* time since she's been in the EMU. And on a *Saturday—*"

"Can't wait to hear about it later," I interrupted in a false-cheery voice, as I watched Sam's face tighten again. "Have her call us when she's ready."

"I love you, Mommy!" Sam suddenly shouted.

We stared at each other after hanging up. "We should celebrate, don't you think?" I said, feeling hopeful again after several bleak days. "Let's tell Nana."

Sam jumped out of my lap and threw open the door to his room, shouting for Nana. "Quietly," I said in a stage whisper. "Remember Sadie." I stayed on the carpet, picking at the loops of fabric and staring out the window at the blue winter sky, crisp and cloudless. Sam spoke in excited tones, and Ellen responded in a quiet but upbeat voice. My body felt lighter than it had in weeks, months even, and I tipped my head back against the soft comforter that covered the lower bunk. One more step done. One step closer to the end, to Casey's return, to the return of our life.

CHAPTER 17

Casey

I lay in the hotel bed, moving my arms and legs as if making a snow angel against the smooth white sheets, enjoying the size of the mattress, the reassuring weight of the blanket, so different from the bed at the hospital. Gray, dry glue from where my electrodes had been littered the area around my head and shoulders. The glue proved more difficult to get off than expected: even after two showers remnants of the flakes remained on my scalp, shedding onto my shoulders as I moved.

Yesterday, Dr. Alem said that the department needed more information before deciding if I was a surgical candidate, and that meant SEEG testing. He came with the neurosurgeon, Dr. Hernandez, a woman with thick, dark hair, and she explained the SEEG procedure that I already researched during the EMU lonely nights: fifteen holes drilled into my scalp at predetermined places decided by the St. Lutheran's neurosurgery department and Dr. Alem. I'd been released from the EMU and scheduled for SEEG implant surgery tomorrow morning. Then more seizures, more EMU time, and brain mapping, whatever that was.

But for now, with one day free from the EMU, I alternated between naps and television. Before I fell asleep around noon, Holly left for the business center in the lobby, and said she would return around four with pizza. I glanced at the clock. Three p.m. Time to work. I sighed as I grabbed my laptop case from the floor and slid the computer out.

Scanning work emails, I didn't notice anything too urgent. A few from Doug Randall, the first few asking, the more recent ones demanding me to call him. He must be displeased with the documents I'd produced before I left. *Well, he can wait.* I smiled as I imagined him seething in his office, already angry that this case had progressed as far as it had.

Holly came in, holding a large pizza, some paper plates, and two beers. The smell of the cheese mixed with fresh dough was intoxicating.

"You okay?" she asked, putting the pizzas on the desk and pulling off her parka. She popped open a beer and handed it to me: the bottle was ice cold, and condensation dripped over my hand. "It's five o'clock somewhere," she said, raising her beer in a cheers. The smell of fresh hot pizza crust and pepperoni wafted through the air, filling every corner of the room as she opened the box. She slid a piece onto a paper plate and passed it to me.

I took a bite of the best food I'd eaten in over a week; the cheese slid down my chin, and I barely caught it with the plate.

"I have to call Harold," I said, wiping the grease from my face. "Need to do more damage control on the Kellan case." After taking a long swig of my beer, I put down my plate, and grabbed my phone from the nightstand. The picture on the home screen showed Sam and Sadie with their arms around each other, grinning mischievously the moment before they jumped into the pile of yellow, red, and brown leaves in front of them. As I stared at the image, I tried to remember how it felt to hold them, and yearned to wrap my arms around their small, soft bodies. I entered my passcode, and the picture disappeared, the sentiment dissolving as I pressed Harold's name. I leaned back against the padded headboard and stared at the ceiling. Holly turned away and tactfully pretended she wasn't listening.

He picked up on the second ring. "Are you out of the hospital?"

"Yes," I said. "For now."

"What do you mean '*for now*'?" His voice hardened. "You said two weeks. If you're out, aren't you coming back to Portland? It's two weeks this Friday."

"They need more information, so they're going to do more testing," I said, settling into the puffy hotel pillows, dusting away more flaking, leftover glue. "I'm going back tomorrow morning for an operation and to begin the second round of testing." I didn't have the energy to get into the medical details of the surgery, and I doubted Harold would care.

I was right.

"So, you won't be back this week?"

"No."

"Huh."

"Something wrong, Harold?"

"Kathy Kellan called yesterday," he said. "God, she's touchy."

"You *spoke* to her?" I sat up straight in the bed. "What did you say?"

"I essentially told her to calm down, stop being so hysterical—"

"You called her *hysterical*?"

"Well, she was crying. Something about being scared about depositions—"

"Oh my God." I shook my head in disbelief. Harold truly had a negative emotional intelligence level. "Harold, you aren't allowed to talk to her anymore. And before I go back into the hospital, I want to get a few things straight. The Kellan case. I know we went over this last week, but here it is again: Kristin and the others are not to have any contact with other attorneys on the case. Violet can direct any calls to my voicemail or my e-mail. And, Harold, if Kathy or any of the other women call, Violet can give them my cell phone number. If you want to keep this case—and I know you do—I'd advise you to not call Kathy Kellan or any of the other women 'hysterical' or upset them. I'm sure we're not the only firm happy to take this case, and Kathy at least knows that."

"If they call, I'm going to talk to them—" Harold began.

"No, you're *not*," I said with an energy I didn't know I had. "Do. Not. Talk. To. Them. Violet will give them my cell phone number. They'll feel special, they can call me, and I can talk them out of whatever they are upset about. This is *my* case, Harold. Leave it to me. If you mess this up, they will walk."

Silence on the other end of the phone, whether from the force of my words or the message, I didn't know and didn't care.

"I'll email Violet with instructions," I said, breaking the wall that had grown between us.

"Think you'll be back by Thanksgiving?" Harold asked.

I cringed, and tears came to my eyes. I'd thought of that. Thanksgiving was still almost three weeks away. I couldn't imagine being gone three more weeks, but with the difficulties I'd had in the EMU last week making seizures come, I didn't know.

"I think so."

"Good," Harold said. "I do have to plan. And one more thing."

Oh, this should be good.

"About last week. You may be a senior associate, and this may be 2016, but I don't accept cursing from my lawyers."

There were so many ways to answer. 'I'm sorry.' 'It won't happen again.' 'Please forgive me, Harold.' But that Casey was gone.

"Harold, just to refresh your memory from last week, you called *me* in the middle of a hospital stay *three times*, and — give me a break — I may be an associate by name, but by this point, we both know that it's only a formality reserved for business cards." *Also, fuck you.*

Holly had swiveled her chair around, her eyebrows raised, a half-smile on her lips, amused by my tirade.

I could feel my brain asking for a rest, demanding it, letting me know that it was not quite ready to jump into the world of litigation and office politics just a few hours after being let out of the EMU: I was a computer almost drained of battery, running out of energy, a car low on gas. My head started throbbing; time to end the call, my brain said, and I felt it closing up. "I'll keep you updated on how things are going here." *Just what he wants.*

I looked over at Holly, who was now leaning back in the chair, wide-eyed and suppressing a smile; she seemed the picture of angelic innocence. "So, how'd it go?"

"You heard." I said, unsure of how to follow up the sentence. *I'm going to leave the firm. I'm done with Harold. I want to litigate on my own terms, with my own cases.* There were too many thoughts swirling in my mind, but one came to the forefront—an immediate practicality. "Look, Holly, we both know that I'm going to be here for a while longer than we thought."

Holly moved over to my bed and lay next to me, flicking away some of the remaining gray glue-dust on a pillow. "I've already extended our stay in the hotel until the end of the month," she said. "In this place people stay for, like, six weeks sometimes, and they had an extended-stay rate. The front desk people were so nice about it, I—"

Looking over at her, guilt rushed into my body like a pound of wet cement. "Holly, you don't have to stay with me. I'm sure Rob misses you, and you probably miss him, and—"

"I'm staying," she said firmly, turning to meet my eyes with the glare that I had seen for decades when she was determined to do something, be it score an 'A' on a chemistry test, win a soccer game with a penalty shot, or get a job. That look meant that her mind was made up, and she was not taking no for an answer. "I told you that I would stay with you as long as you needed—"

"Which we *thought* was fourteen days."

Twisting her body towards mine, she leaned on her arm and softened her tone. "Casey Louise Scott, I'm staying until they get those probe things out of your head, and we figure out what to do next. Rob and I FaceTime at night. He's fine. You, my friend, are stuck with me." She picked a piece of glue off my shoulder, flicked it away, and we watched it flutter to the carpeted floor. "But you should probably shower again. Leave the conditioner in and I'll try to comb this shit out."

I leaned back on the pillows, more of the electrode glue dust falling around my head. "Okay," I said, feeling relief, comfort, and support. My partner in crime since the sixth grade could stay.

The surgical center sat two blocks from the main hospital building, four long, snow-covered blocks from the hotel. With my surgery check-in scheduled for 5 a.m., walking in the dark with the freezing wind and ice pelting our faces was out of the question, so we used the hotel's shuttle. When the large van pulled up to the squat, gray building, we rushed inside through sliding glass doors and checked in at the front desk. The woman behind the counter gave Holly a small pager that she said would beep anywhere on campus when my surgery was over. Directed to the second floor, we hurried up the stairs to a waiting area where people sat quietly in small, gray chairs throughout the large room. We found seats, and Holly put her hand on my thigh. I laced my shaking fingers over her steady ones.

"Casey Scott?" A tall nurse in blue scrubs called my name.

With a deep breath, I stood and hugged Holly. "See you soon," I whispered into her hair.

"See you soon."

I followed the nurse through a short, tan hallway until she stopped at a door on her left and ran her badge over a black square next to it. I heard a click, and she opened the door into a large room where thin beige curtains separated patients from each other, providing some privacy, but very little. Men and women in various colored scrubs bustled up and down the lanes in between the make-shift rooms, entering with cheery voices while introducing themselves to people they would soon either drug into unconsciousness or cut open.

The nurse slid a curtain to the side, revealing an area with a small bed, covered in a tan sheet, a monitor for heart rate and oxygen, and a shoulder-high laptop. A see-through plastic bag with white string at the top lay on the bed next to a thin blue robe.

"Change into that," she said, pointing to the robe. "Everything off. The bag is for your clothes."

"And they'll bring my bag of clothes in the OR?" I asked, grasping for any details about my belongings from outside the hospital to normalize the situation.

"They'll be in your room when you're done with surgery," she said, a tinge of impatience in her tone. "The tech will be in to insert your IV soon, and then you'll see the anesthesiologist and the surgeon." She tugged the curtain closed, and I listened to her clogs thump down the hall.

As I held the plastic bag limp in my hand, I felt reluctant to undress, to replace my jeans, shirt and sweater with that thin piece of cloth on the small bed. Slowly removing my shirt, my skin erupted with goosebumps. I pulled off my sneakers, socks, jeans, underwear, and slipped on the dress-like garment that tied around my waist. The bed looked somewhat soft, and I sat hunched over, trying not to shiver while I waited for the next step.

"Knock, knock," said a female voice, opening the curtain simultaneously. A woman with short brown hair and large eyes rimmed with thick eyelashes approached with a smile. "I'm Dr. Morgan," she said. "I'll be your anesthesiologist." She noticed my curled-over position. "Didn't anyone offer you a heated blanket?"

"No."

She left, returning with two thick white blankets. Their warmth permeated my body, and I lay back on the bed, its top part raised, as she tucked the blankets around my torso, feet and legs.

"Knock, knock," said a male voice, opening the curtain. Dr. Morgan looked over at the man in green scrubs and nodded in welcome. "I'm here to place your IV."

I sighed, knowing what this could or could not entail. Dr. Morgan noticed my tension.

"He's good," she said, as the tech started studying my hands and arms, looking for a vein. "I have a few questions about any history with anesthesia."

The interview was quick, the IV tech was, as promised, good, and soon Dr. Hernandez came into the room. Pulling up a stool to the side of my bed, she laid her hand on top of the blanket that covered my forearm.

"Today should go smoothly," she said. "I wanted to make sure that you knew that we have to shave part of your head to put in the SEEG probes."

"No, I didn't know that," I said, suddenly more tense than when I entered the building. "How much?"

She squeezed my arm gently. "About half."

My stomach clenched as if someone had punched me. "Excuse me?"

"We need a clean slate to place the SEEG probes," she explained. "So, we'll need to shave about half your hair off."

"Oh," I said softly. "Well, there's nothing I can do about it now, I suppose." I wanted to ask how long it would take to grow back, to bargain for just a few areas to be shaved. But vanity wouldn't get rid of seizures, I realized, and the words died in my throat. Jonah would love me with or without hair. And Sam and Sadie... in a year or two, they wouldn't even remember this uneven hairdo.

"Are you ready?" Dr. Hernandez asked. "I'm going to walk with you to the OR."

Ready? For holes to be drilled in my skull? For half my head to be shaved while I lay in a drug-induced sleep? I didn't know the answer to those questions, but the one thing I knew was that I was working towards getting my life back. I was ready for that. "Yes. Let's go."

A man in blue scrubs put the sides up on the bed and rolled it down the hall. The blankets began to lose their heat, and I tucked them tightly under my chin to retain the fleeting warmth. Dr. Hernandez walked with her hand on the left rail as we moved deeper and deeper into the bowels of the surgical center, passing ORs on our left and right. Finally, we stopped at a large metal door. The man pushed it open with his back and pulled me in.

"I'll be right back," Dr. Hernandez said, leaving me in a gray room with bright lights and a thin metal table that looked much less comfortable than the bed I was currently riding. Several people in surgical masks and caps stood close to the table, some others busy in different areas of the room. I recognized Dr. Morgan behind her surgical mask and cap, and found her eyes comforting in this sterile environment. The man in blue scrubs removed the now-lukewarm blankets. I shivered.

"Why is it so cold in here?" I asked.

"ORs are generally cold," Dr. Morgan answered without expounding. "Let's move her." She counted to three, and I was pushed and pulled from one flat surface to another. "Lay back, Casey."

I tried to relax on the hard surface, squirming to get comfortable, while various people arranged me under a bright circular light. Dr. Morgan busied herself filling vials with clear liquids from different containers, placing each carefully on a tall metallic table.

Turning back to me, she connected one vial to my IV. "This may feel warm for a second." As she pushed the liquid into the IV, I felt the promised warmth course through my veins and, gazing into the reassuring brown eyes of my anesthesiologist, fell asleep.

CHAPTER 18

Jonah

I paced around the house like a caged tiger. Ellen recognized my stress — my worry about Casey's surgery — and took over the morning rush. At 7 a.m. in Portland, 10 a.m. in Cleveland, Casey was already in the OR.

We spoke last night, and I woke up to a text from my wife that said *"I love you. I will talk to you later today. Wish me luck!!"* and a text from Holly saying, *"She's in the pre-op area. Doctors say it'll be about a 4 hour surgery. They'll call me when she's out."* I felt sick with nerves as I read Holly's text again and again. Casey was in. During her most important, and, in my opinion, most dangerous, hospital time so far, I was not there. And so many things could go wrong in that OR.

"Get your shoes on!" I yelled at Sam, who dawdled by the front door. His mouth shook, and he blinked back tears as he pulled on his yellow Velcro sneakers. I could not find it in me to apologize and walked away, hearing Ellen's voice comforting him, trying to explain my mood without giving details. Even with Ellen's help, I was starting to crack.

"Daddy's just a little stressed today," she said. "Let me help you with those..." The rest of the sentence was buried beneath Sam's sobbing.

I turned around to see Sam's face hidden in the side of Ellen's neck and Sadie standing, dumbstruck, next to them.

"I have shoes on, Daddy," she said, pointing to her feet. "No more yelling about shoes!"

"Get in the car," I said slowly, almost shaking with anger that was really stress manifesting itself in the worst way.

"Jonah, you go to work," Ellen said gently. "I'll take them."

"Just get them in the car," I snapped at her, and stormed out of the house. I heard Ellen grab jackets and hats that the kids for once did not fight when asked to don. The drive to daycare was quiet and tense: Sadie sat stock-still and barely seemed to breathe; Sam sniffled a bit and occasionally wiped away a remaining tear.

"I'm sorry, Daddy," he said, as I pulled him down the brightly colored hallway to his classroom. "I didn't mean to be bad. I'll be better next time."

I stopped in the middle of the hallway and looked down at him; his young eyes seemed so earnest and sincere. Taking a breath, I rubbed his head. "It's not you, Sammy. I'm just—" *Worried? Stressed? Angry that your mum has to be gone? All the above?* "I'm sorry. I shouldn't have acted like that. I love you very much. And you're a wonderful boy, you know."

He opened the door, currently covered with a floor-to-ceiling paper turkey, and smiled at me while waving goodbye. I forced a smile, hoping to leave him with the feeling that everything was just fine. My white-knuckled grip on the steering wheel and clenched jaw as I drove to work under metallic gray clouds and over brown river water reinforced the knowledge that it was not.

Arriving at G&H, I hurried up the stairs to my office and closed the door to call Holly.

"Hey," she answered on the first ring.

"So? Any news?"

"Nothing new. She's in. Been in for a few hours. You know, St. Lutheran's really has this surgery thing down. Instead of just waiting in a room in the hospital with uncomfortable chairs and no internet for hours on end, they give you a pager, take your cell number, and the pager goes off when she's done and you can come back to the surgical center to be with her. You can't leave the campus, but, Jonah, you should see this place. It's huge. Anyway, I'm in a lobby area in the main building doing some work while she's in there. I mean, four hours—I might as well."

My silence was audible.

"Jonah, she's going to be fine. You should see these doctors. The neurosurgeon trained in Spain, France, *and* here. She's brilliant, like, literally a genius. Trust me. Casey and I stalked her on the internet. You—" she paused. "You—are you okay?"

I had known Holly since Casey and I first started dating, always known the bond between them: sister-like, something so rare that I almost envied it. But only almost. And now, as Casey lay unconscious in a sterile room where doctors took control of her brain, deciding where to place probes in her cerebrum, I was thankful for their bond.

"Thank you, Holly," I said, my voice filled with anguish. "Thank you for taking care of her." I realized at that moment that, with Holly by her side, Casey, the woman I loved most in the world, would have the comfort she needed on this journey.

Holly cleared her throat. "Jonah, you know I would do anything for her."

"I know."

"I mean, we've been there for each other for decades. Especially this decade." Her voice finally broke, and I knew she was thinking about the miscarriages, the IVF, the over-lengthy, expensive adoption procedure. The final decision to move on. Casey had told me. "I mean, in life there are always problems, but they don't tell you that as you grow up, the problems become more significant, bigger. When you're a kid, you just want to be older, but no one ever tells you of the darker side of getting older. You just see the shimmering lights, the freedom. But, it's not just that, is it?"

I shook my head; an answer she could not see.

"No," I said. "It's not."

"I'll call you when she's out," Holly said, regaining the self-control that she usually displayed.

We hung up, and I reviewed the schedule for the day. Team meeting in five minutes with a B of A pitch to review, J.Crew's newest campaign to unveil at one, and Portland Airbnb ads to finalize. *Then I'll check in with Holly again. Or hopefully she'll have texted me.* None of the team knew that Casey was having surgery today: I kept my work life and home life separate. Very separate, as if I was two different people. But today they intertwined, and Casey's brain surgery made all the G&H work seem trivial, almost not worth doing.

A knock on the door brought me back to the present. Jonathan smiled as he walked into my office.

"Bad time?" he asked.

"I have a team meeting in a few minutes," I said, smiling back, "but always time for you."

"What room?"

"St. Johns."

"Let's walk together."

"Of course." Hiding my nerves, I gathered my laptop, and we navigated through the building, making sharp turns around wooden walls that matched the lobby, passing glass doors and windows to each conference room and office.

"How's it going?" Jonathan asked cheerily.

"Fine," I said. *My wife is currently having probes put in her brain in Ohio, and I yelled at my children this morning like a madman, but — other than that — swimmingly.* "You?"

"Oh, good," he said. "Same as always. Busy, busy. And this Kevin retirement. It's hard to determine the right replacement." He stopped walking and faced me. "There are a lot of things to consider. Have you thought about what we discussed in the interview?"

Scrutinizing his face, I tried to think of an appropriate response. Today, I realized, I was completely off my game. There could not have been a worse time for this conversation.

"Jonah? Did you hear me?" Jonathan looked confused.

"Yes, sorry—I did. I'm just a little distracted today." This, I knew, was not the answer to give someone trying to decide whether to hand you a serious promotion based on your assumed promise to dedicate evenings and weekends, your life, really, to his company, but maybe today was the day to mix work and home. "Casey's in Ohio, having some surgery. She's in the OR right now. We're trying to get control of her epilepsy, and it's just—it's…" I took a breath. "It's a stressful day on the home front, you know."

Jonathan put his hand on my shoulder. "I get it. You should take the day off—"

"No," I said firmly. "There's too much to do here."

"Dwayne can handle it."

Oh, that's just *what I want.* "No, I don't think he can. But thanks for the offer."

He seemed pleased with my answer, not realizing that I needed work to keep me sane today, and that this was not an indication of my answer to his question of dedication to the company through more face time.

"Well, I just wanted to let you know that it's down to you and another candidate. There are a lot of things to consider."

"I'm sure." We arrived at the St John's conference room. "I hope we can talk more about it at the next interview," I said, my hand on the doorknob.

"Definitely. We'll see you this afternoon." He smiled again. "I hope everything goes well with Katie."

It took all my restraint to walk into the conference room without grabbing Jonathan around the neck and throwing him to the ground. *Casey, not Katie.* Maybe I had kept my life a little too separate. And what was this afternoon? I pulled out my phone and looked at my emails. I had missed one from last night, too exhausted after putting the children to bed to do my normal late-night check.

RE: *Second Interview*

Dear Jonah,

We are delighted to extend you an invitation to the final round of interviews. Yours is scheduled for tomorrow, November 10 at 4 p.m. in the Tilikum Room.

Sincerely,

Lynn Foster
Head of HR
Grossman & Howe

Rolling my eyes, I shoved the device back in my pocket and opened the door to the room. The team assembled around the table fell silent as I entered.

"What?" I snapped. "Let's get going, then." I may have been the only one who was five minutes late, but I knew I was also the only one whose wife was in an OR 3,000 miles away at the moment. "We have a lot to do and not a lot of time."

·   ·   ·

The neurosurgeon said that it all went well, Holly texted. *Going in to see Casey in a minute.*

I reread the text again and again. It all went well. Good news to bring home. Vague news, but good news, compared to the alternative. *Went well.* Something to tell Ellen, to tell the children. "Mummy's surgery 'went well.'"

Armed with this knowledge, I walked slowly to the Tilikum Room at 3:55. I knew who the other candidate was, everyone knew who it was: Dwayne. I did not really care; this was not about competition anymore. I had my angle, my personal pitch. It was good, and I was going to sell it.

I knocked on the door, smiling in my confidence. After we shook hands and the pleasantries were over, we got down to business.

"Like we said in the last interview," Jacob began, "you're an asset to G&H. What's holding us back from just handing this to you is concern about your dedication and willingness to put in the time at the office, to lead by example."

"I heard your concerns about my time commitment at G&H, and I want you to know that as Director of Marketing, I won't fail you. Yes, I'm a family man, but in this day and age, that doesn't mean you can't be as devoted to a company as someone who stays until eight, nine, ten, and comes in on weekends. It's *because* I have a family that I get things done quicker, better, and smarter than anyone else—look at what I do in eight hours at the office compared to what some other people do in twelve. The same amount of work, the same quality— better, in fact—but more efficiently. And I'll show the people I lead how to do the same—how to work quicker, better, and smarter. Good leadership is about inspiration and results. I've shown that I can inspire and lead, and I've shown that I can get results. *And* I've done it in a way that truly embodies the G&H work/life balance."

I stopped and smiled. How's *that* for a pitch? I wanted to tell Casey, to tell *someone*. To hear someone outside of this room say, "That's brilliant, Jonah. Well done."

But Jonathan and Jacob received the message stone-faced, and I realized that I had just tried to convince two workaholic men over the age of sixty the idea that you did not have to be in the office to work. I realized too late that my angle was the equivalent of trying to sell an Adidas shoe to the CEO of Nike.

"Thanks for coming in, Jonah," Jonathan said without any emotion, rising to shake my hand. "We'll let you know."

I screamed in the car on the way home, trying to let out all my fury before I saw my family, to avoid taking it out on them.

CHAPTER 19

Casey

This time, the seizures came fast and furious — two, both the day after the surgery: the world going black, coming back into focus with my body aching, my head pounding, leaving me crying, wishing for Jonah, whispering Sam and Sadie's names while Holly stood next to me and rubbed my shoulder, telling me everything was okay.

"Your brain is more vulnerable right now, more susceptible to changes in medication, in sleep patterns," Dr. Alem explained during his visit that evening. "The seizure recordings are complete." He seemed almost ecstatic. "Tomorrow we will begin brain mapping."

I watched him through my half-closed eyes, silently envying his health, his ability to move freely from room to room, to think such complicated thoughts, unaware that he was doing it. The thick bandage wrapped tightly around my head had slipped slightly to the right during the second seizure, and I could feel prickles on my left side where long, soft hair had been hours before.

"You're back on your normal dose of meds now," Dr. Alem said. "You should feel better in the morning." Pulling a chair close to me, he patted my arm. "This is the home stretch, Casey. You've been so strong, so brave. Tomorrow we will get the final information, and then we will know our options." His large hand moved to my sore, bruised, IV-abused one, currently having a break from needles as the veins healed from overuse. The weight of his hand and thick fingers folding over the back of mine comforted me.

"Just stay brave for a few more days," he said before he left.

I was back in the same room that I occupied during my previous stay, which was encouraging in a way: a bit like coming back to an old bedroom in the house you grew up in, if that house made you anxious and sad, and was actually a hospital. But I'd asked for this room because of the view, and luckily it was available. I peeked in other rooms when I first came to the EMU, and again when I left: most just had a view of the side of another building, and there wasn't much one could do with that for hours on end. This room had a view of a large lawn with a sidewalk going from the main building to a parking garage. The outlook provided a small amount of entertainment because every morning before Holly arrived and every evening after she left, I watched the migration of workers changing shifts. The crowd came for the day shift at around 7 a.m., leaving close to 7 p.m., with a new, smaller replacement crew coming to work through the night. During the day, I could watch people coming and going, and had invented several games: Male or Female, Count the Pink Parkas, Match the People Arriving and Leaving. It kept me busy in the slow times, and was less depressing than staring at a brick wall.

After Holly left for the night, I watched the evening shift appear in the waning, pale sunlight. *One, two pink parkas, none of them Holly's, and another that could almost be called pink, but is really more red.* My mind wandered to the office, to the Kellan case. Kathy was out of prison, but the other three women were still in there, and I wondered what they did to pass the time. Cards, maybe. I knew the general layout of the prison from other cases: the common areas, the attorney/client rooms, the location of the supervisors' offices, the shop area, and the grounds. The lack of privacy in that complex overwhelmed me. When I got back to the office, I would hit the ground running, defending those women with everything I had — that was my plan. At least for now. With depositions in the middle of January, four women to prepare, and

Doug Randall frothing at the mouth to soothe his bruised ego from the loss of the hearing last month, I had to be ready. I would be ready.

Another pink parka made an appearance: three. *What a strange color to be so popular.* In the fading light, all the coats moving across the lawn began to look black. I leaned back in my bed, adjusting the dense wrapping around my skull. My constant headache still needed oxycodone, and I pushed the nurse call button to ask for another dose.

Glenda came bustling into the room. For a second, I felt envious of her long hair, the same length on both sides.

"Feeling better?" she asked. She passed me a small paper cup with the pills and a plastic cup of water.

"Getting there." Moving my bed into position with that familiar whir, I curled up on my right side, away from the holes in my skull, and waited for the medication to dull the ongoing pain.

•   •   •

In the morning, Dr. Alem arrived with a short, mousey-looking woman named Natalie, whom he introduced as the Fellow working on my case, and a man named Jeff, the tech who would work the SEEG machine. They settled on hard plastic chairs, and stared at me, as I sat in my partially- raised bed, my half-shaved head still wrapped tight in layers of surgical bandages. Holly had moved her chair to the corner of the room, turned off her laptop, and silenced her phone. Tension filled my body, and I tried to sit up a little straighter, adjusting the angle of the bed, pulling nervously at my V-neck.

"Now, Casey," said Dr. Alem, "today we're going to stimulate some electrodes and see what happens. We may get through them all today, we may not. For some of them, I don't expect much to occur. For others, you may find that certain things do occur. We'll see. The goal of brain mapping is to find out what areas in your brain control speech, motor skills, and what area may provoke a seizure."

I clenched my jaw. *Another seizure today?*

"We're going to start the stimulation for each electrode on the lowest level, and we'll slowly keep increasing stimulation until either something happens or the stimulation becomes uncomfortable for you, whichever is first."

My heart beat faster. I hadn't considered the possibility that the testing could be painful.

"Are you ready to begin?" he asked.

"Yes." *No.*

Everyone in the room looked very serious: even Dr. Alem didn't smile or make a joke. He sat back in his chair and glanced at the paper in his hands. Natalie leaned forward, grasping her clipboard and a pen, her pallid face eager.

The SEEG machine resembled a large black computer with holes in the side. The wires from my probes plugged into the holes, each location carefully reviewed for accuracy by Jeff, Natalie, and Dr. Alem.

Dr. Alem turned to Jeff. "N15, level 1."

Jeff pressed a button on the machine. I braced myself for an uncomfortable twinge or shock, but none came.

"Do you feel anything?" Dr. Alem asked.

"No," I said. "Should I?"

"Not necessarily. Okay. N15, level 2."

Jeff pressed a button again, and again the doctors stared at me: I felt like an animal in a zoo or the circus with spectators that had paid good money expecting a show I wasn't providing.

"Now?" asked Dr. Alem.

"No. I don't feel anything." I almost followed up with *I'm sorry*, but just shrugged my shoulders and glanced at Natalie. She gave a tight, close-mouthed smile.

"N15, level 3," said Dr. Alem.

The left side of my brain vibrated-not an unpleasant sensation, but something I knew wasn't normal.

"Stop that," I said. The words came without thinking, and I pulled at my bandages, trying to get rid of the vibration.

It stopped.

"What did you feel?" asked Dr. Alem.

"A vibration in my brain, back here." I gestured to the back of my skull. "I didn't like it," I added, and blushed as I realized how child-like that sounded.

Natalie took rapid notes, and Dr. Alem looked pleased.

"Good," he said. "Let's move on. N14, level 1. Casey, please point to the window with your right arm."

I pointed to the window as Jeff pressed another button.

"Okay. N14, level 2," said Dr. Alem. "Point to the window, Casey."

This is silly. Then, trying to point to the window, my right arm would not lift.

"What? Why won't my arm move?" I looked at Dr. Alem with wide eyes. My arm lifted. Shaken, I kept looking at Dr. Alem, rubbing my arm to make sure it could feel, stretching out my fingers and massaging my hand. "What happened? Why wouldn't my arm move?" I asked louder.

Natalie hunched over her clipboard, taking copious notes. I wanted to rip the entire thing — clipboard, paper, pen — from her arms and throw it against the wall. *Tell me what is going on!*

"That electrode is evidently connected to the motor skills area of your brain," explained Dr. Alem, his tone even and calm. "Now we know at least one area that would be inoperable. Would you like to take a break?"

I stared at my right hand, moving my fingers one by one. I hadn't expected that this testing would entail shutting off parts of my brain, piece by piece, or what that meant. I hadn't realized the potential severity of the surgery I was hoping for: one wrong cut, and I could lose the ability to move my limbs forever. "No. Let's continue."

As they worked their way around my brain, I became accustomed to the small tingling when the electrode was stimulated too high, and stopped them each time I felt the vibration.

Dr. Alem passed me a book sitting on the counter next to the sink behind him and asked me to read it out loud. "N7, level 1," he said.

Looking at the book, the pages were blank. *That's strange. Why would he have a book of blank pages? This must be a trick book.* Then, words simultaneously appeared on the blank pages in my lap, emerging together as if all written at the same time.

"How did you do that?" I demanded, confused, alarmed, afraid. "Have those words always been there?"

"What did you see?" asked Dr. Alem.

"The pages were blank when I first looked down, and then..." I trailed off, realizing how ridiculous I must sound.

"And then?"

"Then, the words appeared. But they couldn't have, could they?" Scrutinizing the face of every person in the room, I searched for an explanation. "Could they? How?"

"We found another part of your brain that would be inoperable," said Dr. Alem, nonplussed by this information.

I passed the book back to him silently.

Natalie leaned over and whispered in Dr. Alem's ear, who nodded and frowned at her words. I glanced at Holly; she smiled reassuringly.

Natalie returned to her paper, pen, and clipboard. Dr. Alem looked at me, and shifted in his chair.

"Here we go. N8, level 1. Casey, what is this?" He held up a pen.

"A pen."

"Good. N8, level 2. Casey, what is this?" He held up the pen again.

A pen, I tried to say, but my mouth wouldn't make the words, my vocal cords didn't move: they didn't receive a message from my brain that they should. Fear flushed through my body like a flood; a panic greater than I'd ever felt. *A pen! A pen! A pen!* I thought wildly. "Pen!" I finally shouted. "Pen! Pen!" Shaking from adrenaline, I wrapped my arms around my torso, and rocked back and forth, staring at my lap. "It was a pen."

Holly came over and rubbed my back.

"We found your speech area," said Dr. Alem.

"Yes, you did." I giggled uncontrollably, a sound which quickly turned into hysterical laughter. "You did." Still shaking, the mad laughter morphed into huge, wracking sobs, and I sucked in air with deep breaths between my tears. "That was so scary," I muttered over and over, continuing to rock back and forth, my arms clutched tightly now across my chest. "So scary, so scary. It's like torture, this. Just like..."

Holly pulled her chair over to the bed, and put both arms around me while I continued to weep desperately. "So scary, so scary," was all I could say, over and over and over.

"Let's take a break now," Dr. Alem said, gesturing to Natalie and Jeff to follow him out of the room. "We'll come back in a bit to see if you are up to continuing today." They filed out of the room, talking in low tones.

I was left with my tears under the florescent light, Holly's arms wrapped around my rocking torso.

"I'll tell you that would have been fascinating if it hadn't been happening to you," she said, hugging me tighter.

I gave a watery smile through my ragged breaths. "Unfortunately, it *is* me," I said, wiping my face with the back of my hand, my body slowly calming in Holly's warm embrace.

•　　•　　•

When they returned, Dr. Alem assured me that most of the electrodes left would not have the same effects as the ones they had mapped out in the morning.

"I don't anticipate any more loss of speech or motor skills," he said, glancing at the paper in his lap. "But, we'll see."

I felt bitter from the morning's events, feeling that a little more detail of what to expect had been warranted. Had I known that my loss of speech was imminent and temporary, maybe I would have been able to react with reasonable laughter instead of losing myself in hysterical sobbing. The vague "finding the speech and motor areas" description hadn't prepared me for upcoming traumatic events — traumatic, really, because of their surprise and because I didn't know how long each event was going to last. Now, tense and angry, I sulked in my bed, acting immature and not caring.

"Let's get started," I said, quietly furious.

After testing N5, N4, N3, and N2, I felt worn down. The emotional rollercoaster of waiting to see what power each electrode held left me fragile and fatigued. I didn't want to be a lab rat anymore. I'd tired of people staring at me to see if my brain would do something awful when the tech pulsed extra electricity into it.

"Very good," said Dr. Alem at the uneventful end of N2. He looked down at the papers in his lap. "Let's see. Where were we…"

Natalie pointed to a spot on her clipboard, leaning over to share some secret information with him. He nodded slowly.

"This is the last one," Dr. Alem said. I felt the energy between the doctors shift, both suddenly very serious and tense, as if they expected some sort of terrible event. "N1, level 1."

A moment later, I knew why. The seizure struck quickly, my body instantly thrashing on the bed, out of my control. *Medicine*, I pleaded silently, as my head turned sharply to the right. *Give me the rescue meds.*

I could see Dr. Alem and Natalie now standing around my bed, and felt embarrassed as the seizure continued, like I was a sideshow freak in an old traveling carnival. Ten cents to see the girl with the brain that blows up! Anger replaced the embarrassment. *Stop staring at me. Medicine. I know you have it.*

The seizure subsided, and I lay in bed, twitching, limp, and panting, my eyes darting wildly around the room.

Dr. Alem and Natalie continued speaking to each other quietly, and I couldn't understand them. Holly crouched next to my bed, her hand on my shoulder, whispering in my ear, "It's okay, Casey. It'll be okay."

I tried to lift back to a sitting position, but failed. Moving my head to the side, I gazed at Holly, who continued to whisper reassurances, and stroked my arm.

Dr. Alem stood at the foot of the bed. "Casey, can you hear me?" he said loudly.

Yes. Yes. Just give me a second. Just a second. I nodded almost imperceptivity, but Dr. Alem seemed to notice.

"We're done, Casey." He squeezed my foot, his kindness returning with a smile. "Brain mapping is over. I'll come in later to check on you. Rest." Natalie and Jeff followed him like ducklings as he left the room.

Holly turned off the lights in the room, closed the curtains, and pulled up a chair next to my bed. "Sleep," she said. "I'll be right here."

I turned on my right side, facing the SEEG testing machine. *Stupid machine. I hate you.* I stared at the black rectangular contraption that had caused so much pain, pushing down an impulse to smash it on the floor. Squeezing my eyes shut, I curled up into a ball and prayed that when I opened them, I would be at home, and this would have all been a bad dream, a realistic nightmare: something that I could report quickly to Jonah before getting out of bed and starting my day. But, of course, as my headache and aching body reminded me, the nightmare was real—very real, indeed.

CHAPTER 20

Jonah

"It was terrifying, Jonah," Casey said. "Imagine if you just suddenly lost your power to speak, and didn't know why, didn't know if it was coming back, didn't expect it."

The lighting in her hospital room emphasized the bags under her eyes, the shadows of her cheekbones. The thick white bandages wrapped around her head contrasted with the brown wall behind her, making them stand out on the computer screen.

"I'm so sorry, darling," I said, putting the laptop on the dining room table. With dinner complete, and the children and Ellen watching a show on the telly in the guest room, Casey and I had a moment together. "It sounds terrifying."

She looked down and shook her head in response.

"You made it through, though."

She seemed far away in every way, withdrawn into a place where I could not comfort her, at least not how she needed. "What're you thinking, Case?"

"Just reminding myself that every minute that passes is a minute closer to getting home." She stared at the camera, and I saw the fight come back to her eyes. "Getting back to you and the kids."

As if on cue, Sadie's quick, small footsteps sounded on the stairs, and she burst into the room, wearing her pink-dotted pajamas, her eyes wide and happy.

"Mommy!" She ran over to the table, hopping on my lap with rabbit-like speed. When she looked at the screen, her mouth dropped open, and she turned her face away, burrowing into my sweater. "*Mommy?*" Her voice was muffled by the fabric.

Neither of the children had seen Casey since her surgery. Although I had described their mother's appearance, Sadie was too young to turn my words into the correct mental picture: Casey's new bandages were twice as thick as her previous ones, and there was no hair peeking out from the bottom. To a three-year-old used to her mother having long, dark hair, this woman on the screen probably seemed foreign and frightening.

"Hi, Sadie," Casey said, waving cheerily. "How are you, sweetheart?"

Sadie didn't answer.

"Sadie?"

I nudged Sadie. "Honey, it's okay. That's Mummy."

"Why does she have the hat?" Sadie whispered to me. "I don't like the hat." She kept her face away from the computer.

I heard Sam and Ellen coming downstairs: Sam's small voice continually talking, punctuated with Ellen's brief responses.

"Sadie, it's okay," Casey said. She touched her bandage-turban, so thick that it looked like the cap of a mushroom on her head, and patted it on the sides and the top. "Can I show you my hat?"

"Mommy!" Sam ran towards the dining room table at the sound of his mother's voice, as his sister had done. When he saw Casey's image on the screen, he stopped. Glancing at his sister, still buried in my lap, he seemed to assess the situation quickly. Ellen stood behind him, her hand on his shoulder.

"I don't like her hat, Sammy," Sadie said.

Sam's gaze moved between Sadie and his mother. He leaned closer to the screen to examine Casey's face and head.

"Look, Sammy," Casey said. "It's a really thick bandage. Like, lots and lots of them."

Sadie's face turned towards the screen, curiosity overcoming surprise and fear. Casey showed the children around the bandages that encompassed her head. "And they just kept wrapping the bandage around and around to keep the little electrodes in place," Casey explained. She poked at it, and Sadie smiled. "It's so thick, I can barely feel that."

"You going to wear it at home?" Sadie asked. Wrapping my arms around her soft body, I could feel her tension; whereas usually she was relaxed and pliable, she was now stiff, almost rigid.

"No, Sadie," Casey said. "The doctors will take it off before I get home. I promise."

Ellen leaned over my shoulder to get a closer look at the screen and her daughter's appearance. "How does it look underneath?" she asked.

This was an opening for a new discussion. We had not told the children about their mother's half-shaved head, mostly because we did not know what it actually looked like, so we were not sure how to describe it. If Sadie was this upset about the bandages, she would need some time to get used to Casey's new haircut.

"I'm not sure," Casey said. "But, guys," she spoke to the children, "I think that it'll look pretty different than when I left."

"How different?" Sam asked, picking nervously at his striped pajama shirt.

Casey moved her mouth from side to side, a sign that she was thinking about how to answer. "They shaved about half of it when they did the surgery."

The children's faces, wide-eyed and serious, reflected their feelings exactly.

"I'm sure it's going to look different, but still lovely," I said with false enthusiasm. "Lots of people have partially shaved heads. Especially in Portland."

"That's right," Ellen jumped in.

Sam seemed to force a smile. "I'm excited to see it, Mommy."

"Me too," Casey answered, laughing.

Sadie stayed quiet, but her body had relaxed since the tour of the bandage wrapping.

"Time for bed," Ellen said, pulling Sadie from my lap and taking Sam's hand. The children's voices faded into the background, and Casey and I were left alone again.

"Dr. Alem came back this evening," Casey said. "They're going to discuss my case Monday at their department meeting, and then we'll know for sure. No more brain mapping. He said that I'll get the electrodes out Monday afternoon, and then I can be released. So, just hanging out in the EMU over the weekend."

The end was in sight. We both knew there was no more testing they could do. Monday's conversation would tell us our options, not just Casey's, but as a family unit, where we could go from here. She would come back to Portland on Wednesday or Thursday, we decided. There was no mention of Harold or going back to work, but I was sure she had thought about it. Screens do not provide the best forum for debate, so I did not ask when she planned to go back to the office. *Just give us the weekend at least.* I could see her trying to get to the office the morning after she returned to please Harold, kissing the children goodbye, and hopping in her car. But maybe not. There would be time to talk about that later.

"I'm glad you made it through today, Case," I said. I heard Sadie calling for me, and could see Casey's energy fading. "I have to go."

Walking into Sadie's room, thoughts ran through my head like racehorses. *We're on the home stretch. There's an end date. Monday we'll know.* I knelt by Sadie's toddler bed, holding her little fingers. The pink seashell nightlight by the chest of drawers cast a soft glow around the room and on my daughter's face. Her eyes were wet.

"I didn't like the hat, Daddy," she whispered shakily. "Why the hat?"

"Mummy just needs it right now. It'll be gone soon." I picked Sadie up from bed, and took her over to the stuffed rocking chair in the corner of the room. Covering her with a fleece blanket, we rocked back and forth in the darkness until Sadie's even breathing told me that she slept.

CHAPTER 21

Casey

This was it: the final meeting. I waited anxiously, just like last Monday, for Dr. Alem and Dr. Hernandez to tell me my options. Or lack thereof. Today, these doctors would let me know how I could change my life, or if I had no options but to keep trying to survive. In a few minutes, I would know if Dr. Alem had the keys to my cage. Last night, I dreamed that Dr. Alem came in and said, "Ah ha! We found it! We can take out that part of your brain, no problems, and you won't ever have a seizure again!" I woke up in a sweat, realized that it had only been a dream, and broke down, sobbing angrily into the thin hospital pillow.

Thinking back to the beginning of this journey, I couldn't believe how naïve Jonah and I had been.

"It's only fourteen days," we'd said over and over. And we believed it. Then, there was the realization, at first unspoken, that it could be longer than just two weeks, and, finally, the discussion when we had both come to the understanding that I didn't know how long I was going to be in Cleveland. We'd stopped making deadlines, just coping day by day.

Watching the few parkas moving through the biting snow under the gunmetal gray sky, I remembered how I thought that the pre-surgical workup could be easy — in and out. I hadn't expected fifteen holes drilled into my skull; I hadn't expected leaving Cleveland with half of my head shaved; I hadn't expected finding it so hard to have a seizure in the hospital, my boss being the final nail in the coffin, the one missing trigger. And I hadn't expected losing the ability to speak, to move, to read — skills I'd taken for granted, that I assumed would always be available to me. It appeared that was not necessarily so.

Whatever Dr. Alem said today, I would get these electrodes out this afternoon and be discharged tomorrow. After resting in Cleveland until Thursday, Holly and I would fly home and resume our lives. Even if they could do surgery, they wanted my brain to recover first, Dr. Alem explained. The doctors had what they needed from me right now. It was time to go home.

Home. I told Harold earlier today that I would be back in Portland on Thursday, emphasizing again and again that my flight would only land around midnight, and I would need rest from traveling.

"Will you be in the office Friday?" he asked, as if he hadn't heard these words.

I was tempted to say yes. Pre-Cleveland Casey would have made such promises. But, my seizures had taken so much time away from the people I loved, I knew my new answer. I thought of the look on Jonah's face, my mom's face, the faces of Sam and Sadie, if I arrived late Thursday night and told them that I had to be at the office at 8 a.m. Sam and Sadie's expressions confused because they had waited for me, wanted to spend time with me, missed me as much as I missed them — so much that it physically hurt. My mom's expression of subtle disappointment that I would leave the family I hadn't seen in weeks for a man who caused me to have a seizure. And Jonah, shaking his head and turning his face away, the distance between us growing greater than the practical distance now. I gave the new Casey's answer.

"No, Harold. I'm going to take a few more days to get settled, recover. I have fifteen electrodes drilled through my skull as we speak, so I'm sure you understand that I need a few days. Probably next Monday or Tuesday."

"We may need someone to take over your caseload if you're going to need time to recover. I think that things are falling behind with you being gone for a whole week longer than you said originally — with me giving you two weeks already."

My heart rate rose as I watched the monitor next to my bed. "Harold, I get back on Thursday, then it's basically a weekend. Everything has been handled so far. I haven't heard from the Kellan women, Doug Randall's emails can wait until Monday, and every other case is in a good place. You don't need to have someone 'take over my caseload.' Give me a break."

He grunted, realizing his threat failed, and, as any rant couldn't bring electrodes out of my head sooner, there was nothing he could do.

"So, thank you for your understanding of my ordeal in this difficult time," I said, and hung up.

Holly doubled over in her chair next to my bed with silent laughter. "He's a sociopath," she said. "How you deal with him, I don't know."

"I don't know either." Staring out the window at the lawn below, I knew what I was going to do, and that Holly knew as well: I was going to leave Harold's firm. I would wait until after the Kellan case was done, but I was leaving. I'd toyed with the idea before, but since being in Cleveland, I'd officially decided. After the Kellan case, I was out.

This case, these women, had become my lifeblood at work, the reason I would continue to show up every day, the reason I stayed. I would use the firm's ample resources — the firm's money, space, everything I could — and avoid any arguments about whose case it was by staying through a settlement or the trial. My plan was simple, but required time. So, I would wait to tell Jonah. After I got home, I would tell him, but not immediately. I didn't want to start another argument about when I should leave the firm. I just wanted to go home to his embrace and support. I wanted his smell, his touch, his kiss. I wanted peace between us.

He hasn't talked about his work much. That means that either everything is fine or it's all a shit show and he doesn't want to tell me. I think it means it's all fine. We don't keep secrets like that. I realized that I hadn't even heard any comments about Dwayne Richards' behavior, which was a bit odd, but perhaps warranted in this situation. Dwayne Richards' petty actions were less important than the emotional scarring from brain mapping.

Aware that my time of watching life separated by glass was ending, I smiled. Tomorrow I would be on the other side of the window, one of the hundreds heading away from the hospital. Today, time ticked by as slowly as drops of sap from a maple tree.

Hearing a shuffle by the door, I glanced over at Holly. She walked quietly to the open door, and smiled as she came back.

"It's them," she said.

I called Jonah, putting him on speaker.

"They're here," I said in a loud whisper. "I think they're coming in just now." Leaning forward in bed, I caught sight of a flash of white coat in the corner of the doorway, heard a deep voice talking, and my stomach turned. Holly held my hand, her eyes anxious yet excited.

Dr. Alem and Dr. Hernandez strode into the room. Back to smiling as usual, Dr. Alem held a model of a brain in his hand.

"Good afternoon, Casey, Holly," he said.

"Jonah is on the phone," I said, pointing to the table. This meeting was already reminiscent of the meeting last week, which seemed like decades ago.

The doctors found chairs in the room and pulled them up to my bed.

"I'm sorry we're so late," said Dr. Alem. "We just got out of the department meeting. Your case took a while to discuss."

"Oh," I said. "Why?"

Dr. Alem grimaced before taking a breath. "Casey, your brain is the most difficult case that I have ever seen in my entire career."

I felt the air leave my lungs. *No, no, no. This is not how this conversation is supposed to start.*

"You see," he continued, "we can't pinpoint exactly where your seizures originate, as we see at least two sections — the frontal lobe and the parietal lobe—are so closely connected that it is difficult to determine which is leading the other." He gestured to the front of the brain and the left side of the brain as he spoke. "I feel that we can make a case for the frontal lobe being the leader, as when we stimulated it you had a seizure immediately, whereas, when we stimulated the parietal lobe, you didn't have a seizure. However, not all my colleagues agree. There were some that thought we shouldn't do anything—no surgery—and that we didn't have a definitive pacemaker."

I tried to digest this news without showing any emotion. Another meeting with a doctor where tears could come later; now was the time to be the woman who didn't cry, who stayed in control.

"What was the split?" I asked. *Please make it small. 80/20. 90/10.*

"About 50/50," said Dr. Alem. "But Dr. Hernandez and I were on the side of surgery, as was Natalie, who is very informed about your case. We think that looking at the seizure you had with the EEG testing, along with the results of the SEEG testing, we can make a strong case for the frontal lobe as the leader. Now, we can't operate on the parietal lobe—that might affect your ability to speak or read or write—but we *can* operate on the frontal lobe without many, or perhaps any, issues. The surgery that I'm suggesting, if you decide to do surgery, is a laser ablation. This is a surgery where we use a laser to destroy a small section of the frontal lobe that I believe starts the seizures. It's a minimally invasive surgery, and I'm recommending it instead of a resection because we can just take a small amount of tissue, and there won't be any cognitive deficit."

Looking down at my hands, I realized they were shaking, and I hid them under the blanket. *Just breathe, breathe.* "And, fifty percent of your colleagues thought this was a bad idea, why?"

"They were worried about potential cognitive deficits and weren't convinced that an ablation would help you. Some thought the parietal lobe was the pacemaker, but I don't agree." Dr. Alem sounded impatient with the idea.

For the first time since I arrived at St. Lutheran's and started making decisions about my testing and care, I didn't know what to do. I wanted someone else to decide for me, to tell me if I should burn out part of my brain or not. I stared at the doctors' faces, trying to see what they felt, but couldn't read them. Dr. Hernandez looked sympathetic as always, and Dr. Alem looked serious. I supposed that discussing the destruction of a part of one's brain was a conversation that required some gravity.

"I know that it's a lot," said Dr. Alem. "And you're welcome to go home, talk about it with Jonah, and call us when you decide. I know that it's not an easy decision to make."

"No," I said forcefully. "*No. I'm* not leaving here without a decision made." I could feel my brain getting tired, and knew that I couldn't maintain this level of thought for much longer. This wasn't a surprise: I hadn't slept properly in almost two weeks, had been on and off my medication, and currently had fifteen holes drilled into my skull. But, I knew that I didn't suffer to walk out of this room without a plan, without knowing how I was going to proceed in life, how I was going to fight these seizures. I felt strongly about that, rational or not. Digging into my pitiful energy reserves, I tried to focus.

"Dr. Alem and Dr. Hernandez," I said, staring at both of them with pleading eyes, praying for guidance, "if I was your daughter, your wife, what would you advise me to do? Would you advise me to have the ablation?" *Just tell me what to do and I will do it.*

"I would advise you to go through with the ablation," Dr. Hernandez said, nodding.

"I would as well," said Dr. Alem. "It's currently your only chance of being seizure free. And it's a good chance."

Seizure free: there was that term again. I didn't even ask Holly and Jonah for their votes; I knew what they would be.

"I'll do the ablation," I said. My brain relaxed, sensing that all the thinking and decision-making was done.

Dr. Alem smiled. "Good choice, Casey," he said. "I really believe it's our best option right now. You know, I have a patient who had an ablation, became seizure free, and he told me that it was like having music turned off in his head that he hadn't even known was on."

I processed this information: a quiet brain. I couldn't imagine what that would be like, but I knew that I wanted it. More than anything, I wanted to have the music shut off.

CHAPTER 22

Jonah

In the deep quiet of the evening, I opened my laptop and Face Timed Casey.

"Holly?" I said, as her face appeared. "Shouldn't you be at the hotel?"

"I couldn't leave her that early tonight. She's still a little groggy after the probe removal. She asked me to stay a bit. Want to talk to her?"

I nodded. Holly turned the screen around to show my wife. She looked tiny without the giant bandage wrap of the last few days, and, on the left side of her head, all her hair was gone.

"How are you, Case?" I asked.

"Ok. Tired. Ready to go home." Her words were slurred, as if she'd had one too many beers.

"You get to leave the hospital tomorrow. You're so close to being done."

"I know." Her eyes moved away from the screen, looking at something beyond. "I know. How're the kids?"

"Fine. We've made it through, your mum and I. I honestly don't know what I would have done without her. She's been brilliant. Did you know she said she'd stay through Thanksgiving?"

"Oh, thank God," Casey breathed. "I thought she was going to leave almost immediately, and I don't think that I'm going to be one hundred percent for a bit."

"Case, we could always just have hot dogs and chips for Thanksgiving dinner. And spend the day watching sports, like most of America."

"No one in my house is having hot dogs instead of turkey on Thanksgiving," Casey said firmly. She took a deep breath. "I'll talk to my mom about it when I get home."

The light drew attention to the shaved part of her head, and there were black sutures where the probes had been from the front to the back of the left side of her scalp. She caught me staring.

"Does it look awful?"

"No. Not at all."

"Liar."

"No, *really*. I mean, I'll need to see it closer, inspect in person, you know, but on screen it looks just like it's supposed to—the haircut of someone who just got out of brain surgery."

Casey laughed. "Well, that's good." She paused and her eyelids drooped. "I'm tired. Talk tomorrow after I'm discharged?"

"Yes, darling."

As I closed the laptop, I realized that we had done it. I could almost measure the end in hours. Seventy-two hours. Casey was coming home on Thursday.

Home on Thursday, I thought again as I turned off the light on my night table. I faced Casey's side of the bed and rubbed the empty sheet. "Come home," I whispered. "I need you here. Right here."

·　　·　　·

Waiting nervously in the meeting area of the Portland airport, I passed time pacing, counting the patterns on the trademark green carpet, and checking my watch against the computer screens that updated the flight information. Finally, almost at midnight, her flight arrived. Casey was back in Oregon.

At my first glimpse of her coming out past security, I barely recognized my wife: she wore a green head covering with pink flowers that encompassed the front of her hairline to her shoulders, hiding the shaved part of her scalp and the sutures, the result being that she resembled an Orthodox Jew. Holly told me that Casey was barely eating in the hospital, and she came to me gaunt and fragile-looking. When I hugged her, she felt breakable, like a tiny bird.

In the car, she and Holly chatted about the weather in Cleveland in the winter, and the kindness of Dr. Alem and Dr. Hernandez. Casey told light-hearted stories about getting drunk in the EMU and her interactions with the night nurses on duty.

She scratched at her head covering. "I'm going to take this off. It's a little itchy," she said, and gently maneuvered the fabric over her scalp and down what remained of her long hair.

The results in person were much more dramatic than on screen. The surgeon was not a hair stylist—all the hair on the left side, from the front to the middle of her scalp to the back of her left ear, was gone. In some areas, the shave was so close it looked like she had no hair at all. As she still had hair on the right side, she looked like two different people. A few strands fell over the shaved section, giving it less of a medical look and more of a fashion choice, but the sutures gave it away: fifteen little black knots dotted the left side of her head. Casey tried to hide the area with her hand.

"Don't," I said, pulling her hand down. I kept my eyes on the road and we zoomed down the almost-deserted highway in silence.

"Personally, I think it looks hot," Holly said, breaking the quiet tension. "And once you get those sutures out, Case, you'll blend right in with all the twenty-somethings who do that as an actual choice this year."

"What do you think the kids will say?" Casey asked. She had Face Timed with Sam and Sadie while wearing the head covering Holly bought her, but finally she took it off so that they could see what she would look like when she came home. Sadie immediately asked her to put it back on, and Sam asked her why she had spiders on her head, which, to be honest, was what the black sutures resembled.

"They're going to be so happy to see you, they'll get over it almost immediately," I answered, knowing that this was true.

We arrived home close to 1 a.m. Ellen sat on the sofa in the living room, waiting. Upon seeing her daughter, she cried, and the two sobbed into each other's shoulders as they came together in a hug. Exhausted, Casey dragged herself up the stairs; I followed with her suitcases, putting them down as she sat on our bed.

She patted the space next to her on our mattress. We held hands as she spoke about the darker side of Cleveland: the loneliness, the pain of the various needles, the sound of the wind and ice against her hospital room window, and never-ending hiss and release of the leg compressors—little things that compounded until, together, they created an enormous weight on her heart, and left her broken and splintered on the floor. She spoke evenly, recalling the events and details as facts, and I sat, listening in wonder to the woman I married, a person stronger than I ever could have imagined.

Eventually, she slid out of her clothes, and slipped under our covers. As she pushed herself against my body, I wrapped my arms around her waist and we fell asleep.

•　　•　　•

The pancake batter sizzled as it hit the hot pan. With the children sitting expectantly in their seats at the counter, Ellen leaning against the pantry door, still in her satin-flowered pajama top and bottom, with her mug of coffee, and me making breakfast, there was a sense of peace in the Scott household. Casey slept upstairs, but she was back, and the equilibrium restored.

"Who wants blueberries in their pancakes?" I asked the waiting crowd.

"Me!" the children trilled, shooting their hands into the air.

I heard noises from upstairs: steps moving across the floor, then water running down the pipes. "I think Mummy is awake," I said.

Sadie struggled to get out of her booster seat to no avail.

"Can we go see her?" Sam asked, smiling wider than he had in weeks.

"Let's let her come down," I said, sliding a pancake onto his plate. "She's had a long night."

Footsteps came slowly down the stairs, and when Casey turned towards the kitchen, the children screamed, unable to help themselves.

"Mommy!" Sam leaped from the kitchen stool and ran towards her. I unbuckled a wriggling Sadie from her booster seat, setting her loose on her mother. Casey crouched down to hug them, wearing a different head covering, this one purple with blue swirls that matched her light blue t-shirt.

"Mommy! Mommy! Mommy!" Sadie screamed, jumping up and down, her fuzzy nightgown bouncing around her ankles. "Daddy! Mommy's here!"

"That's right, sweetheart," Casey said, stroking her daughter's hair. She turned towards her son. "Hi, Sammy." A single tear ran down his plump cheek, and she wiped it away. "Sammy, darling. I'm here now. It's okay. I'm here," she whispered into his ear. "Everything is okay."

He nodded, and she kissed his cheek, wrapping her long arms around his small body in a tight squeeze. I could see that he had closed his eyes, and, smiling, returned his mother's embrace.

"Hi, Mom," she said, rising from the floor, and hugged Ellen. She walked over to the stovetop and wrapped her arms around me as I flipped pancakes. "Hey, you."

"I can't believe you're home," I said, putting down the spatula and passing her a cup of decaf.

"I know." She leaned her head on my shoulder as she took the cup. "I missed you so much."

"What about me?" said Sadie. "Miss me too? And Sammy? And Nana?"

Casey flashed the children a mischievous smile. "I missed you *all* so much." Taking a seat at the counter, she pulled them to her, one child on each side of her lap. "Now, tell me everything. *What* has been going on for the past few weeks?" She kissed their faces all over, and blew raspberries into their little necks, hugging them tighter and tighter.

"Mommy read book?" Sadie asked, hopefully. "I get book."

"Pick an easy one," Casey called, as Sadie ran around the corner towards her bedroom. "Mommy's head is still a little tired." Casey rubbed her temples, and I glanced at Ellen with a look that said, *Maybe she should go back to bed.*

"You okay, Mommy?" Sam asked, noticing our worried glances.

"Just a little tired, Sammy."

"You can go back to sleep."

"I might in a bit, Sammy," she said. "But right now—" Casey kissed him on the top of his head. Sam pushed himself closer to her body.

Sadie hurtled back into the kitchen, holding a Mo Willams' Elephant and Piggie classic. Thrusting the book at Casey, she scrambled onto the left side of her mother's lap, and snuggled in next to her brother. Casey opened the book, took a deep breath, and began to read. As I flipped another pancake, the Scott household seemed back to normal.

CHAPTER 23

Casey

After dinner, I sat in bed, sifting through my work emails, and prioritizing them in order of urgency and importance. The eerie quiet from Harold since I was discharged from the hospital on Tuesday was unnerving, especially as I emailed him yesterday to let him know that I was coming home and would be in the office on Monday. I called the office before boarding the plane and Violet sent me to his voicemail, claiming that he was in a meeting. I didn't see a meeting on his calendar. His uncharacteristic silence since I told him that I wouldn't be returning as soon as I got home was likely a sign of sulking and anger, rather than respecting my right to recuperate in peace. I knew he'd sensed his control over me slipping away. If this was his way of dealing with my not coming back to the office the day after I set foot in Portland, I wasn't surprised.

With the children now asleep, I could hear the domestic sounds of my mother cleaning up dinner and talking to Jonah. Closing my eyes, I breathed in the scent of my house: one so familiar, yet almost forgotten after a few weeks surrounded by the sterilized aroma of the EMU.

I rubbed the back of my hand, where the bruising from the IVs had almost completely faded, now only a sickly yellow-brown color remaining. Last night, I woke up at 3 a.m., panting, covered in sweat, after a nightmare where I had to do brain mapping again. I jolted awake just as Dr. Alem was about to start the electrode that caused seizures. Jonah felt my movement, and soothed me back to sleep: a heavy, dreamless slumber until breakfast.

As a celebration of my first day home, Jonah kept the children out of daycare, and had taken a vacation day himself. They needed this time; I needed this time; we needed this time as a family. Now, staring at the emails, I felt the free time coming to a close.

Shutting the laptop, I leaned back against our headboard and closed my eyes. I was having trouble reading, losing my place, and tiring within one paragraph. True, I had been out of the EMU for barely four days, but I wanted to make sure that this wasn't a permanent side effect of brain mapping. If there was one skill that an attorney needed, it was the ability to read and comprehend a lot of documents.

I heard Jonah's footsteps on the stairs, and opened my eyes, watching as he entered our bedroom.

He flopped down next to me on our bed, and settled his head sideways on a pillow. "How's work?" he asked.

"Fine. Under control. I'm going to go back to the office on Monday." I scrutinized his face, waiting for some reaction.

"It's up to you. If you're sure you're ready for it."

"I am."

"And how's it going with Harold?" He started tracing a figure-eight on my leg, and avoided meeting my eyes, staring at my thigh instead.

"Oh, Harold." *This might be the time. Quiet, rested, and alone together. This is the time.* "He was a pretty big dick while I was in Cleveland. It made me think a lot."

Jonah stopped tracing the figure-eight, and looked up at me, staying silent.

"It made me think about how I don't want to work there anymore. I mean, I could start my own practice or, I don't know, go to another firm, but just not work there." I could feel the tension between us, but couldn't quite read it: it was as if he was holding back—his breath seemed a little shallow, and his shoulders set. "I don't want you to get too excited, though. It's not going to happen this week or anything."

A smile broke on his face, softening his eyes. "It doesn't have to happen this week. I think you could definitely find a position with another firm or even open your own place. You're a brilliant attorney, Case."

His support and lack of judgment surprised me, made me relax and open up. Having expected a battle, a push to quit the firm right now, I put down my sword and shield, and outlined my plan.

"I'm going to see this Kellan case through—use the firm's resources, money, all of that. Trial is set for spring—if we don't settle before—and I have to finish it, Jonah. It's *my* case, the one I care most about. I just can't seem to separate myself from it. The other cases I'll leave at a good mid-point for someone else to pick up—or for Harold to deal with, although I doubt he'd handle them alone." I tried to imagine Harold working on all my cases as well as his case load. "No, he'd need to hire another associate."

Jonah turned on his back, folding his hands behind his head. "Shame. That poor associate. Is it legal for you to warn this person, then?"

We laughed and kissed. I felt lighter, the future brighter now that Jonah knew my plans. His support without pressure made me feel that we were a team again. I slipped off my shirt and slid on top of him. He stroked the shaved side of my head, avoiding the sutures.

"You know, I've never shagged a girl with a shaved head," he said. "It's kind of hot."

"Glad to hear that," I said, unbuttoning his jeans. "Get used to it."

·　　·　　·

I rolled towards the windows, taking in the evergreen trees against the lightening morning sky. When I went downstairs, the mayhem would begin, so I planned to take my time getting ready.

The weekend had been relaxing, exactly what I needed, but now, Monday morning, I knew Harold would look for me in the office.

Examining my head closely in the bathroom mirror, I ran my fingers over the stark shaved area, touching the hard ends of sutures scattered across my almost-bare scalp, and then brushed the other side, still long and straight. There was almost enough hair left to make it look like a fashion statement, and this haircut — the half-shave — *was* popular in Portland at the moment. Dr. Hernandez said I could have the sutures removed ten days from the surgery. Until then, I'd wear a head covering.

I had yet to tell Harold about this new look. Turning on the shower, the water warmed up over my hand, and I wondered how the exchange would go. I took a deep breath of steamy air to calm myself.

When I finally went downstairs, I found Jonah already dressed and pouring the kids their cereal in the kitchen. He swooped over with a commuter mug of decaf and gave me a kiss.

"You ready for today?" He sounded upbeat, but his eyes were full of worry.

"Ready as I'll ever be." As much as I didn't want to deal with Harold, I felt a thrill pulse through my veins, knowing that I'd be returning to the Kellan case. I missed the fight, and wanted back in the ring.

My mom walked in, coifed and clean. She smiled, and came towards me to adjust my head covering. "I like the blue flowers," she said as I pulled away scowling, and winced at the pain of the sutures moving. The last thing I needed was a reminder of the ridiculous fabric that shielded the world from the fifteen black knots holding my almost-bald scalp together.

Jonah gave my shoulder a reassuring squeeze and went to help Sadie out of her booster seat.

"Oh, I forgot," he said in a light voice. "I didn't want to worry you before, but there's the G&H holiday party in a few weeks. I think it's about three weeks after Thanksgiving. Holiday slash honor for Kevin's retirement." He put Sadie down and looked over at me, smiling broadly.

"Do I have to go?" I could just imagine all the G&H employees and their dates staring at me and my unintended half-shave. It would either be 'That's so cool' or 'She's trying to look younger. Ew.' or 'Does she have cancer?'

Mom tactfully left the room to corral Sadie into day clothes.

"In a way, yes," Jonah said. "It's the annual holiday party. Everyone is expected to go — and bring their spouses. You know how we joke at the office about how it's 'optional', but *they* notice — Jonathan and Jacob. Somehow, they notice if an employee isn't there."

"But do *I* have to go?" I asked again, pointing to my head. "I'm not exactly in a partying mood — "

Jonah wrapped his arms around my waist and kissed me. "You look great, first of all. Second of all, I could go stag and explain to them the situation, but let's see how you feel in a couple of weeks." He released me and stepped back, his voice still light. "I shouldn't have brought it up. Don't give it another thought. Just have a good day back at work. Try to take it easy, won't you?"

I nodded and turned to leave.

I left the house confused as to how that hadn't turned into a fight, but glad that he'd understood enough to set the issue aside. As I slid into the car, something bothered me — a piece of information casually inserted into the brief conversation. 'Holiday slash honor for Kevin's retirement,' Jonah had said. *Kevin is retiring. Jonah works right under him. Therefore... Therefore what?* My fragile brain tried to come to the conclusion. *I'm missing something. Missing something...* The thought flew out of my head as I started the car and drove out of our neighborhood.

•   •   •

Back in the office, Violet greeted me with a big smile, and a "Welcome back!" trying to pretend that she didn't notice my yellow head covering. I smiled and thanked her.

"Is he in?" I asked.

She nodded, her short blonde curls bouncing up and down.

"And...?"

She knew what I was asking. "I think he's in a good mood today," she said. "With you coming in and all. I think it's a good day."

Entering my office, I put down my briefcase, taking stock of what had changed and what was the same. My office looked exactly as I left it three weeks ago: brown L-shaped desk facing the wall and the window, the large leather swivel chair, the computer on the window-side of the desk, turned off. It didn't even look like any documents had been moved, which was reassuring on some level: I could pick up where I left off. Dr. Alem had said to take it easy for a few weeks, but he didn't work for Harold. I trusted my brain to show me my limits.

Although my office looked the same, so much seemed to have changed in three weeks—mostly my attitude towards Harold. I'd broken out of his control, and he could sense that I wasn't there to please him anymore. I could tell.

I walked down the hall to his office and opened the door as I knocked. He sat behind his desk, which was messy as usual, and appraised me, his gaze wandering up and down, coming to rest on my head covering.

"Casey," he said. "Finally. Are you fixed now?"

I sat in one of the large leather chairs, ignoring the question. Harold either did not understand common courtesy or was just being rude. "I'm going back for the actual surgery in January. I've marked myself out already."

"I see," he said. "Why are you wearing a head covering? It's rather unbecoming."

"I can take it off."

Harold's eyes widened as he took in my half-shaved head with the sutures still in place.

"I just thought it more professional to keep it on," I said, smothering a smile. "At least until the sutures are out. Is this more — what was it—'becoming'?" I tilted my head, waiting for an answer, and enjoying the shock value.

He looked away. "Your decision," he said. "Maybe keep it on when you're with clients. How long is it going to take to grow back?"

"I don't know. Years, I would think. It'll look a little better in a few months. And, of course, after I get the sutures removed. But how are things here? I'm going to start slow. Right now, I get tired easily. My brain seems to need some time to heal and not work too hard."

"Whatever you need, of course," Harold said, the sarcasm and insincerity forefront in the sentence. "Take your time. You know your schedule."

I rose from the chair. "I do. I'll be in my office." Holding my head covering, I strode out of Harold's office, ignoring Violet's expression of surprise and horror when she saw what had been under that piece of fabric.

Shut in the safety of my office, I turned on my computer. I tempered the desire to call Doug Randall and let him know that I was back, and tried unsuccessfully to respond to emails that required attention: sentence structure evaded me and I couldn't recall some words. I needed to speak to Kristin about the Kellan case, but didn't trust myself to hold a lengthy conversation with her about strategy. My head ached, and, after a few minutes of attempting to put together a brief email that confirmed the dates of a phone conference I felt my brain shutting down, letting me know that it was not ready to work today.

Blaming technology for my headache and the stress on my brain, I turned away from my computer and reached for a document on my desk—a request for production in a case that I'd put on the back burner. The response was due on Friday, leaving plenty of time to send back the answer with promises to collect the information. Taking out a pen from my desk drawer, I went through the document line by line, trying to make notes about what we would produce and what we would not. I read slowly, reviewing each request several times before I could make sense of it. By the fifth request, I was reading the document out loud to see if that made it easier to understand. It didn't.

I spent the rest of the morning staring out the window, thinking of my bed, and wishing I had a place to sleep under my desk. At noon, I slipped out of the office without saying goodbye, and spent the rest of the workday under the covers of my bed, in my quiet, dark room, healing.

DECEMBER 2016

CHAPTER 24

Casey

Instructed to dress as if she was going to a job interview and to wear light make-up, Kathy Kellan arrived at the office wearing a long sleeve, pale green, button up blouse and knee-length khaki skirt with loafers. Her interpretation of 'light make-up' was too heavy for a video deposition and her hairstyle too large, but before I could move her to my office to redo her eyes and lips using the make-up I kept in my drawers for just such an occasion, she burst out "What the hell happened to your hair?"

With the sutures removed and a few weeks of growth, it looked almost like a hairstyle someone would choose, but not a litigator in her late thirties. "Remember when I went away for a few weeks in November?" I asked, ushering her to my office to start the makeover.

"Yeah."

"I had some testing on my brain. Ended up, they had to shave part of my head." I rolled my eyes as if it had all been just a minor inconvenience, a blip in my schedule. "I have epilepsy, but I'm having surgery in January, so it'll all be fine." I started combing her bleached hair out of the large 1980s-style curls she wore, struggling to brush through the thick layer of hairspray.

"My cousin has epilepsy," she said. "He just takes a pill though, and he's alright."

Lucky him. "I'm similar," I lied, turning her around to wipe off her lipstick with make-up remover. "Now, let's talk about your deposition."

I gave her the lecture that I gave to every single client when I first discussed their depositions with them, which I found they all forgot and needed to hear again right before their deposition began.

"Listen to his question, and just answer the question," I said, as I applied a neutral color to her lips, and wiped the dark eyeliner from under her eyes. "Don't go farther than the question. Don't offer any extra information."

"Is he gonna be mean?"

"I've only seen him take a couple of depositions before and he can be mean," I said. I moved behind her, and pulled her hair back. "But try not to let that get to you. He might be snide, he might be condescending, or—if he's been hit over the head in the past few weeks—he might be very nice. If that *is* the case, just remember, he is not your friend. He is not working to help you. Understand?" I twisted a rubber band around the ponytail I had styled at the bottom of her neck, and surveyed her new look. "Very nice."

Kathy pulled at the ponytail.

"Any questions?"

"How long's this gonna take?"

"I don't know," I said. "Could take an hour, two hours, could go into the afternoon." Putting my hand on her back, I guided her out of my office and towards the conference room. Doug Randall was already there, checking the video equipment while the court reporter set up.

I entered the room ahead of Kathy, like a mother lion guarding her cub. With the sutures out, I'd stopped wearing head coverings, and had been waiting for this deposition, waiting to see what Doug would say.

I showed Kathy to her seat at the head of the table. She fidgeted nervously, as Doug toyed with the video camera. The videographer stood behind him, arms crossed, while Doug presumed to know her equipment better than she did.

"Morning, Doug," I said, as he moved away from the camera and took a seat at the conference table.

"Casey." His eyes flitted to my hair and then down to his notes. "Interesting haircut."

"Thank you."

"Ready to start?" He raised his gaze, and finally acknowledged Kathy.

She looked over at me, and I recognized the familiar terror in the eyes of a client who has done nothing wrong and doesn't understand why someone thinks she did: the face of a woman intimidated by this situation on so many levels, not the least of which being that she has to prove her story yet again to someone she considers smarter than herself. I patted her leg.

"You're ready," I whispered.

"I'm ready," she said to Doug in a soft voice.

This is how half of the civil rights depositions started: my client afraid, unsure, nervous that she would say something wrong, do something wrong, that, perhaps, according to the law, she *had* done something wrong. But, after the preliminaries, when opposing counsel got to the meat of the issue, usually something clicked inside my client, and anger replaced nerves. At that point, I watched for off-script answers, and called for a break when, inevitably, the client started talking outside the scope of the question in a way that was just taking time, and, like a coach in a football game, I reminded the client to listen to the question, answer the question, and wait for the next one.

"Let's go on the record," Doug said. Giving Kathy a fake toothy smile, he began the deposition.

Although I'd seen Doug in action before, I'd never seen him like this: just as I'd warned Kathy—snide and condescending.

"Who did you tell about this sexual assault?" he asked, attempted smile gone.

"The supervising officers—Officer Gabe and Officer Stilton," Kathy replied quietly.

"And did anything change?"

"They moved Officer Hawkins from Shop to security up front."

"Anything else?"

"Not that I saw."

"Do you know if an investigation was done?"

"No. I don't think it was."

"Did you follow up to ask if an investigation was done?"

"No. That's not really how things wor—"

"So, no."

"No."

Doug made a great pretense of sighing, shaking his head, and looking at his notes. *What a shame,* his body language seemed to say. *You should have done that.*

Kathy looked confused. "Let's take a break now," I said. "We've been going for about an hour and a half."

The court reporter stretched and asked where the bathroom was, and the videographer turned off the camera. I marched Kathy out of the conference room and down the hall to the safe space of my office.

Once there, her outer shell broke, and she began to cry.

"It's not like that in prison," she said, as I handed her a box of Kleenex. "You don't just go up to supervisors and ask them what they've done. 'How's that rape investigation going, Officer Gabe?' They just all kinda stick together, like they've all got each other's backs. The inmates, we're like second-class citizens." She wiped her nose. "That lawyer doesn't get that."

"I've got you," I said. "I'm going to ask some follow-up questions at the end. You can explain it then, okay?"

"Okay."

For the rest of the deposition, Doug stayed away from what happened in the shed, focusing on when Kathy reported 'the incident', as he called it, and who she reported it to, trying to bolster his case that certain supervisors may or may not have known, and, if they knew, they did something about it.

"And that's all I have," Doug said around noon. He reached for his briefcase, and I heard his stomach rumble.

"Great. I've got a few follow-ups," I said brightly. "Let's take ten minutes, and then come back."

"How long are these going to take?" Doug asked, caught off-guard. I knew he hadn't been expecting questions from my side of the table.

"I don't know. As long as they take."

After the break, I started my questions.

"Ms. Kellan, can you explain how inmate access to the guards and supervisors works at Oregon Women's Correctional Facility?"

Kathy explained her access to the guards and the supervisors, and how prisoners were treated. We moved on to what she hoped would happen when she reported the rape, and what she saw happen instead. She explained her relationship to Officer Hawkins, the grooming, and the other officers who never said anything. Together, we tore apart Doug's case bit by bit. Kathy found her groove, and we played off each other perfectly.

We finished in an hour. Ordering the court reporter to send him a copy of the transcript, and the videographer to send over the video, Doug stormed out of the conference room without a goodbye.

"Was he okay?" Kathy asked, as we stood to leave.

"No," I said. "He wasn't. You did a good job."

We walked into the lobby, and she pulled me into a tight hug.

"Thank you," she said. "I'm so glad that you're my lawyer."

I left the office after the deposition, excited to be home mid-afternoon, to tell Jonah the entire story, to pick up the kids from daycare without a rush, and to be present, fully present, for my family. My brain had recovered from a punishing November. It felt quiet. Although Dr. Alem told me about the "implantation effect"—an immediate, but temporary, reduction in seizures after having SEEG testing—I wondered if I even needed the ablation. Today, I realized, except for the comment from Doug and the explanation to Kathy, I hadn't thought about seizures at all.

CHAPTER 25

Jonah

"Are you sure I look okay?" Casey asked as we walked through the Pearl District to the Blue Square, Portland's newest event space and G&H's chosen venue for their 'Mad Men'-themed holiday party. Casey had pulled together a red dress and heels that even Betty Draper would envy, and styled her hair to make the shaved half look cool, not medical. With her shimmery eyeshadow and red lips, my wife looked striking. No one would guess that just over two weeks earlier, she had been in a hospital bed in Cleveland.

"You look stunning," I told her for the tenth time, and squeezed her hand as we walked up the cement steps. Stopping to face her, I smiled. With Casey by my side, this night might be fun. "Come. Let's see what G&H has put together."

The G&H event staff had truly outdone itself. We entered a full-on winter wonderland scene, complete with sparkling "snow"-covered evergreens, and full-size, glistening, fake reindeer, peeking their heads between the trees. Golden draperies hung from the ceiling, lit by subtle lights that gave the entire room a soft rich hue. People milled about, laughing, drinking champagne and other cocktails, following paths winding through the room between the puffy snow. Not only had the G&H event staff taken everything over the top, but the G&H employees fully embraced the theme, wearing everything from bouffant hair and stiff suits to the looser sixties creative look.

Millennials crowded the photo booth area, using the props to enhance their drunken poses, and tall tables were strategically placed throughout the space to encourage gathering, yet leave enough room for movement. A buffet laden with organic, local fare stood against a wall, and bartenders poured out made-to-order cocktails to thirsty employees.

At the coat check, we exchanged our heavy jackets for tickets. Casey stuffed them in her small clutch while I scanned the room for my team, Jonathan, and Jacob. Several emails about the holiday party had gone out the past two weeks, reminding everyone about the time, place, and theme, as well as the fact that this would be Kevin's swan song, his night of honor. The underlying message was, "You will *all* be at the party where we will announce Kevin's successor."

Soon, almost everyone had forgotten that it was a holiday party, and only talked about Kevin. Employees congregated in hallways and spoke in hushed tones about who would replace him. More than once, I caught some members of my team giving me curious looks, as if I knew something more than they did about the promotion. I pretended to ignore the rumors, and hated to admit that I was just as in the dark as all of them. Since the disastrous last interview, I knew that my chance of being chosen as Director of Marketing was as good as gone. It would be Dwayne; I was sure of it, and that knowledge made me furious.

Grabbing Casey's hand, I passed her a glass of champagne, took one for myself, and forced a smile as we entered the throng.

"Everyone's looking at me," she said through clenched teeth. "Do we have to stay long?"

"Just for a bit," I told her as we wove through the crowd to my team. "Just a few minutes of face time. Hello, everyone! Happy holidays!" I held up my glass in a cheers.

For a second, the group froze. Thomas stopped talking mid-sentence.

"Hey there!" he said brightly, almost too brightly. "Happy holidays!"

"You remember my wife, Casey," I said, putting my arm around her waist. "Casey, the team: Whitney, Callan, Kyle, Steve, Thomas, Jose, Anna, and Tara. Where's Dwayne?"

Everyone looked at their drinks, and then I heard it: the honking laugh that was Dwayne Richards.

"Uh, I think he's over there," Whitney said, gesturing to a group across the room.

I looked and my smile faltered: Dwayne stood in a circle with Jonathan, Jacob, Kevin, and their wives, who seemed entranced by whatever he was saying. He looked like the belle of the ball in a bright red bowtie and Don Draper-cut suit. As I watched, the group exploded with laughter when he finished talking.

I turned back to my team. "Well, I think I'll go congratulate Kevin. Happy holidays." I raised my glass again, and they all mumbled 'Happy Holidays.'

Grabbing Casey's hand, I dragged her through the crowd.

"Jonah, what's going on?" she asked. "Are you okay? You never really explained to me more about Kevin's retirement. I actually forgot to bring it up again. Can we just take a second before —"

"I'm fine," I said shortly. "Just fine." We reached the group, all still fixated on Dwayne's continued monologue. "Jacob! Jonathan! Kevin!" I interrupted, smiling broadly while trying not to pant from the speed I just exerted by almost sprinting across the room. "Happy Holidays."

Jonathan raised his glass of vodka on the rocks, his favorite drink.

"Jonah, good to see you. And Katie," he said with a smile. He leaned forward and kissed her on the cheek. "How are you feeling?"

"Casey," she said, somehow still charming in her correction. "I'm feeling fine, thank you."

The rest of the group looked puzzled. Jacob actively frowned.

"Fine from what?" he asked curtly.

"Oh, I just had a little time in the hospital," Casey said lightly. Classic Casey: putting on a face effortlessly when inside I knew it was costing her everything. "Nothing to worry about. Happy holidays.

And congratulations on your retirement, Kevin," she said, turning to the correct person, even though she had only met him once before.

"Thank you," Kevin replied. "I'm looking forward to it. Although, I'll miss the G&H hustle and bustle." He chuckled with Jacob and Jonathan.

"You're welcome to come back whenever you like," Jacob said.

Dwayne grinned. "Of course you are," he said, his face an open invitation that he seemed to suddenly have the power to give.

"You okay?" Casey whispered. I must have been frowning, and quickly set the smile back.

"I'm fine," I replied. "Stop asking."

Jonathan glanced at his watch and then surveyed the room. "Well, let's get this party started," he said. He clapped Kevin on the back. "You ready, friend?"

For a second, I saw some emotion in his eyes as they met Kevin's and realized that they had worked together for almost three decades, and tonight might be painful for more than just me.

Kevin swallowed. "Ready." He kissed his wife, whose Botoxed face barely registered a smile, and followed Jonathan towards the microphone at the front of the room, with Jacob trailing behind.

Jonathan took his place behind the mic. "This thing on?" he joked. Everyone looked to the front.

"Yes!" the crowd yelled.

"Great. Well, happy holidays, G&H-ers. Another year already. And it's been an *exceptional* year!"

From the corner of my eye, I saw that the deafening applause from the crowd made Casey wince, look at the floor, and rub her temples.

"You alright?"

"Just that my head hurts," she said softly. "Can we sneak out when they're done talking?"

"Of course, darling," I said, trying to listen to Jonathan's words.

"Now, as you all know," he was saying, "this is no normal holiday party. Tonight, we're honoring one of our most valuable members of our community as he retires. Kevin Atchinson."

Thunderous applause again filled the room, and, again, Casey winced.

"When we started this company, Jacob and I were in our mid-20s and had no advertising experience besides watching television, seeing what was out there, and thinking that advertising could be so much *more*. Looking at the ads in the late '70s, early '80s, we thought 'If only there was a company that pushed the boundaries and *really* brought these products, these brands, to life.' So, together, we started Grossman & Howe. But, we couldn't do it all alone. I was creative. Jacob was math-business minded, but we needed someone to seal the deals, a pitchman. And one of the first people we hired was this gawky twenty-seven-year-old guy named Kevin." He gestured to Kevin, and the audience laughed at the description.

"Wait," Casey said, pulling at my arm. I looked over at her, anxious to give all my attention to Jonathan. But her green eyes glinted with sudden realization. "Are you going to be taking his position?"

I shrugged. "I doubt it—I—"

"You *doubt* it? I don't understand. How can you not know? Did they interview you?"

"Now," Jonathan continued, "Kevin also had no experience in advertising, but even then he had a way with words—he could sell anything to anyone. He could convince the two of us that even though he knew *nothing* about the advertising business, he was the man for the job 'just because.' And being as young as we were, and being as poor as we were, there weren't a lot of options. So, we gambled and won. Kevin has been working with us ever since."

He clapped Kevin on the back and began to list his many successes. "He has helped us grow Grossman and Howe to the powerhouse it is today, with offices in San Fran, L.A., New York, London, Paris, and Tokyo. And, as the Director of Marketing in our home office in Portland, he has landed some of the biggest clients that our firm has ever seen. Kevin is a master at reading people. He can tell when someone coming into a pitch is a little nervous. He can tell when a client has a few doubts, when a client is thinking 'Is this the direction

I want to go in?' and he knows *immediately* how to work with that client, how to convince them that if this is not their direction, G&H will make whatever they want for them, and he will personally ensure that it is done right. And that's how he lands clients, even clients with a bit of doubt.

"He treats everyone as an equal—you've all seen that. That's how he leads his team, and how he gets his results from G&H-ers. We should all aspire to be as great a leader as Kevin, and we wish him the best in the future. Let's raise our glasses to Kevin, his legacy, and his future. To Kevin!"

"To Kevin!" The room responded with applause reverberating off the walls as Kevin took a bow.

"Jonah, have you been offered a promotion?" Casey's voice was hard, bordering on angry. "We haven't even talked about it." She seemed to analyze the situation, slowly finding the right questions to ask, heading into dangerous territory.

I knew what was about to happen behind the microphone before it was even said. "They didn't offer me the position, Case."

Technically, it wasn't a lie.

Jonathan held up a finger and paused for effect. The room went silent.

"But like Whitman said, 'The powerful play goes on' and G&H must—sadly—go on without Kevin. That's why I'd like to introduce Kevin's successor. This man has been an asset to G&H for about a decade. He has proved that his instincts, like Kevin's, are second to none—"

"Jonah, are you *sure*?" Casey asked. I could see her posture grow rigid, both of our gazes fixed on the microphone and the man behind it.

Oh my God, he's describing me.

Casey clamped a hand on my forearm. "Jonah," she whispered harshly. "What the fu-"

I held up my hand roughly to silence her, motioning with my chin to the podium. "I mean, not officially…"

"Please join me in welcoming our new Director of Marketing..." Jonathan's voice boomed.

My throat constricted as I waited for what, a few minutes ago, had seemed impossible. I stood, fixated on Jonathan, only hearing my heart crashing against my chest wall, again and again.

"Dwayne Richards!"

The words seemed to come in excruciating slow motion, every syllable enunciated, making it that much more difficult to hear. Dwayne pushed his way past me and Casey, sauntered up to the microphone, and waved to the crowd. He heartily hugged Jonathan and Jacob, and then gave a little bow to Kevin before hugging him, too. The applause engulfed the room, as if everyone else agreed that Dwayne the Wanker was the right choice, and I was completely forgotten.

Within seconds, Dwayne Richards had gone from being my direct report to my supervisor.

"Jonah. *Now* can we go?" Casey's sharp voice interrupted my thoughts. "Have we put in enough face time?"

I nodded and turned away from the scene unfolding at the front of the room. "Yes. Let's go home."

"How long have you known that Kevin was retiring?" Casey asked, as we donned our coats.

"A few months."

"Didn't think to tell me?" she said, facing me, her shoulders squared, eyes flaring with anger.

"They didn't offer the position to me, Casey. Let's stop talking about it. Please."

She sighed, and her stance relaxed. Reaching for my hand, we walked side-by-side through the faux winter wonderland towards the door, where real winter was waiting, bitter and cold.

CHAPTER 26

Casey

On Christmas morning, Jonah dutifully rolled out of bed at six to the sound of our kids shrieking, "Santa came! Santa came!"

I clamped a pillow over my head to drown out the noise. I needed my rest, not just to avoid a seizure, but because Jonah's parents had come in three days ago, and proceeded to make the holidays a nightmare. This was the one time of year they saw their grandchildren, and, ignoring Jonah's instructions that we weren't having anyone at the house this year because I needed to recover from Cleveland, they sent their flight number with the expectation of a personal airport pick up. To James and Linda Scott, the fact that their daughter-in-law might not want to entertain Christmas houseguests this year due to her faulty brain was not their problem. Jonah should have married someone else in their eyes, someone British and appropriate, so I resigned myself to five days of judgment by people who never understood epilepsy or took the time to try.

"I can come and sleep on Sam's bottom bunk," my mom offered when I told her that the Scotts were coming. "I can handle them." Holly also offered to run interference, so suddenly we went from having just the four of us to having a full house at Christmas. I'd decided that the stress of his parents' visit was the reason Jonah had been so morose and quiet lately. He didn't enjoy his parents' company either, but he was a dutiful son and it was only five days.

He lifted the pillow and kissed my forehead. "You sleep," he whispered. "I'll handle the presents."

I smiled and nestled under the covers, thankful for the reprieve. I didn't need anything under the tree: my present was getting the rest I needed. I'd see everyone downstairs at nine.

By noon, the kitchen smelled like ham and stuffing, both baking in the oven. Christmas music played softy in the background, filling in the occasional gaps between conversation, laughter, and the children's audible excitement over their presents. Sam and Jonah were already building his new train set near the tree, and Sadie had strapped her Teddy bear into the stroller and was singing "Rudolph the Red-Nosed Reindeer" as she walked it back and forth from the dining room to the couch, dodging the train tracks as she went.

The kitchen was full with my mother snapping the green beans, Linda peeling the potatoes, and Holly, who had come early with Rob, cutting each potato as Linda passed it to her to make it easier to mash after the boiling.

I chuckled to myself. *We look like a magazine cover. As if we'd all put aside our differences and resolved to get along.* Mostly these differences consisted of Jonah's parents' judgment of everything in our American lives, and perhaps the calm atmosphere only occurred because I had learned to make Yorkshire pudding and given Linda a few glasses of spiked eggnog. Whatever the reason, she was contentedly humming "Oh Come All Ye Faithful" along with the Pandora playlist while she peeled the tenth potato.

Sam ran into the kitchen. "I finished the train tracks Grandpa got me! Come see, Mommy!"

"They're BRIO. Amazing quality," James said, as we followed an excited Sam over to his creation.

The set was impressive: twists, turns, bridges, docks, battery-powered trains that ran smoothly around it all. Sam's face glowed as he watched the train move.

"See, Mommy? See—over here it goes to the dock and then you can push up the ship, and load the train and..." he continued to speak rapidly, almost manically, about the system. I patted his head.

"It's wonderful, Sammy."

"And did you see the *other* presents?" Linda asked, suddenly at my side. "We thought their wardrobe might need a little, well, freshening up." She smiled, knowing that I understood the meaning behind those words. I looked over at Sadie, who had dressed herself in worn zebra-patterned leggings and a stained long-sleeved cotton shirt with a felt sun on the tummy.

"Thank you," I said, returning her wintry smile with my own.

She gestured to a pile of boxes that I hadn't noticed, stacked in two neat columns just behind the tree. "Just a few things: some dresses for Sadie—Rachel Riley has beautiful prints—a new jacket for each child, lovely Amaia peacoats. You know, they were almost sold out. I had such a difficult time finding *two*! And then just a few jumpers for each child, some trousers, socks. I didn't know their shoe sizes, otherwise I would have tried to bring some over." She looked down at Sadie's sneakers, a faded pink-gray with the Velcro peeking under the straps.

"Thank you," I said again. "I am sure the children will be very well dressed at dinner. And school."

"Now they will."

Fuming, I walked over to my mother to check on her work with the green beans.

"Is this good?" Mom asked, as I watched her snap each bean carefully to match the others.

"Great. The next step is to put them in that baking dish, then we'll do more in a few hours."

After the potatoes were boiling, and the timer set, we took a break. Before walking over to the living room, I refilled my cider and offered Holly more, which she gladly accepted. We passed the dining table, and I paused to look over the setting, done last night by a strictly supervised Sam and Sadie. In my mind, it was a combination of the past, present, and the future: the gold-plated flatware from my parents' wedding, cut-crystal glasses and the white China plates that Jonah's parents bought us from our wedding registry, new candles, two fresh flower arrangements, and—at Jonah's insistence and the children's delight—Christmas crackers at each setting. The sight brought me a feeling of peace, goodwill, and hope that this coming year would be better than the last: fewer seizures and the miracle cure for my epilepsy.

"Lovely," Holly said, standing next to me, and admiring the children's work. "Really lovely."

"Thanks."

"Sometimes I think that less is more," Linda said, appearing behind us. "Keeps the table from looking so crowded and, well, garish in a way, don't you think?"

No one asked you, I was about to retort.

"It's in honor of Jesus Christ, our Lord and Savior," Holly said quickly, her improv bullshit sparing my mother-in-law my rude reply. "We find it is *so* important to honor Him, especially on this holy day. More eggnog, Linda?"

"No thank you," she said shortly.

As we walked towards the living room, my good mood returned. I took in the scene of family and friends chatting animatedly, and Sam and Sadie playing with their toys on the floor in front of the Christmas tree. With the aroma of warm food hanging in the air, I sat next to Holly, ignoring my frowning mother-in-law, who glowered beside her husband. Turning to talk to my best girlfriend, I felt happier and healthier than I had in months.

•   •   •

The day after Christmas was always a day of relief and relaxation. Sam and Sadie, exhausted from the excitement of the previous twenty-four hours, happily watched television in the guest room while the adults reclined on the couch in the living room, drinking coffee and eating leftovers.

I walked into the kitchen for a glass of water, and heard Jonah and his mom talking in Sam's room. To my knowledge, they hadn't spoken alone her entire visit, and I instantly felt my chest tighten, my antenna go up.

"Well, I just don't think you get enough credit for all you have to do around here," Linda said.

"Mum, that's not true."

"Jonah, from what I've seen, no one is talking about all *you've* done in the past few months—taking care of the children while she was gone, *while* working full time. No mention of it at dinner last night, just a vague toast to 'The value of family and friends.' I mean, really, darling, doesn't it bother you? It should."

"I had plenty of help from Ellen."

"Still. I'm sure you did most of it."

"No. Ellen and I were a team. I don't know how I'd have managed without her. She was really brilliant, cooking dinners, picking up the children from school—"

"And who is checking on *your* health, Jonah?" Linda interrupted, trying another tactic. "All I hear is everyone worried about Casey. There is more to life than just Casey's brain, Jonah. *Your* well-being matters too."

I stood like a statue in the kitchen, unable to move, waiting for Jonah to stand up to Linda, to tell her that I thanked him, that he knew I appreciated him, that he didn't care what she thought.

"It's fine, Mum." I heard him walk out of Sam's room and watched him enter the living room to join his dad and my mom.

With tears of anger in my eyes, I stormed towards Sam's room, finding Linda with a small smile that disappeared when she saw me, quickly replaced with a scowl that made her face seem older than her sixty-five years.

Blood rushed to my head, and my hands clenched so hard that I could feel the nails biting into my palms.

"We're fine, Linda," I snapped. "Jonah is fine. *And* appreciated." *And I swear if you don't come back next Christmas, it'll be the only gift I need.* I stormed out of the room, leaving her, mouth agape, alone.

Rushing into the living room, intending to request that my husband and I speak upstairs, my mind changed instantly as I saw Jonah sitting next to his father, his head thrown back with laughter, eyes watering, happier than I'd seen him in weeks.

"Sit, darling." He patted the space next to him. "Dad was just telling us about a man he had to sit next to on the flight over, and — well, you tell it, Dad."

My frustration and anger melted; I couldn't interrupt this. Sitting next to my husband, I took his hand and tipped my head onto his shoulder, joining him in laughing at the outlandish story that was probably based in the truth but made bigger through a few days of reflection, and funnier with the wry British humor.

Linda finally appeared, jacket on, with her suitcase by her side, and curtly announced that it was time for her and James to leave. Goodbyes were said all around; my mother promising to keep in better touch with Linda, and the kids pried away from their movie to give quick hugs to people they only saw once a year.

When Linda turned to me, I kissed her on both cheeks and whispered, "Stay out of my marriage," before turning her around and escorting her out of the house.

JANUARY 2017

CHAPTER 27

Jonah

Cleveland felt full of wonder and potential, despite the dreary January weather. A lot of it was because I hoped that, soon, Casey would be on the road to recovery and seizure freedom, away from the dire mention of SUDEP that hung over us like a storm cloud. But I was also more than happy to be away from the office for a week—almost 3,000 miles away from Dwayne Richards.

His official promotion start date was not until the end of January, but he already swaggered up and down the halls, acting like a child king of his new domain. It was truly sickening to watch. His new office was a spectacular place on the third floor—the top of the building— half the size of a basketball court, and he would not let anyone forget it.

"Just send the brief up to me in my new digs—you know, third floor," became a familiar refrain, along with, "If you need me, I'll be in my office—you know, third floor."

I thought that *"You know, third floor"* should be chiseled on his tombstone when he died.

Because of the holidays and end-of-year vacations, I never talked to Jonathan or Jacob about the decision. It was easy enough to guess: they thought I did not and would not put in enough time at the office. But if they expected this recent blow-off to light a fire under me and inspire me to come in early, stay late, and work weekends, they were wrong. It had done the opposite. With no prospect of any promotion within G&H, the pressure was off, and I was all too happy to put in the request to take the first week of January off and accompany Casey to her surgery.

After we checked into the hotel, we went to a French café tucked away in the museum district. A waiter with a man bun and a friendly manner quickly seated us at a white-clothed table for two by a large window. Casey and I perused the wine list, decided to be daring and each enjoy a glass with our lunch. We ordered two glasses of expensive Chardonnay, and the waiter swept away to fulfill our wishes.

Over the calm of the atmosphere and the snowy beauty of the surroundings, the ablation seemed a far-off dream: something that might happen to someone someday, but not to Casey this week. We sipped our wine, taking our time with hors d'oeuvres, main courses of salmon and duck confit, finishing with crème caramel and an espresso each. We wondered aloud how Ellen was coping with the children, whether they were behaving. She had volunteered readily for the job, assuring us that she could handle her two grandchildren, as our trip was only five days.

We finished our espressos, and I sat back, watching the falling snow. *Fuck Grossman. Fuck Howe. I'll find a new, better job.*

"You okay?" Casey asked.

I snapped back to reality and stared at my wife. Her eyes held an amused look.

"You looked so deep in thought."

"Just enjoying the scenery." I reached for her hand. She sighed, and the amused expression became serious.

"Guess we should go see the hospital now. Get you familiar with it," she said.

Pushing G&H out of my mind, I squeezed her hand. "I'll call an Uber."

In the car, Casey grew tense beside me. We turned a corner, and an enormous, glass building towered in front of us with a driveway circling a low fountain.

"There it is," Casey said in a low voice. "Come. I'll show you the inside. Maybe we can even see my old room."

We entered hand in hand, and Casey moved closer to me as we walked through the front sliding doors. A mixture of medical personnel and patients bustled around us, a piano played in the distance somewhere, and a sanitized smell permeated the air, reminding the visitor that, although there may be shiny floors and bright light coming through the gigantic windows, this was a medical center.

"Wow," I said. "I've never seen a hospital like this."

Casey breathed deeply. "I'll show you the EMU."

I knew this was therapy for her: a confrontation of the place she had sat, helpless and alone, now returning in control of her own movements, her own clothing, her life. Passing through the impressive front area of the hospital, we wound through less-remarkable halls, tan with florescent lighting, until we reached a bank of elevators. The elevator door opened, revealing a large space with steel handles on the walls.

"That stops the orderlies from bumping into the walls when they're transporting people," Casey said. She sounded bitter, and we rode up in silence.

The doors opened, and Casey strode confidently down the hallway, her memory of the maze to the EMU astonishing. She stopped in front of two large, brown doors with a metal sign reading "N50" attached to the right side.

"Here it is. The EMU ward." She pushed on the door and I stopped her.

"Can we just go in here?"

"Yes."

A low-lit hallway led to a wall at the end. Doors to hospital rooms sat open or partially open on either side. As I followed Casey down the hall, I peeked into each room: men or women lay in the single bed, each one with their head wrapped in bandages of varying thickness. Some patients sat up, watching television, looking at their phones, or talking to a visitor; some slept or seemed to sleep. A heavy feeling of loneliness pervaded the air.

Halfway down the hall, a nurse in green scrubs and a lace head covering stood at a tall counter surrounding a low desk. Behind the desk, black and white videos of each patient played on separate monitors with the number of the room on the bottom left-hand side. The nurse was laughing with a coworker when we approached, and stopped when she noticed us.

"Can I help you?" she asked.

"Glenda? Hi, it's me—Casey Scott?" Casey smiled for the first time since we entered the hospital. "I was here a couple months ago..."

"Casey?" The nurse looked incredulous. "I didn't even recognize you."

Casey ran her hand over the shaved part of her hair, which was slowly growing back, now soft instead of spiky. "I'm back for an ablation. Just thought I'd visit the old EMU."

Glenda's eyes drifted to me, and Casey gave the introduction. "This is the nurse who was so good at putting in IVs," she said.

"After a few hundred, you figure it out," Glenda replied, waving away the compliment.

An alarm went off, a mechanical wail filling the hallway, and a light started blinking next to one of the doors. Nurses came running from a back area and flew into the room with the blinking light.

"Good to see you," Glenda said, as she followed the crowd. "Good luck!"

"Someone pressed a seizure button," Casey shouted over the continuing wail. "We should go."

We exited the hospital through the sliding glass doors in the lobby. I could feel Casey's mood immediately lift as her body relaxed and her gloved hand slipped into mine. The snow fell softly as we walked towards the hotel, and the hopeful feeling of earlier in the day returned.

•   •   •

"This was rated the best fried chicken in Cleveland," I said, putting the large brown paper bag on the desk in our hotel room. "So let's try some of Cleveland's best."

Casey closed her laptop and slid off her bed. Smiling, she piled a paper plate with greens, mashed potatoes, a biscuit, and a fried chicken breast, pulling a thin paper napkin and plastic utensils from the greasy bag.

"Harold's not making any noise," she said as she returned to her place on the bed, balancing the plate on her lap.

"That's good." I faced her from the other queen-sized bed, my plate also precariously resting on my crossed legs. *Work should be the furthest thing from your mind, Case,* I wanted to say, but changed the subject instead. "How did it make you feel, going back to the hospital?"

She pushed her mashed potatoes around her plate, silent and contemplative. "I felt like I just shut down for a bit. It was good to see that nurse, but I think of everything that happened there and..."

"And?"

"And I don't know why I wanted to go back to the EMU. It's like visiting a trauma site for me. But I think that I just wanted to show the space that it didn't beat me." Shaking her head, she took a bite of greens. "That doesn't make sense, but I walked out feeling like I'd done something. Something brave."

"You're brave, Case."

"I'm scared of this surgery is what I am."

"Being scared doesn't mean you're not brave, you know."

Sitting across from each other, eating our dinner in the quiet hotel room, tomorrow and the surgery felt far away. We moved on from talk of the hospital and the EMU to non-medical topics: cases at the firm, rehashing the lunch, laughing about the waiter with the man bun.

"Then again, I have almost half my head shaved, so who am I to laugh?" Casey grinned as she cut into her chicken breast. "And this chicken is fantastic."

We ate in silence until Casey wiped her hands on the napkin and looked up at me.

"Everything going okay at G&H?" she asked. "Weird that Dwayne got that director position. Did they interview you for it? You worked right under Kevin."

"Well, they interviewed several people," I said evasively, trying to keep my tone light. "It appears Dwayne was the best fit."

Casey narrowed her eyes, studying my face as if trying to determine the truth of my statement. "Why would they interview a bunch of people when you're Kevin's direct successor—"

"I don't know, Case." I struggled to keep my calm, but I was not about to be cross-examined by my spouse, especially about something I had withheld from her, which would now probably start a fight about secrecy or team decision-making, and escalate into a discussion about career trajectories. Not now, the night before brain surgery. "Who knows why Jacob and Jonathan do anything, right? They just make decisions based on—well, I don't know what, really."

She looked more confused.

"Anyway, oh, I know!" I said before she could speak. "Let's call the kids! We can tell them all about the day, and they can tell us how they drew trees or colored balloon pictures or how Gemma got sent to the office for scraping her elbow."

"Jonah!" Casey threw a pillow at me, laughing. "Okay. Let's call them."

I buried my guilt as we called home and, as expected, received reports from our offspring about crafts, coloring, and preschool drama.

CHAPTER 28

Casey

I opened my eyes with my head throbbing and tried to remember where I was. I was in a bed. Beige curtains hemmed in the bed on the sides, but left an opening in front to an area busy with people in black scrubs working purposefully at computers or talking to each other.

A woman with a long, black braid sat on a three-legged rolling stool, her back to me, talking to another woman over the counter in front of her. *I've been here before. This is a hospital. Hospital. She is a nurse. And my head hurts because...* The reason was just beyond reach. I groaned and the black-haired woman turned around.

"You're awake," she said.

Awake. Awake after... After...

"The doctor said that your surgery went well." The nurse walked over and glanced at the numbers on the screen next to me. "Vitals look good," she said cheerily. "How do you feel?"

I shook my head. *It will hurt too much to speak.*

The nurse's smile disappeared. "In pain?"

I nodded slightly, the most movement that my head could make without me screaming.

"On a scale of 1 to 10, where would you say your pain is?"

Now I would have to talk. "Ten," I breathed softly. "Ten."

"Ok," said the nurse. "I'll be right back with something to help you."

Through half-closed eyes, I watched her move away, and prayed for the pain to stop. She returned quickly and pushed some clear liquid into my IV. The throbbing subsided, and, slowly, the room faded to black.

•   •   •

My eyes opened again, and I placed where I was quickly. *Hospital. Surgery. Ablation.* My head still pounded, but slightly less, and something about the space was different, a noise that hadn't been there before. Looking to the side, I saw Jonah sitting in a chair, tapping away on his phone.

"Hi," I whispered.

He looked up and smiled. "Hi. Dr. Hernandez came by while you were sleeping. She said the surgery went well."

"That's good." Then I remembered, stopped and listened. My head felt eerily quiet through the pain. "Jonah, I think the music has stopped."

Jonah leaned forward, his eyes intense and hopeful.

"I don't know," I said, "but I think." I began to notice parts of my body besides my aching head: my mouth felt as if the inside was covered in sand. I was hungry, but nausea overrode my desire to eat. "I'd like something to drink."

The nurse with the braid sat on the moving stool with her back to my bed again. I wished I could raise my voice to let her know what I needed, but I knew that the pounding in my head only allowed for whispering without repercussions. "Jonah, could you...?"

Jonah understood and talked to the nurse.

"How about some ice chips to start?" she suggested in her overly loud voice and bustled off to fetch them.

Anything. The inside of my skull felt as if it were on fire, as if my brain was angry with me. I touched the left side of my head and felt a small piece of gauze close to the front with staples to keep it in place. "No turban," I whispered.

The nurse returned with the ice chips in a Styrofoam cup, and I started sucking on them immediately. They cooled my mouth, and I stuffed in more as the first batch melted, moving them around my tongue, my cheeks, and my gums before swallowing them. In a minute, they were gone. I passed the empty cup to Jonah, and laid back on the bed. My nausea increased rapidly, as if the ice chips were an unwelcome visitor in my body. I closed my eyes, trying to hold off the acrid liquid rising in my throat.

"Jonah," I said, feeling the cold sweats that usually preceded any vomiting, "get me a trash can. I think I'm going to..." Clamping my hands over my mouth, I bent forward; the still-cold fluid crawled up my esophagus. Frantically, Jonah searched the area. Finding a trash can tucked under the head of the bed, he held it over my lap.

I leaned over the black plastic bucket just in time: the thin liquid was clear, intermingled with some small chunks of ice. With an empty stomach, there was nothing else to come out, but I continued dry heaving, even after my gut expelled all the ice chips and water. The contractions came relentlessly, as if my body wanted to punish me for putting it through this ordeal. When the retching stopped, I closed my eyes, feeling exhausted and still in pain. I cried silently and prayed. *Dear God, if you are even there, please let this ablation work. Please. Help me.*

The nurse took the trash bucket and gave me a pill for nausea. As it dissolved on my tongue, I curled into a ball, pressing on my midsection and pointlessly willing the bilious twinge in my stomach to subside immediately: it was almost as terrible as the pain in my head. I breathed shallowly through my nose and reached for Jonah's hand.

"It's okay," he said helplessly. "It will all be okay. You'll see."

While I waited for the pill to work, I continued putting pressure on my abdomen, breathed in rapid, shallow breaths, and tried to decide whether I could still hear music that I hadn't even known was there.

FEBRUARY 2017

CHAPTER 29

Casey

The party came together seamlessly. Clusters of purple and silver balloons floated next to the couch, and Trader Joe's finger foods, pink champagne and pink lemonade decorated the dining table. Sam and Sadie chased each other around the house.

I sat in the living room, resting from another dull headache and annoyingly persistent aura. Dr. Alem and his team had assured me that frequent auras were common in the weeks after an ablation, nothing to worry about, so I'd learned to ignore them.

After almost a month back from Cleveland, I still needed at least a brief nap during the day. I found working from home easier, a concept foreign to Harold, who regarded anytime not present in the office as a day off. The ablation recovery had been slower than the recovery from the SEEG electrode removal, and I was getting impatient with my limitations.

But a small birthday party for a three-year-old I could put together. Two weeks ago, when I asked Sadie who she would like to invite to her party, her list was surprisingly short.

"Nana, Holly, Rob, you, Daddy, and Sam," she'd recited in a sing-song voice.

"Any friends?" I asked.

"No."

"Why not?"

"Because then they might take away attention from me on my special day," she said, and asked if she could go play. So, a few phone calls to the important adults in Sadie's life, and she had the party she wanted.

The doorbell rang, and Sadie ran ahead of me in anticipation of who could be there. Holly and Rob stood on the porch, huddling together to avoid the rain that blew sideways. Sadie's gaze bounced from Rob to Holly for some sort of gift, and landed on the large, beautifully wrapped box tied with a pink bow in Holly's arms. Her jaw dropped.

"Happy birthday, Sadie," Holly said, putting the box in Sadie's waiting hands.

"Come in," I said, pulling them inside and closing the door. "It's too wet out there."

Trembling with excitement, Sadie looked up at me with the silent question of 'Can I open it now?' I gave her a little nod, and she tore the beautiful wrapping away from the box, the pink bow discarded like last night's trash, until all that remained was the present itself, the thing that I had told Holly was Sadie's deepest wish: a baby doll with eyes that opened and closed.

Sadie's face lit up, her disbelief matching her excitement. I barely finished the "What do you say —" before she threw herself at Holly, almost crushing the box that protected the doll from the world. She wrapped her arms around Holly's knees and squealed, "Thank you! Thank you!"

"You're welcome," Rob said in mock acceptance.

Sadie threw herself at Rob, hugging his leg with one arm, the other clutching the precious boxed doll. "Thank you, Uncle Rob!"

She stared at the doll in the cardboard box behind the plastic protection: green eyes with dark eyelashes, a plush body with a vinyl head, arms, and legs, wearing a pink beanie that matched its removable onesie.

"Open for me, Mommy?" Sadie asked. She held out the box, her eyes full of hope and the magic that comes with being young and innocent.

"Sure, babe." Taking the box, I walked into the kitchen to find scissors. "You know, it's a pretty small party—just you guys, us, and Mom. It's been so helpful having her here while I've been recovering. I can't believe she stayed when we got back. I didn't realize how much we'd need the extra help."

Cutting open the box and the hard plastic ties that held Sadie's new baby in place, I pulled the doll from the safety of its container and placed it in the arms of its new owner. Sadie ran off, calling for her brother to see her newest toy.

Jonah came into the kitchen and broke off with Rob to sit in the living room, which left me and Holly alone.

"How've you been feeling?" she asked, leaning over to see the shaved side of my head. "Can I touch it?"

"Sure. I thought I'd heal faster like last time, but I guess your brain doesn't like having a part of it burned out. I've had to take it easier than I thought I would."

She rubbed the side of my head. "It's growing back."

"It'll take time." I sighed. "I think a lot of time."

"It's just hair," she said, shrugging.

"Then you shave part of yours, and we can stand here saying how 'It's just hair,'" I snapped. The hurt look in her eyes made me immediately remorseful. "I'm sorry, Holly."

"It's okay. No harm done. I get it."

This was part of what I loved about Holly: she meant that. My little snaps in the EMU, my impatience, imperfections over the past few months, and no harm done.

We joined the group in the living room, and I told the kids that they could help themselves to whatever food they liked. Sam took this responsibility seriously and showed all of us the choices he'd made—how he'd balanced between what he considered 'healthy' food and sweet food. We praised his efforts, and he sat on the floor, putting his plate on the coffee table with a smile, proud of his accomplishment. Not to be outdone, Sadie showed us her plate, laden with sweets, and received the same praise. They gobbled their food and ran into Sadie's room to examine and play with her loot.

Jonah stroked the long side of my hair. "Time for cake yet?" he asked.

"I think so. I'll get it." I heaved myself out of the comforting depth of the couch.

"Want help?" Holly called as I walked towards the kitchen.

"No. I got it."

The round cake from the local bakery sat on a glass cake holder. Decorated with a white unicorn head sprouting a rainbow horn, "Happy 3rd Birthday Sadie" written in purple cursive, and pink piping lining the top and bottom edges, the cake was truly a work of art. As I picked up the cake holder from underneath, I felt an aura coming. I stood still and waited for it to pass.

Another aura, the familiar wave from the back of my brain to the front, followed on the heels of the first. My body turned in a small circle.

"Ahhh," I said in monotone, not of my own volition. "Ahhh." The cake holder slipped slightly from my hands.

"Casey?" I heard Jonah's voice as I continued to turn in a circle. I could see Jonah, Rob, Holly, and my mom jump up from the couch and rush towards the kitchen. The cake half-slid off the flat glass, and Holly grabbed it and the holder, setting both on the counter. Everyone stared at me as my feet made small steps, round and round, and the sound emanated from my throat.

"What do we do?" I heard my mom ask in a voice bordering on panicked.

"I don't really know. I've never seen this before," Jonah answered.

Suddenly, the turning stopped, as did the noise. I glanced at the cake. "Glad it's okay," I said. "Nice catch, Holly."

"What was *that*?" Jonah asked.

"I don't know. I feel fine, though." *Fine.* As if whatever that was never happened. "How strange."

Hearing Sadie's voice, we all knew that the party had to continue, uninterrupted by whatever this had been.

"Really. I'm fine. I feel just like I did when I walked over here." I grabbed the candles and pushed them into the cake. "Hold this," I said, passing the cake to Jonah.

Reluctantly, and studying my face for any sign of pain or fatigue, Jonah held the cake as I lit the candles with a green lighter. Looking around, I saw everyone still staring at me. A strained silence filled the room like air in an overfilled balloon.

"Come on, guys," I said, smiling. "I feel *fine*. It's probably just my brain settling down more. Let's not let that ruin Sadie's birthday party."

My mom smiled, a false, positive energy in her eyes. "Alright, Casey. Let's sing, everyone. Sadie! Sam! Cake time!"

The children barreled into the room and sat side-by-side at the dining table, waiting expectantly for this main event.

"Happy birthday to you," I sang.

"Happy birthday to you," Jonah, Holly, my mom, Sam, and Rob joined in, "Happy birthday, dear Sadie, Happy birthday to you."

Jonah placed the cake on the table in front of Sadie, and her eyes shone as she took in the wonder before her.

"Make a wish!" Mom said.

Sadie closed her eyes to make her wish, opened them, and blew out the candles in one breath.

•　　•　　•

Up in the comfort and privacy of our bed with the party over and both children finally asleep, Jonah and I discussed the event in the kitchen, trying to decide if it was an actual seizure. Dim light came from the lamps on our night tables.

"It's not any seizure that I recognize," Jonah said.

"I mean, they burned part of my brain out. That has to be pretty traumatizing for it." I tried to soothe the fear building inside me as I remembered the wheelchair-bound woman in the waiting room and my loss of speech during brain mapping. "I bet all the auras and strange things go away after it settles down."

"We should set up a virtual visit with Dr. Alem. Just to make sure. I'm not sure that was just an aura."

"Well then, what was it if you're such an epileptologist?" Unwanted thoughts continued to creep through my mind like shadows. The shawl of darkness peeked out, hopeful again.

"I don't *know*." Jonah took my hand from under the comforter and stroked the back rhythmically. "I just think we should find out from Dr. Alem, tell him about it."

"Fine," I said, angry at the possibility that this whole experiment might have failed, that my hope might be shattered. I flipped away from Jonah and glared at the wall, furious with the world.

"Casey." Jonah's voice was almost pleading. "It might not mean anything. It might be a normal part of healing, just like the auras, you know?"

"It might be," I said, and, turning back to face him, I tucked my head under his chin.

He kissed the crown of my head and stretched his arm over me to turn off the lamp on my table before rolling over to switch off his light. We fell asleep huddled together, holding each other in the night.

CHAPTER 30

Jonah

We sat in silence at the dining table in front of Casey's laptop, waiting for Dr. Alem to connect to the visit. We had spent the past week discussing what the event in the kitchen might mean, why Casey was having such frequent auras over a month after the surgery. Did the ablation fail or was her brain still getting used to this new set-up? Would she just be having auras all the time from now on? Round and round we went until we realized that we did not have any answers.

The screen changed from our faces to show Dr. Alem's, our picture now stamp-sized up in the right corner. He sat in his office, wearing his white coat and tie, and smiled when he saw us.

"Hello! How good to see you!" he said.

"Likewise," Casey said. "I miss Cleveland."

"Oh, yes, it's beautiful this time of year," he joked. Through the windows behind him, the clouds were light gray and looked fluffy, as if dirty cotton balls covered the sky.

I wanted to move the conversation along, to get to the point, but I knew that Casey had a slower, more personable way of talking to her doctors, so I remained silent and tense.

Casey sensed my impatience. "Dr. Alem, I don't know how things are going over here. Jonah and I are a little confused. I've been having lots of auras since the surgery, as you know."

Dr. Alem nodded, taking notes on his computer.

"Last Saturday, we were in the kitchen and something strange happened." She described the turning, the involuntary sound, the quick finish and immediate recovery. "But I could go on with the day, as if nothing had happened. Was that a seizure? Does that mean the ablation didn't work? Or is it maybe just my brain still working things out? It's only been just over a month." She stopped talking when she saw Dr. Alem's face.

No, no, no. Don't say it, Dr. Alem. Say it's just a normal part of the healing process.

But I knew, and, I think at that moment, Casey knew, what his answer would be. She grabbed my hand under the table, and I almost cried out as her desperate grip rubbed my bones together.

Dr. Alem looked at Casey through the screen; his eyes had lost the sparkle of moments before. "That *was* a type of seizure, I'm afraid. It seems the ablation didn't completely work. It looks like the surgery *did* interrupt part of the epileptic network in your brain, but it didn't completely eliminate the pacemaker, if there is one. You remember that the department was split as to whether the frontal lobe was actually the pacemaker; sometimes it seemed that the parietal lobe was starting a seizure a millisecond before the frontal lobe joined in, but we weren't sure. But the way the seizures were presenting themselves physically lead us to believe that the frontal lobe was the leader. Perhaps we didn't take enough tissue, perhaps seizures could begin from another area. But it looks like the ablation did not completely make you seizure free."

"So, we gained nothing?" Casey said, blinking away tears. "After all that, that time, that pain, the being away from home — all of it? I still have to worry about SUDEP? About dy..." Her voice shook, and she stared at the man on the screen. "All of it for nothing?"

"No," Dr. Alem said forcefully. "We did *not* gain nothing. We gained a significant amount of information on how your brain works and where your seizures come from. We know more now about your brain than we ever have before."

"Is there something else we can try, now that you have that information?"

"At this point, no. But we can take this information into the future and use it when new technology comes out. As for SUDEP, you have gone several months without a tonic-clonic seizure, *and* we seem to have interrupted the seizure network, so it's likely you won't have tonic-clonics anymore. We can put the SUDEP worry to rest. If we can keep on this timeline and your seizures are less severe, well, that is a good step."

Casey started crying.

"I think, Dr. Alem, we were just so hopeful that the ablation would make her seizure free," I said, rubbing her back. She stared at her lap, not even trying to communicate. "It's quite disappointing."

"I understand," said Dr. Alem. "We'll keep your case on hand, Casey, always looking for something that can help you. I promise you that."

Casey wiped away her tears with the back of her hand and looked at the screen. "I know you will," she said.

"I'm sorry for this news. I had hope too. But, my new hope is that the seizures will be less frequent and less severe because of the interruption in the network. And, I think," Dr. Alem's face lightened, "this is possible."

With a plan for another virtual meeting in three months, I clicked the "END VISIT" button. Casey rubbed the left side of her head.

"How disappointing," she said, staring out the window. Except for the red house across the street, the view was full of dark gray and black: all the leaves on the trees lining the sidewalk had died by this point.

"Let's focus on the positive." I turned her chair towards me. "The new goal is fewer seizures and less severe seizures. The SUDEP threat seems to be gone. Can you believe that, Casey? *Gone.*" I couldn't tell if she even registered my words, but I continued, hoping for some acknowledgement. "*And* the Cleveland doctors have all the information they currently need to find something else, and Dr. Alem said he'll keep your case in mind, didn't he? These are all good things." My eyes searched her face for an opening, a show of some sort of emotion, an agreement that there were many encouraging things in this situation, a smile, a "You're right, Jonah."

Nothing. She sat, staring back at me, her eyes pits of sadness, and I knew what she was thinking: her seizures were still there. Maybe changed, maybe less severe, but not gone.

"How about some tea?" I rose to turn on the kettle. "We have some of the turmeric ginger you like—"

Casey shook her head, stood, and ran up the stairs to our room, slamming the door behind her. The children were on playdates, and the emptiness and silence of the house felt heavy, as if even the space was grieving after Dr. Alem's meeting. I stood by the kitchen counter and watched the kettle, lacking the energy to pick it up when the click of the button showed the water was ready. Instead of making tea, I turned away, plopped onto the sofa and put my head in my hands, wondering where to go from here.

•   •   •

I was not planning on bringing it up, but after the visit with Dr. Alem, at some point, Casey's working for Harold had to be addressed.

We go into marriage expecting to roll with the highs and the lows. Today had been a new low for both of us, and I knew better than to make it worse. Today was not the time for that discussion, I decided.

She said it on her own.

"I'm quitting," she said as we lay side by side in the darkness of our bedroom that night.

Funny. The same words almost left my mouth at work yesterday. I do not think it was a surprise to anyone that I quickly came to hate my job. The tension in the team felt so thick you could reach out and touch it: it was almost a civil war, with Dwyane outnumbered but somehow still winning. He was a terrible leader, his new-found power inflating his already overly-large ego. But now, he gave the orders, and everyone else looked at me as an example of how to react. My apathy must have spread like a virus to the rest of the group: I simply came to the office, did the bare minimum, and left at five.

And yesterday was almost the breaking point after I received an email from Dwayne.

Hey J,

I'm noticing a little shift in your attitude, and your work of late has been below your usual standards. I don't think I need to remind you that the Performance Improvement Plan exists to help those employees who are struggling at G&H. If you're having an issue, let's talk, before it gets to that.

Dwayne Richards
Director of Marketing

I smiled wryly as I read the email over and over. They only used a Performance Improvement Plan at G&H when someone made some sort of significant professional misjudgment—like smoking pot in the bathroom or blowing a pitch that resulted in the loss of a huge client. A PIP meant, *'We're giving you thirty days' notice that you're fired.'* I powered off my laptop and sauntered out of the office, unperturbed and amused. Putting *me* on a Performance Improvement Plan. *I dare you, Dwayne.*

Now, I rolled over to face my wife's back in the blanket of dark. She was saying the words I dreamed of saying to Dwayne, but also dreamed of hearing from her. "You are?"

"I'm done, Jonah. It's the only thing I can do now. You were right. The stress, Harold. I shouldn't have pushed myself. I did too much. I made it worse. And now…"

"What about the Kellan case?"

"Why do you even *care*?" she snapped. "This is what you wanted, isn't it? You should be happy. You get what you want."

"I'm not *happy*, Case." I tried to wrap my arm around her waist, but she tensed and brushed it off. "I know it's not what you want. But—"

"But it'll be good for me," she said, pulling the words out of my mouth in a sarcastic tone. "Good for *us*, right?"

"Casey..." I began, and fell into silence.

"You were right," she said finally, sounding less bitter, more resolute. "The work, the cases, Harold—it was all too much." Her voice cracked. "And quitting the firm is... good. It'll be good." She sounded like she was trying to convince herself. I was not part of the conversation anymore.

"It'll be good," she said, and I heard in her voice something I had never heard before: a note of defeat.

CHAPTER 31

Casey

When I walked into the office, I refused to think of the partner position, of how close I'd come to the opportunity I'd been chasing since graduating Stanford. I refused to think of Judge Woo's words, said so long ago; words that I used to bolster my confidence, used as a crutch to ignore my worsening seizures.

"I expect your litigation career will be long and successful," she had said to my twenty-six-year-old self. *If only she could see me now. Thirty-six and walking away from everything.*

I went to my office and stared at the papers on my desk, my computer, all things that after this morning I'd never need again. The boxes of documents from the Kellan case. Who would protect those women now? I tried to keep my mind on Jonah, Sam, and Sadie. They needed me, and staying could ruin my brain. Little by little, but eventually things could, and likely would, get worse. *This is going to be a good thing.*

I knew Harold's schedule was empty this morning, and, taking a deep breath, I strolled towards his office. I opened the door without knocking. Harold sat behind his desk with his morning cup of coffee and seemed momentarily surprised to see me.

"Yes?" he said.

The sky was a bright blue behind him, unusual in February, and the view from his window was still fabulous. A view that now I would never have.

Or.... Somehow, the words stuck in my throat. The sentence I had practiced so long in my head, practiced out loud to the mirror for months while getting dressed, said in the dark while I had fifteen electrodes drilled into my skull, would not come. Yes, I'd planned to say it, but only after the Kellan case was done. And the Kellan case wasn't done. *Maybe this is a sign. What if I stayed?* In my job, I fought for people who didn't have the voice to fight for themselves—why shouldn't I keep doing it? Jonah would understand. Eventually. Maybe. The kids would understand. I mean, they wouldn't have a choice. And these seizures would, well... Who knew? What if they didn't get worse?

"Something wrong, Casey?"

Then I remembered my conversation with Jonah last night. And Sam and Sadie—the stress of work, the auras, the seizures that took me away from them. I couldn't trade my brain for a view and a business card that said "partner." Pushing my ego down, I found the words.

"Harold, I resign." The sentence emerged painfully from deep in my body. I half-wanted to take it back, to grab the phrase and shove it back into my mouth, but I stood still, my gaze fixed on Harold's flushing face.

"You what?" He asked, his eyebrows drawing together.

"I resign. It turns out that the surgery failed. My seizures are back. And the stress from litigation is just going to make my epilepsy worse. It's—it's impossible for me to continue here." *Or anywhere*, I wanted to add.

He put down his coffee mug and spoke quietly, which was almost worse than yelling. "Just like that, huh?" Then his voice gained volume. "What about the Kellan case? You're going to just leave those women and—"

"I know. I wanted to see it through. But I need to listen to my brain. And my brain says I need to stop." I swallowed the lump in my throat.

"Well, I can't have quitters in my office," he said. "But, to be honest, I thought you were tougher than this." He glared at me from behind his desk, that famous look powered by intense anger that made most people give in. But I didn't give in. His attempt to stare me down didn't touch me anymore. Instead, it lit a fire inside me, and I said the first words that came to my mind.

"Harold, we both know I'm not a quitter. I'm leaving here and I doubt you'll find anyone as good to replace me. But I'm putting my health first, my family first. You should try it. Maybe you'd be able to keep a marriage for more than five years."

I grabbed the two pictures of my family from my office, left the building, and called Jonah to let him know that it was done.

"How do you feel, Case?" he asked.

"Fine," I lied. "I—well, fine."

"Okay. I'm proud of you. I love you."

When we hung up, I realized that his words disgusted me. Proud of me for what? For leaving my job? For giving up? For being too scared to go on?

"Fuuuuccckkk!" I yelled as I crossed the bridge from my office for the last time. Then the question that had lingered in the back of my mind suddenly shoved its way to the front, and my breath caught: if I wasn't a litigator, what was I?

I realized that I didn't have the answer.

CHAPTER 32

Jonah

Sitting in Dr. Duncan's examination room, nothing in the room had changed: the posters were the same, the table was in the same place, still covered with thin white paper, the two chairs against the window were the same, as was the rolling doctor's chair. But Casey was different; I was different. We had changed in the past six months. We were not the same people as before Cleveland, for many reasons, and it was surreal that this room seemed to have paused in time.

Casey quit her job two weeks ago. She relaxed the first week as she unraveled from the stress of work, but I could tell by the second Monday she was feeling restless, lost.

"Go for a walk," I suggested, as I packed to take Sam and Sadie to daycare. "The weather is lovely today."

She stood in her pajamas and stared at me, frowning, as if I was speaking a foreign language. "To where?" she asked. "With who? You mean just go alone? That's not fun."

"Call Holly?" I suggested. Casey glared at me, and I did not offer other ideas. I did not have any to offer, anyway.

We held hands as we waited for the doctor, but did not talk. We both hated Dr. Duncan. His lack of bedside manner—much less any common courtesy—left a bitter taste in both our mouths, but Casey needed a neurologist in Portland, he was also the only one in-network on my G&H insurance who specialized in epilepsy, so we swallowed our pride and here we were, back to update him on our new lives.

As before, he entered abruptly, without knocking, immediately sitting on the stool and logging into the computer.

"How's it going?" he asked. "How was Cleveland?"

Casey waited to answer until he turned to look at her, his face expectant with a slightly impatient tinge in his upraised eyebrows.

"We did a lot of testing. I was there for about three weeks," she said. "Ended up doing SEEG and had an ablation in January. It didn't work. I'm still having seizures. They're just different."

He pushed back his stool. "Of course it didn't work. I mean, really, what do we know about ablations? They burn a part of tissue out, but if they leave just a little bit, you're still going to have seizures. You probably shouldn't have done it."

"The doctors there said that they would tell their family members to do it, though," Casey said. "That it might make me seizure-free –"

"Ha!" Dr. Duncan laughed harshly. "Those guys over there are known for just wanting to cut. All those Middle-Eastern guys, they're so insistent on surgery. And the surgeon – what's his name?"

"Her."

"Her name?"

"Dr. Hernandez."

"Right. She's from Mexico?"

"Spain," Casey said through thin lips. I glanced over at her and saw that her face had gone pale, her eyes wide, but not with sadness – with fury.

"Well, I mean, show me a Spaniard who isn't aggressive. And this SEEG stuff? What information does it *really* give you? But Cleveland docs just *love* using that technology." He shook his head and turned back to the computer. "Of course the ablation failed."

I felt Casey tense up, and knew things were going to go very badly, very quickly.

"*You sent me there,*" she spat. "You told me I could die and then fucking *sent* me there!"

The curse word caught Dr. Duncan's attention, and he stopped typing.

"And where were *you* when I was sitting in a hospital bed with fifteen electrodes in my skull, trying to decide whether to burn out a part of my brain? Huh? Where the was your grand opinion *then*? And don't talk about the doctors like that. They're all better than you'll *ever* be, which is why they work in one of the best hospitals in the country and you're in this shitty little practice." She turned to me. "We're done here. I'll meet you at home." Standing up, she grabbed her keys and purse.

"Wait a sec." Dr. Duncan pointed to her keys. "You're not still driving, are you?"

"What? Yes. No one ever told me not to."

"Yes, I did."

"Actually, I've only seen you once before and, *no*, you *didn't*." She looked at me for confirmation.

"He didn't," I said.

"How did you think I was getting here?" Casey asked.

Dr. Duncan shrugged. "Well, you can't drive anymore. It's against the law."

"What? How am I supposed to get around?"

He shrugged again. "I don't know, but you can't drive."

"What's the law?"

"Three months without a seizure. So, you might as well just turn in your driver's license because, with your case, you're never driving again."

"You're the worst doctor I've ever seen!" Casey shouted. "What is *wrong* with you?"

I stood and put my arm around her waist. "If I hadn't been here, I don't think that I'd believe a doctor would say any of these things. This is the most unprofessional meeting I've ever witnessed."

I walked a shocked Casey out of the hospital to the parking garage. "I'll meet you at home," I said. "You can at least drive there." She stared at the keys in her hands and then back up at me. "And then we'll figure it out. It'll all be fine."

I heard her Subaru beep as she unlocked it, and watched her drive away. I sat in the driver's seat of my car, while Dr. Duncan's harsh words looped in my mind. Then, the practicalities of our new reality sank in and the stress in my body built. After Casey told Harold what I had wanted her to say for years, I realized what that meant for me: I had to keep my job at G&H. The only way for her to stay at home was for me to work. Casey's income had been good, but we were fine with just mine; however, we could not both be out of a job. And that meant I could not get sacked.

I took time from work to go to this appointment with Casey, but I knew that Dwayne, Jonathan, and Jacob were watching me, monitoring my work, and that I was one slip away from being put on a Performance Improvement Plan. So, I needed to smile, to stop sulking, to take orders from Dwayne as if I was just fine with the new hierarchy, like the sting of being passed over did not exist.

We all made sacrifices, adjustments in our lives because of Casey's epilepsy, I realized as I pulled out of the hospital parking lot. Casey left her favorite case, her job, and walked away from the potential partner position. Now I had to make sure that I stayed employed at G&H. I had to park my ego and get on with it.

MARCH 2017

CHAPTER 33

Casey

I lay on the floor of Sadie's room, staring at the ceiling. A full bucket of laundry sat beside me, the clothes ready to be put away, but the act of finishing the laundry seemed too difficult. I would have to sit up, grab a shirt or socks, and then fold it. *No. Better to just lie here on the carpet and stare at the ceiling.*

The house was quiet, almost echoing with silence. The children were at daycare; Jonah was at work. He seemed to work more now, or perhaps it was just that I wasn't working and was alone most of the day, so his hours were more noticeable.

The pressure of depression in my chest was especially heavy when I was alone. The hole in my heart since the seizures came back, since I stopped working, stopped driving, wasn't healing at all; instead, it seemed to have expanded, as if construction workers took careful time to dig it deeper and wider. The worst part of having this chronic illness and having a failed brain surgery, I found, was not necessarily the heartbreak from the failure, although that was bad, but it was the afterwards, when people stopped calling, emailing, texting to see how you were: when everyone else went on with their lives, and you were left on the floor, unable to fold the laundry, with a broken heart where hope had been.

I found the silence unbearable now, so I listened to music constantly. I would call my mother, Jonah, and sometimes Holly, but besides those connections, everyone had other responsibilities, and didn't have time to talk during traditional working hours. Now, I filled the empty space with a somber playlist: music that matched my mood.

I stopped trying to explain my depression to Jonah, who thought I could just "enjoy being home."

"Maybe find a hobby of some sort," he suggested. "What about a book club? Or yoga?"

"And how would I get there?" I looked at him with angry eyes.

"I don't know," he mumbled. "Just trying to help, Case."

I knew he wanted to help, but my bitterness and anger had to land somewhere, and he was the closest and easiest target. So, now we lived in a parallel universe: roommates who mostly avoided each other. We hadn't had sex since I quit working; he didn't even try to touch me, and I was fine with that. Most of our time together was now spent either in silence, bickering, or watching television on opposite sides of the couch.

To everyone else, everyone outside our home, I was "fine."

"Oh, you know," was my party line whenever an acquaintance from the outside asked, "I'm hanging in there." No one wanted to hear the truth. It was too sad, too intense. *Well, my seizures are coming every ten to fourteen days, the ablation didn't work, I had to quit my job because my brain found it too stressful, I can't drive, and I'm so depressed that I can't get off the floor and fold laundry. And how are you doing?* "It's fine" was all anyone had time for when I saw people outside the house, which was limited to neighbors, and only when I dragged myself to walk down the street for exercise.

I watched as rain hammered against the windows, and listened to a song about someone who tries to commit suicide, and the person who finds them pleading with them to hold on, not to die. I cried at the chorus. *Hold on, I still want you. Come back, I still need you.*

The floor vibrated. I plucked out my earbuds and wiped my face. "Hello?"

"Hi." Jonah's voice came from the entryway. "It's me."

I pushed myself to a seated position and tried to smooth out my greasy hair that I had fashioned into a high bun. Pulling one of Sadie's shirts from the laundry basket, I started to fold it as Jonah walked towards her room.

"Just folding the laundry," I said, holding up the small shirt as if providing proof.

"Okay," he said, and stopped in the doorway. Dressed in a designer t-shirt and tapered jeans over Blundstones, he looked so put together, the opposite of what I felt and looked—unshowered in gray sweatpants. "I thought I'd just come home for lunch quickly. I don't have any meetings this afternoon, and left the team with instructions on some projects. Do you want some lunch?"

"Sure. What do you want?"

He hadn't come home for lunch in over a month. I hoped he would offer to make it, so that I didn't have to cook as well.

"I don't know." He turned to the kitchen. "Let's take a look, shall we?"

I pushed myself to standing, torn between annoyance that I had to move and appreciation for the company.

Jonah pulled out one container after another of leftovers: rice, chicken, Brussel sprouts. "Would you like some of these?" He put a pan on the stove and turned on the gas.

"Sure." I sat at the kitchen counter.

We stayed in heavy silence: Jonah pushed the chicken around the pan and I watched him. When the food was hot, he divided it between two plates, and sat at the counter next to me.

"Thank you." I poked at the food.

"So, what have you been up to today?" he asked.

The dreaded question. *I wonder what he would say if I told him the truth?* 'Well, I got out of bed and, after sending the kids off to school and you to the office, I got back *in* bed, stared at the ceiling and thought about killing myself because I had several auras and I'm out of my rescue medications. Instead, I got out of bed again, pulled on a clean t-shirt, put what remains of my hair in a bun, and managed to bring the laundry basket to Sadie's room. I listened to depressing music as I lay on the floor and had a few more auras because it's been about ten days, so I don't want to leave the house. Only my mom and Holly called to check on me because the only other person who did that regularly — you — seems annoyed with me for not enjoying this time at home, and everyone else has other things to do. I thought about putting the laundry away, but it seemed like it took too much effort, so I stayed on the ground until you came. Now I'm faking normalcy, which I know you can see right through.'

That might be too much, considering where we were on the communication scale. I sugar-coated a partial truth:

"Not much. Just did some house stuff, and now I'm doing laundry. You?"

"I had an initial meeting for a new client, a start-up with a large budget," he said. "Nothing on schedule for the afternoon, but still a lot to do. You know how it is at the office." He ate his rice quickly, not waiting between bites or putting his fork down, so he didn't see me wince at the last part.

I stared at him, wondering what he thought of what his wife had become. Even though he was just six inches from me, I couldn't bring myself to touch him, to caress his hand. My emotions had shut down: I was out of commission at the moment, and unsure if I would ever be fixed. *He still cares. Probably.* I still cared for him, but I was too caught up in the unrelenting seizures and depression to show it.

I was having thoughts I wanted to tell him, but was too ashamed to say out loud: a darkness he might not take as seriously as I needed him to, that he would just brush off as getting used to being home. He was either too stressed, too clueless, or too apathetic to initiate a conversation about feelings. I couldn't tell. But now, he had a wife who couldn't even muster the energy to get showered and dressed. A wife who couldn't drive, didn't have a job, who lived in the invisible cage of epilepsy and had forgotten how to express her anger and sadness to the person who was supposed to be closest to her.

Jonah pushed away from the counter, his plate empty, and slid it into the dishwasher. "Are you going to get dressed today?"

My eyes welled with tears, and I studied my hands in my lap. "I don't know," I whispered. "It's so hard."

"You should try to get dressed, Casey," he said in a cold, hard voice, sounding like a professor reprimanding a truant student.

"I know, *Jonah*," I said, my bitter tone matching his. "I'll try."

"Alright." He walked towards the front door and grabbed his car keys. "See you this evening."

I heard his car start and drive away. The unbearable silence returned, but I stayed at the counter and stared at my food. Finally, I got up, leaving the plate of uneaten food behind. I walked over to the knife station and stared at the handles sticking out of the wooden block. The rain had eased up, no longer a hammering, now tap, tap, tapping on the kitchen window. The gray light from outdoors fell through the window onto the stove and kitchen counter, leaving the knives in shadows.

Looking at the black handles, I wondered how much it would hurt to slice my wrists. How much it would bleed. Would it make a big mess? I wouldn't want to leave Jonah with a large mess to clean up. Did people slice up and down or sideways? I stood and stared at the knife block, hands by my sides, listening to the rain, and considered my options.

But Sam and Sadie. Sam and Sadie. No, I couldn't leave them. How does someone grow up if their mother commits suicide? *And my mom.* She'd never get over losing her only child. Jonah would grieve, but he could move on, marry someone else, someone with a cooperative brain, someone who could run, drive, climb mountains, ski. If it was just me and him, well...

But it wasn't just me and him. Turning away from the knives, I quickly left the kitchen, returned to Sadie's room, pulled another shirt from the pile of laundry, and slowly began to fold.

CHAPTER 34

Jonah

I drove from our house to a small coffee shop on Division, a favorite of mine and Casey's, before she seemed to fall apart. Sitting at the corner table, I looked out the window through the drizzling rain, watching for the familiar red bob to appear. The baristas busied themselves with drinks that included Moroccan spices, and the scent infused the air. Their tattooed-sleeved arms moved quickly as they poured espresso shots into tall paper cups, always asking the customer if they would like a milk substitute.

Holly rushed in from the rain, pulling off the hood of her jacket. She quickly scanned the white-walled space and waved at me as she moved towards the table.

"Be back in a minute," she said, taking off her wet black raincoat and hanging it on the light wooden chair across from my padded seat at the wall. "What're you having?"

"Moroccan mint tea."

"I'm more of a latte girl myself," she said. "Be right back."

When she returned, she took a sip of her drink before speaking. "What's up?"

"It's Casey," I began. "I just don't know what's gotten into her."

"What'd you mean you 'don't know what's gotten into her'?" Holly frowned. "She's depressed, Jonah. And she has every right to be — the ablation didn't work, she quit her job because of these seizures and has no current prospects for another—again because of the seizures. Everything she's worked for all her life, hoped for—poof, gone in a matter of weeks. Your wife is not meant to sit at home day in and day out. And that prick doctor said she can't even drive anywhere. What the fuck do you *think* is going on? All of that. That's what's 'gotten into her.' I've tried to talk to her about it, but she just clams up. Even to *me*. 'I'm fine.' 'It's all fine.' Bullshit. She should probably see a therapist."

"Therapy? What? No. We can handle this by ourselves." I shook my head and stared at my tea. "She doesn't even shower or get dressed, Holly," I said, my voice breaking. "Sam's sixth birthday is coming up next week, and she's barely acknowledged it. And you know how she loves planning parties."

"Have you tried to talk to her about any of this?"

I wrapped my hands around my warm cup, turning it between my palms. "I mean, I've asked her to shower, to get dressed. What am I supposed to say? She won't talk to me about anything. We just talk about what we're having for dinner and the children. And she's so testy, we just, I—I just—we've sort of stopped talking, in a way. I never know what to say, you know?"

"Jonah, you're a smart guy," Holly said. "Can't you see that not taking care of herself is a symptom of something bigger? *Much* bigger. Your concern can't just be limited to showering, dressing. It's bigger than Sam's birthday. Those are signs of a bigger problem. She needs professional help."

"Maybe."

"*Maybe*? What's so wrong about seeing a therapist?"

For some reason, the thought of a therapist made me feel uncomfortable, as if we were admitting defeat. When I was a child, no one went to a therapist for their problems. You kept quiet and just got on with it. "I don't know. It just seems... extreme. Help me, Holly. What am I supposed to say?"

"How about 'How're you feeling, Case?' 'Seems like you're a little depressed. Wanna talk about it?' or, even better, proactive, 'Let's talk about it.'"

I stared at my tea again. "Like I said, we seemed to have changed how we communicate, you know? We're not like that anymore. And things are stressful for me at work, and—"

"So?" Holly seemed amazed at my words, and not in a good way. "This is your *wife* we're talking about, not some Nike pitch. What would you say if she came to you and said 'Jonah, I'm so depressed. I miss working. I'm stuck in the house, and the seizures are still coming. I don't know what to do.' What would you say?"

"She hasn't done that, though. I've told her to enjoy this time. Relax. Just rest her brain. That there's more time now with the kids, less stress in the house. I told her that I'd *love* to just be able to stay home. She got furious with me, said I didn't understand, but she never explained what I didn't understand." As the words left my mouth, I thought, through the hiss of warming milk from behind the coffee bar, that it might have been the wrong thing to say, especially to someone like Casey, who used to define herself by her job.

"Did you ask what you didn't understand?" Holly asked.

"No."

"So, you're just going to watch her spiral downhill and not do anything? Your life partner, your wife. You're just going to sit back, ask her to shower, tell her to be happy, and not talk to her about what's *really* going on?" Now the tears were in Holly's eyes. "This is Casey, Jonah. *Our* Casey. She needs help, and now." She took another sip of her latte. "You really should look into therapy for her. Maybe even couples' therapy."

I sat silently, remembering how Casey's laugh used to sound, realizing that I hadn't heard it on over a month. "Maybe the therapist is a good idea," I conceded. "It's worth a try." This was not Britain. And if one of the strongest women I knew was telling me that my wife needed a therapist, then maybe, I supposed, it was worth a try.

"You have to give her a break," Holly said. "I know she still loves you. She would have told me if she didn't." She glanced at her watch. "I have to go. Meeting at two." When she looked at me, her expression softened. "Jonah, please, talk to her. *You* have to be the one to do it. Promise you'll talk to her."

"I promise."

"Good." She slipped on her raincoat and flipped the hood over her head. "Therapy. You can't fix this all on your own." A blast of cool air hit the customers in line as she left the shop. Turning my now lukewarm cup round and round in my hands, I contemplated how far Casey and I had fallen in the month since she left work, and how I could fix it.

CHAPTER 35

Casey

On the carpet next to my leg, my phone vibrated. *Probably Holly or my mom.* Looking down, I was shocked at the name: Kathy Kellan. Slowly, I put down the shirt I had been folding, and picked up the phone.

"Casey Scott."

"Casey?" Kathy's voice held a note of panic.

"Kathy? Are you okay?" She'd never called me on my personal phone, even after Violet gave her the number while I was in Cleveland. "What's wrong?"

"Did you get fired or something? Why aren't you on our case anymore? Harold said you don't work at the firm. Did you change jobs? Where you at?"

I sighed and stared at the green laundry basket next to me. *At home, folding children's t-shirts.* "No, I'm not with another firm. I had to quit for health reasons. It's—I wanted to stay—but it's my epilepsy. Turns out I can't just take a pill and be fine like your cousin. I had to leave. But I wanted to stay." I rushed the last part. "Who has your case now?"

I heard Kathy take a deep breath. "Harold." Her voice was bitter and hard. "He took over."

Ah. Now I understood the reason for the call. "And how's that going?" I asked, trying to keep my tone light.

"He's horrible, Casey! Horrible. The other girls agree with me. His attitude, it's like we're bothering him when we call. Had some sort of media—no, what's it called?—meditation?"

"Mediation?"

"Yeah, that. Had that last week. Didn't work. I didn't even know what was going on. I'm sittin' in a room with Harold, and this person keeps coming in and out—I think it was a judge—and saying 'Well, this is their number,' and Harold kept saying, 'Nope. This is our number,' and then just looked at his phone when we were alone, and didn't even try to explain what was going on. Kept saying something about 'need at least the prayer,' and juries giving 'putative damages.'" She sounded furious.

"Punitive damages."

"Well, I don't know what the hell that is, but I sure wasn't about to ask *him*. Can't you just come back? We want *you*."

'We want you.' And I wanted them. I wanted this case. But my brain. I almost screamed in frustration.

"We're gonna go somewhere else if we have to keep dealing with Harold. The girls are treated bad enough down in prison. And I don't need one more man in my life acting like I don't count. We're gonna find a good woman lawyer, like you, and go with her. But we really just want *you*."

My heart ached for them. I knew how Harold could be, especially with women; that's part of why he assigned the case to me in the beginning.

"Just hold on a second. Don't leave yet. I can't go back full-time—I don't even know if Harold would take me back," I said with a harsh laugh. "But it might be possible to come in as co-counsel."

"So, you'll come back? Take our case back from that asshole?" Kathy said, her voice lifting.

I bit my lip as I thought. I'd told Jonah that I was going to quit after finishing this one case. He couldn't be too mad about me doing what I'd planned to do anyway. "When is trial?"

"About three weeks from now. Little over. Starts April 17th. Do I have to go up on the witness stand? What do I say?" Now the note of panic returned, replacing the excitement of a second ago. "I don't want to ask Harold—"

"Okay, okay. I'll call Harold. We'll see what I can do."

"Thank you, thank you, Casey," Kathy said. "We just can't deal with him anymore."

"I get it. I'll call you back in a bit." We hung up, and I sat on the floor, contemplating my next move. Thoughts swirled around my head. I knew how to get Harold to take me on as co-counsel—that part was easy. This was an exceptional case—easily the most potentially lucrative he'd had since 2010—and the clients wanted to deal with *me*, not him. All I had to do was tell him they were going to go somewhere else, and then stand firm while I named the terms. Easy.

The harder part would be telling Jonah. But, suddenly, I felt alive again. I felt the dark cloud that inhabited my body dissipate. If I could explain this to him, make him understand, then everything would be okay. In a perfect world, I'd talk to Jonah before calling Harold, but, I mean, I didn't want to bother him at work. He'd seemed stressed lately, and, since Dwayne got that promotion, a little grouchy when he came home. And three weeks was not a lot of time to prep for a trial on a case of this magnitude, although I remembered the information inside and out.

I picked up the phone and called the office.

"Office of Harold Charles Williams, Jr.," Violet's nasally voice said.

I smiled at the familiar sound. "Hi, Violet. It's Casey."

"Casey!" she said. Then her voice dropped to a whisper. "How *are* you? Are you calling to speak to *him*?"

"I'm okay," I said. "And, yeah. Is he available?"

"He's free right now," she said. "Just, he might not take your call…"

"Tell him I'm calling about the Kellan case. And if he says to send me to voicemail, tell him that I've just talked to Kathy Kellan."

A second later, his gruff voice answered. "Casey?"

"Hi, Harold."

"Why is Kathy calling you?"

"It's interesting, Harold. Seems she's not that pleased with how you're treating her. She's talking about taking her case elsewhere."

"Bullshit."

"No. Not bullshit. But she'll stay with the firm if I work her case."

There was a pause on his end. I could almost see his eyes narrowing, his face turned towards the ceiling of his office as he leaned back in his chair. "So now you want to come back? I don't think so. She'll stay. No one is going to take this case three weeks before trial."

"She won't stay. She'll find someone else. There are plenty of attorneys around who would take the case and get the trial date moved. Everyone in the state wanted this case. And you're losing her."

"So, what do you want, Casey?" he asked. He knew everything I said was true.

"I've got a proposal for you," I answered. And I laid out my plan. Now it was his turn to listen.

·   ·   ·

When Jonah and the kids came home that evening, dinner wasn't made, laundry wasn't put away, the dishwasher wasn't empty, but I was smiling.

I'd been on the phone for over an hour with Harold, laying out my plan to come on as co-counsel and the terms: I'd try the case—not him—I'd decide, with the clients, whether to accept any settlement offers, I'd deal with all the press, and we'd split the money from a settlement or verdict: his firm would get one-third, and I'd get the rest. At first, he'd tried to push back, but I wasn't negotiating; I was telling. The alternative to one third, I explained, was zero because when I got off the phone with him, I was going to call Kathy and let her know whether he was amenable to working with me. When I ended the call, I felt like the old me, the me before seizures ruined my life; I felt better than I had in over a month. I felt, for the first time in a long time, the slightest bit of control over my destiny.

While I kissed the children and helped them take their jackets off, Jonah walked past me and looked around the empty kitchen.

"Guess we're ordering in?" he said.

I nodded. "I think so. Thai?"

"That's fine." He started looking at his phone for a menu. "Alright, so, how about some noodles for the kids, and — what would you like? Curry?"

"That sounds good. Look, Jonah, I'm sorry I didn't cook. I was just busy with some other stuff — "

But instead of giving me the disappointed look so common as of late, he crossed the kitchen and wrapped his arms around me. It was the most intimate we'd been in months, and it felt foreign, but welcome. I leaned into his body, savoring his affection.

"It's okay," he said. "You don't have to explain."

I closed my eyes and stayed in his embrace, wrapping my arms around his waist. "Jonah, I have something to talk to you about, but maybe after the kids are down. Maybe we could have tea in the living room?"

He pulled back and smiled. "I'd like that. I have something to talk to you about, too." Our eyes met, and his look was loving, a feeling I hadn't seen for what seemed like ages. I swallowed and pushed down my nerves, wondering how this conversation was going to go and what he had to tell me.

•　　•　　•

After the last goodnight to Sam, I tiptoed over to the couch where Jonah sat with two cups of tea: just like the old times, when I was still practicing law, before everything fell apart. What used to be a nightly ritual felt strange, but familiar, like the hug earlier. I took the tea and sat next to him.

"So, who goes first?" I asked.

"Can I go first?"

"Sure."

He took a deep breath and put down his mug, adjusting his pose to completely face me. My heart rate sped up as he reached for my hand, his expression serious. *This could be bad.*

"Case," he began, "I think you're depressed. I understand that—being in the house all day alone, not being able to drive or work. I get that all of it adds up, I do. I think we should go to therapy. Couple's therapy. I don't know how to change what the situation is right now, and will probably be for a while, but I don't want you to feel sad or alone anymore." He took another deep breath. "What do you think?"

My eyes widened, surprised. Jonah was suggesting therapy? Since when did he even think about therapy?

"Well, that's an interesting idea," I said evasively. "And, you know, maybe. I mean, yes, I've been depressed. I have." Tears came to my eyes, and the tight rubber band of anxiety pulled at my sternum as I thought about my days since I quit working. The shadow that followed me returned. "It sucks being here alone all day—you're right. I hate it, actually. And not being able to drive, or work... Especially work."

He squeezed my hand. "So, are you game, Case? Because I am."

"Well, like I said, *maybe.*" I paused, trying to decide how to phrase the coming information. "The thing is, part of the depression is that I'm not working, and I think that I'm going to be less depressed for a while at least."

He looked confused: his mouth turned down, and he cocked his head. "What does that mean, Case? You can't take on a full-time litigation job."

"Right," I agreed, licking my lips. "So, it's not going to be a *full-time* litigation job. It's just going to be one case. The Kellan case."

In the low light of the living room, he looked even more confused. "The Kellan case? I don't understand. You're going back to Harold?" He pulled his hand away and crossed his arms.

"No. *No.*" I explained to him about the call from Kathy and my arrangement with Harold. "It's just this one case. I always said that I'd stop after the Kellan case was done. That was it, that was the deal. The case isn't done, and they need me, Jonah. I'm needed again."

"So, you're essentially going back to work."

"Only for about three weeks. That's it. Trial is in three and a half weeks, and then—"

"And *then*? Then what? You go and find another case? And another?"

I felt tears run down my cheeks, leaving warm, wet lines. "Jonah. This is not working for me." I said. "Being at home. Alone. Every single day. I hate it. I need something more."

"Which is why I'm proposing therapy. So we can figure out what that more is or could be." He leaned forward again. "Litigating a multi-million dollar case isn't the solution. It's going to bring the stress back, the seizures—"

"The seizures are going to come whether I work or not!"

"They'll come more if you work!" His voice rose slightly and his eyes hardened. "How could you be so selfish? You couldn't even call me?"

"Because I knew you'd say no," I admitted. Now it was my turn to be defensive, to cross my arms and glare, blinking back the tears. "Because I knew you'd tell me to just stay at home. 'Shower, Casey. Get dressed, Casey. Rest, Casey.'" I imitated his accent cruelly, and it gave me some satisfaction.

He lowered his eyes and his cheeks flushed. "I'm not going to say that anymore. I'm sorry."

"Three weeks and a half weeks, Jonah," I said, softening. "That's all I'm asking. Your support while I finish what I started, what I always meant to see through. *Then* we can go to therapy. *Then* we can talk about the next steps." I reached for his hand, but he pulled it away and shook his head. "Jonah," I was almost pleading now, "please. I need to feel useful again."

"I can't support this. You can't do this to us." He pointed towards the kids' rooms.

"I've been considering suicide." *There.* The feelings I hid for so long, felt ashamed of having, saw as a weakness, were now out. *Do with them what you will, Jonah.*

"Casey. No." He moved over and pulled me in, kissing me on the cheek, the neck: desperate kisses in a desperate hug. "No, Casey. No."

"Please, Jonah. Please. Just through this case," I whispered into the crook of his neck, feeling his tears on my cheek, his chest heave. "Then we can do all the therapy you want. I'll chill out, find something to get me out of the house. I just need to finish this one case."

"Fine. Finish the Kellan case," he said, wiping his eyes as he let me go.

I smiled.

"I've missed seeing you smile," he said. "It's been a long time, hasn't it?"

"I know," I said. My mind wandered towards courtroom strategy: witnesses I would need, possible cross-examination questions.

"Casey?"

"Hmmm?"

"I'm going to lose you to this case, aren't I?" He said with an annoyed look on his face.

I shook my head. "No. I'll be here. Present." *At least I'll try.* "It's just three weeks, Jonah." I smiled again and rubbed the back of his hand with my thumb. *Therapy.* The idea reeked of Holly, which I found vaguely amusing and comforting, but I knew that working on the Kellan case — the case of a lifetime — would be all the therapy I needed for right now.

CHAPTER 36

Jonah

I spent lunch researching 'Couples therapists Portland.' There were hundreds of them. How was I supposed to pick? Maybe I would go through the list with Casey once she was back from—I meant, done with—the case. Holly responded as expected when I told her the day after Casey dropped the bomb:

"Well, it's not a terrible idea. I mean, that case was keeping her going throughout the EMU, after Cleveland, even after the ablation. Now she can finish what she started and always meant to finish."

"But, her seizures—"

"Jonah, they're not going anywhere. Just give her the three weeks. At least she agreed to the therapy."

"Sort of," I pouted.

"Maybe you should go to some sort of support group or therapy yourself."

"It's impossible to choose a therapist. There are thousands of them."

"Then look for an epilepsy support group. Maybe one for caretakers. There can't be thousands of *them* in Portland."

Another option I had not considered: support groups. What were support groups, anyway? Too embarrassed to ask Holly, I hung up, promising to keep her updated.

"Knock, knock." Dwayne's voice came from behind me, and I turned to see him opening my office door. "Bad time?"

I quickly closed my browser. "Not at all." I smiled, trying to push the hate down in my chest. "Take a seat."

My office was large, with room for an L-shaped standing desk and two monitors, a small sofa, and a couple of large, puffy, angular chairs. Dwayne sat on the sofa, close to the door. I sat across from him in a chair.

"How're you doing?" he began with a disingenuous grin.

Oh, Lord, is he serious? "Wonderful. Thanks for your email. I hadn't realized how much I had drifted since the new year."

He waved his hand in the air, as if dismissing the idea that a P.I.P had ever been mentioned. "Well, you're back on track now. That last pitch was great, and I'm glad to see you've been socializing more. Community is really important at G&H, as you and I both know."

"Very important," I said, gritting my teeth. I knew this trick: get the adversary on your side by finding some common ground. I used it on some of my younger direct reports to get them to work harder. I had also used it on Dwayne when he first started, and as he progressed at G&H, to cut through his hostile attitude.

"How're things going at home?" he asked with what I could easily recognize as contrived concern. "How's Casey feeling?"

Terrible. Or better. One of the two. "She's fine. Thanks for asking." I kept smiling, and my cheeks began to ache from the effort.

"Great." Dwayne rose. "Well, I just wanted to check in, let you know that we on the third floor are very impressed with your work and effort over the past few weeks. Keep it up."

"Will do." My words disgusted me. I had traded in my self-respect to keep my job.

"Are you coming to the auditorium to watch the talk at noon? Jonathan brought the TED Talk guy in—the one who talks about how not to procrastinate? The one with the monkey drawings? It's going to be hilarious." Dwayne chuckled, the chortle that grated on my nerves.

"I might drop in, but I've got so much to do here. Better to work than to watch a talk about procrastination," I joked. He did not smile. "I'll be at the early happy hour after the Samsung pitch, though." *But, I've got* kids *to drive home and I have a family and* – I knew all these words would just fall on deaf ears, as they had with Jonathan and Jacob. Family before G&H: the wrong order in their eyes. "So, I'll see you then."

As soon as he left, I went back to my computer and Googled 'Epilepsy Caretaker Support Groups Portland.' There was one this Wednesday at noon at a hospital four blocks from the G&H building. *I think I'll check it out. Maybe someone else has a spouse or someone like Casey. Even though there's really no one like Casey.* It would be good to hear other stories, other people's similar struggles. I could just listen. Maybe this could be the beginning of my therapy.

I marked myself out Wednesday from noon to one. I would try the group for one week, and see if I liked it or not. When I thought about telling Casey, my torso tensed and I realized I did not want to. I could not quite place my finger on the reason, but I could just see Casey's reaction: a confused look on her face, the long half of her hair cascading over her shoulder, the short half fuzzy around her ears, with the question in her eyes coming from her mouth:

"Why? Do you feel like a *caretaker* for me?"

"Because I want to see what other people feel" would be my response. And I knew that would not give her the details she wanted.

•   •   •

Entering the support group room, I noticed people milling about a tan plastic table with water, a large carafe of what I could only assume was hot coffee, and a plate of pastries. There were about ten people, some sitting in chairs arranged in a circle. They seemed to know one another. The clock said 11:58. I avoided the refreshments, and picked an empty chair on the far side of the room. I was not eager to make friends; I just wanted to see what this was all about.

A woman with a shoulder-length bob in her early thirties sauntered over from the table.

"Is this taken?" she asked, pointing to the chair on my right. Her voice was husky, and the question almost sounded sensual.

"Uh, no. No. Not taken," I stuttered.

She smiled and slid into the chair. I suddenly felt edgy and shifted my chair slightly away from her. *I shouldn't be here. I should have told Casey.*

The room fell quiet as a lanky Hispanic man in his late 40's took a seat. He looked at each person, deliberately making eye contact with them one-by-one. "Thank you all for coming," he finally said in a rich, deep voice. "Welcome to the Epilepsy Foundation Caretaker Support Group. I'm so glad you could all make it."

Most people mumbled a 'You're welcome,' including the woman next to me.

"Let's go around the room quickly, and you can introduce yourself if you feel comfortable, and how you're connected to the epilepsy community. I'll go first. My name is Anthony Ramirez and I have a fourteen-year-old daughter with epilepsy." He looked to his right where a balding man slouched in a chair. "Would you like to introduce yourself?"

"I'm George Oreaky. My mom has had epilepsy for thirty-one years, and lives with me and my wife." George stared at the floor and spoke quickly, as if he just wanted to get the introduction over with.

Everyone went: some had siblings with epilepsy, parents, children. No spouses, though. Now, the woman next to me spoke. I started to sweat.

"I'm Rachel," she said. "I have a sister with epilepsy. She's in a home near where I live. She needs round-the-clock care, and—oh, that's more than you asked for right now, isn't it, Anthony?" She giggled, and the group laughed with her obligingly.

I stole a glance at Rachel. She wore a tight t-shirt that emphasized her breasts, which I doubted was an accident. Her pants were also snug and ended in black Doc Martens.

"And you?" Anthony was asking me. I ripped my eyes away from Rachel's legs and tried not to blush.

"I'm Jonah. I have a wife with epilepsy. She's a lawyer."

The group nodded, impressed. I gathered from the response that most of their loved ones were not as functional as Casey.

After the introductions, Anthony began. "Of course, as we all know, caregiving comes in many forms with many roles. We have parents here, siblings, a spouse." He nodded to me. "And then every person with epilepsy has unique needs and desires for your role, and *you* have unique needs and desires for your role. This is a safe space — let's establish that first. I'm curious: what does a day in the life of your caregiving look like? And anybody can chime in whenever."

Sitting here, I realized that I actually had it pretty easy. Parents talked about always thinking about the next medication, special diets, the next activity. Grown children talked about role reversals: some of them did not see the caretaker role coming, some of them always knew it would be a part of their lives. And then Rachel spoke.

"Well, I'm somewhat of the primary caretaker for my sister, and somewhat not, so I'm stuck in that in-between place. Our parents died in a car wreck last year, so then her epilepsy landed on me. I mean, she was already in the home, but Mom always took care of getting her meds, went and sat with her all day, helped her through seizures. I..." She paused as her raspy voice broke. "I can't do that, you see. I have a job. I want to have a life. I want to find love. But, I feel like I need to go see her every day. And I feel, I feel..." She began to cry.

I was not sure what I was supposed to do. Rub her back? Comfort her? Luckily, Anthony took over.

"It's fine, Rachel. Feel your feelings." The group murmured in assent. "Guilt is a common feeling among caretakers. No one judges you in this room." Again, common assent.

"Jonah?" Anthony turned to me while Rachel gathered herself, relying on the box of tissues that seemed to appear out of nowhere.

"Oh. Right. I have a wife, Casey, and she was a litigator. Is a litigator, I suppose. And one of her main triggers is stress, so she had to quit her job—litigation isn't a very low stress career." I got a few chuckles out of that one, including from Rachel, and felt a little bolder. "But now she's back on a case, somehow. Anyway, last year, for the first time, I started keeping things from her, things that are stressful to me, and would be stressful to her, for us, and I didn't want to make her more stressed. It's hard because sometimes I feel like not telling her about my life, my job and things like that is lying, but it would just add to the stress on her brain, wouldn't it? Maybe it would leaed to arguing. Maybe she wouldn't get a good night's sleep because of it, and that's a worry, isn't it?" I searched the faces for any support and found it in every single one.

"That sounds hard for you," Anthony said.

"It *is*," I responded. I suddenly realized how long I had been keeping secrets from Casey. Secrets that I thought would trigger her brain, or add to the stress she received from Harold and her clients every day. "I used to tell her everything, and then her epilepsy got worse, and she left for the hospital, and I just stopped. Stopped telling her. I just..." I could not finish the sentence. Rachel patted me on the back.

"It's okay," she said. I looked over at her and met her eyes. They were dark blue, like two deep lakes. "I understand."

I could not remember the last time I heard that sentence. *I understand.* Not at work, not at home, not from my wife, not from my parents. *I understand.*

"Wanna go get a coffee or something?" Rachel asked after the meeting wrapped up.

"Sure," I said, trying to keep my eyes from wandering below her neck. G&H could wait.

We walked out of the hospital and started a conversation about being caretakers that did not stop until we had to part because of a meeting I had at work. Rachel understood me, and I understood her. The challenges, secrets, stresses—I could tell her all of it without judgment. I gave her my number, went back to the office, pitched Samsung their new summer campaign, and waited for a call or text that, when it came, made me both excited and uncomfortable.

CHAPTER 37

Casey

The Kellan case became my life, as Jonah and I both knew it would. It also became the constant source of our bickering, which sometimes made me want to scream at him "This extra stress is not helping!" but, I stopped short of screaming during these arguments, reminding myself that in just a few days, the case would be over.

"Help me make dinner," he said as he stood over my shoulder, watching me flip through documents in a frenzy.

"I am. I mean, I will. I just have to—"

"There's always an 'I just have to—', Casey. Come help me make dinner."

I sighed and gave up on finding the document for the moment. "Fine. What are we making?" I slammed my chair back and stood up from the table angrily.

"Well, if you don't want to—"

"Jonah, do you want me to help you with dinner or not?"

"I want you to *want* to help me. I want you to think about it. I want—" He paused. "I want a wife."

"You have a wife."

"These past few weeks, it hasn't felt like it. I *knew* this would happen. You'd leave all of us behind for this case—"

"Jonah, this is going to be my last trial. There's no way to be a part-time litigator—we both know that. As long as things keep going as

248

they are, after this trial, unless something else comes up to fix my brain, that's it for my legal career. This is what I have left." I pointed to the laptop and documents scattered on the table.

My voice reflected how I'd felt inside when I'd realized the implications of my decision to leave Harold and the limitations I now faced. The Kellan case was going to be my last case for the foreseeable future, and with these seizures, maybe my last case ever. The case started gaining traction in the press over the past few weeks: at first just small articles in the *The Oregonian*, mentioning the trial, but each bigger than the last. Then, suddenly, it had gone national: the AP, CNN, MSNBC started doing stories about it, calling Harold's office, asking for quotes.

"Tell them 'No comment'," I instructed Violet. "And do *not* let Harold on the phone with any reporters, big or small."

The pressure built as the press focused on the state of prisons and sexual assault within prisons, all over the United States. Panels on evening news shows discussed "the situation of incarceration within this country," and, suddenly, this case had become a beacon upon which all other prison cases would stand. Or fall.

So, now, I had to win it, and I would win it. I'd go to the mat, win, give the reporters the statement that they were all craving, comfort my clients as they cried with happiness in front of millions of people, and then come home. As I explained this to Jonah, his face changed, losing the stress and tense look it held for who knows how long.

"We're making spaghetti," he said, taking my hand. For a moment, our arms swung back and forth, and emotions inside me mixed like ingredients for a potion in a cauldron: anxiety, relief, stress, focus, all intertwined in different parts of my body.

"Ok. I'll sit and watch while you boil water," I said, squeezing his hand.

During dinner, his phone pinged from his messenger bag.

"Looks like work needs *you* more now, too," I said, tilting my head and smirking. "I'll get it." I rose to report the text to him. "Password the same?"

He blushed. "Yeah, but you sit. I'll get it. Sorry, everyone. They know not to contact me after work until at least 7:30. Must be an emergency." He stood up from the kitchen counter we were currently using for every meal, as I'd commandeered the dining table for my mission control, and took his phone towards the entryway. After a minute, he didn't come back. I could hear him tapping a return text near the front door.

"Excuse me, kids," I said, putting my napkin on the counter. "I just need to bring Daddy back."

When I walked over to him, he was smiling at the screen, lost in the virtual conversation in his hand.

"What's going on?" I asked. "Are you done?"

He looked up, almost guiltily. *Yeah, Jonah, you can't give me shit for working hard when you're getting texts from the office at six.*

"Sorry. Team member text chain. They needed to know — anyway, I'm coming back now. And — look! I'm putting the phone on Do Not Disturb." He slid the phone into his work bag, and put an arm around my shoulder as we walked back to the table.

·　　·　　·

The settlement offer came late Wednesday afternoon: four days before trial.

"Doug Randall on the phone for you," Violet said hesitantly. "Do you want me to — "

"Put him through."

He offered the prayer plus a small amount more. "The offer's good until tomorrow at five," he said curtly, and immediately hung up.

Mulling the amount over in my mind, I called Harold.

"Randall called with a settlement offer."

"And? What is it?"

I told him the number.

"Not bad," he said, slowly. "Not bad at all. They're scared. It's the public pressure. The press is even asking the President about the state of prisons."

I stood up and stared out my front windows, knowing that Jonah and the kids would be home at any moment. The trees in our neighborhood had started to tentatively blossom: small green buds attached to previously claw-like branches. The settlement offer was good, but I knew that for this case, no offer would be enough. I had to try this case.

"Talk to the clients," Harold said. "I think you should counter with—"

"I'll talk to them, but we're not countering." I said, rocking back and forth on my heels. "We're not settling."

"You think a jury is going to give you more than Randall is offering right now?"

Calmly, I turned away from the window and looked at the table that had become the center of my universe. "Yes."

"Bullshit. Counter and settle the damn thing. Get the convicts their money and—"

"I'm trying the case, Harold. I'll tell the clients the offer, but I'll see Randall in court on Monday," I said. "You can come and watch. It's going to be a bloodbath."

CHAPTER 38

Jonah

Because of some problems with the proofs for an account's social media campaign, I showed up late to the Epilepsy Support Group meeting, but I did not have to worry. Rachel saved me a seat, and I had not missed much. The meeting went the same as always— Anthony gently encouraged us to share our stresses from that week. I did not say more than a few words because while the group's nodding in understanding was nice, the real help, I found, came from Rachel.

Afterwards, she slipped on a hooded sweatshirt and said, "Our regular place?" with a wink.

I had plenty of rituals that bound me to Casey. I should not have had any with another woman; I knew that. Guilt pulsed through me, but I tamped it down, telling myself this time with Rachel was innocent, nothing. Just talking. It was good for my relationship with Casey, if only to have an outlet, a third party to unload my troubles on, so I would not bring them home to her.

"She didn't stop working last night until eleven," I mumbled, shaking my head as I brought the tea to my lips. We sat in our regular booth at the coffee shop, if three visits counted as regular. "*Eleven*. And she thinks this is good for her? It's not. It's as if I'm the only one who sees it, though. Sometimes I feel like I'm the only one of us who cares."

"I hear ya," Rachel said.

"And then I can't even bring myself to talk to her about the stress at *my* work, you know? The drama, the pressure. How angry I am..." Last week, when I told Rachel everything that happened in the past six months at G&H, she had nodded, listened, been supportive and understanding. "Six months of frustration, and where would I even begin to tell Casey?"

"Totally. I'd never tell my sister how much of my life I'm missing. She keeps telling me to go out, have fun. But how can I? A cute guy asked me out at the supermarket earlier this week, and I had to tell him I was busy."

"You did, did you?" I raised an eyebrow, wondering why I was so relieved to hear she had turned a date down. "You could've gone out with him one time at least. Shame."

"Yeah, well, you know what happens. One date becomes two, and then three, and next thing you know, I have to have that talk with them—the 'I come with a disabled sister who needs daily attention' talk. And they never understand. They don't get it. You're the only one who does."

She gave me an expectant look, veiled by her long eyelashes, and a long moment of silence passed between us. I felt heat building, and realized that I needed space to cool.

"Yes, well," I said, checking my phone as I slid out of the booth. Fresh dread leaked in as I remembered that Dwayne was waiting on a new billboard copy for the Apple account. "I've got to get back to work."

"Oh. Okay. Yeah, I have to go too," she said quickly, gathering her things.

But after we walked out of the coffee shop, our conversation again became so easy that she strolled with me the four blocks to G&H. When she waved goodbye, I found myself smiling after her.

As I walked up the curved staircase to my floor, my uneasiness grew. I was journeying farther and farther away from the person I trusted as my place of refuge: my wife. Instead, I found the Wednesday meetings were my only escape into a community that understood me, to a *person* who understood me. For a moment, I wished I could reverse back to a half-hour ago and stay there, frozen in time with Rachel, away from work, from home, from life.

My phone pinged, and I pulled it out, heart racing, but I already knew who it would be.

Rachel: *You're so easy to talk to. I feel like I can tell you anything.*

I texted back: *Same.*

For the first time in a long time, I entered my office in a good mood.

•   •   •

That evening, when Sadie, Sam and I came home, Casey greeted us perfunctorily in her dining room "office." She moved towards the sofa to take a call, her face grave.

I put my finger to my lips, motioning for them to be quiet. "Shhh. Mummy's still working. Go to your rooms and play for a bit, okay? I'll make dinner."

I listened to their feet retreating into their separate areas, and walked to the refrigerator, pulling out the ingredients to make a stir-fry. When I turned on the stove, I heard Casey say her goodbyes.

I watched her as she sat on the sofa, her fingers gently massaging her temples: the classic posture she assumed when an aura was coming on. Hunched over, she looked smaller. Stressed. I crossed the room, and sat next to her; annoyance flitted across her features for the briefest of moments. I had clearly disturbed her.

"Busy?" I asked.

"Yeah. A settlement offer came in today, and we rejected it. So, that's it. The trial's a real go for Monday."

She dragged her hands down her face, and started telling me about the details of the settlement, but 'We rejected it' stuck in my mind. Casey had a way out, a way to get these women justice. The other side was offering what seemed to be an insane amount of money, and yet that was not enough for her. She had taken the harder road, the gamble that would satisfy her ego.

"So, now I'm just working through witnesses, trying to decide order. I think I'll start with the first woman who reported the rape, and then—"

"Casey, why are you doing this?" I asked. "Seriously. It's so stressful for you. How many auras are you having lately?"

She did not answer, but it was clear: too many. She would never tell me. We both had our secrets now.

"Settle it," I said. "Take whatever money they offer and settle it."

"I talked to the clients already and told Randall. It's done. We're not taking the offer, Jonah. And You. Are. Not. Helping. What *would* help is for you to tell me if this trial strategy seems to work."

"Casey, are you even listening to me? This trial has become about *you*, not your clients. You could've settled and—"

Just then, my phone pinged. *Rachel*. I instinctively reached down to grab it from my pocket, but Casey stopped my hand.

"Jonah. Look at me."

I had no choice but to look into the eyes that had melted my heart from the first day we met. The eyes of my wife.

"Just let me get through this trial, and I'll come home." she said, wrapping her arms around my shoulders. "I promise."

I felt my body collapse, tension seeping out of every pore. My phone pinged again, but I ignored it, instead pulling Casey in for a long kiss. A long overdue kiss. "Alright," I said afterwards. "I love you, you know. I just want what's best for you."

She set her face in my neck, the familiar lemon scent from her hair filling my nostrils. "I know you do," she said. "Just a few more days."

I promised to support her, but a little part of me wondered what Rachel's texts would say. My heart quickened, and I pulled my wife closer to me, as if by holding her tight the guilt I knew I deserved to feel would run from my body and disappear into thin air.

CHAPTER 39

Casey

Sitting in our bed, bent over my laptop, I barely heard Jonah's voice in the background until he said louder, "Casey."

I looked up, dragged from the world of revising my opening statement and annoyed.

"Did you hear what I said?"

"Um, no," I admitted. "Just working on my opening. It has to be perfect –"

"*Casey* – what the fuck? It's almost noon. I asked you if you wanted lunch."

"Oh. Uh, yeah." I looked at my opening. "Just give me, like, fifteen minutes."

"Fifteen minutes. Fine," he said, his voice was somewhere between a fact and a threat.

He left the room, and I returned to getting the wording to hit hard, but not argumentative. Statements of fact. Well, there were plenty of those. *Supervisor Stilton and Supervisor –*

Jonah's phone pinged, and my chain of thought broke. *Who could be texting him now? What could G&H want so urgently that they have to talk to him on a Sunday?* I reached over, entered his password, and looked at the text.

RACHEL: *Wanna get coffee again after group this week?*

Rachel? Who was Rachel? Probably someone on his team wanting to brainstorm, but why would someone on his team be texting on a random Sunday? I scrolled up through the texts.

And I almost vomited all over my laptop.

The texts went back over three weeks, and there must have been almost a hundred of them. My jaw dropped as I read through them, and it became hard to breathe.

RACHEL: *You're so easy to talk to.*

JONAH: *You too. I feel like I can tell you anything. Things I can't say even to Casey.*

RACHEL: *I understand. Group helps, but this is helping so much more. Our time together.*

JONAH: *Yeah.*

RACHEL: *Good morning! How's G&H today?*

JONAH: *Ugh. Same as always since Dwayne took charge. How about your day?*

I continued to stare at the phone, confused. Group? What group? My mind raced, and I did the only thing I could think to do: I called Holly.

"Hey," she answered. "What's up?"

My voice shook, a mixture of fear, confusion, and rising anger. "Hi. I, well, I found some texts on Jonah's phone. It just pinged, and I thought it was G&H, and you know how we have each other's passwords—you know how he's sent you some of those ridiculous texts over the years?"

"Yeah." I could hear her smiling. "Like the one 'I'm going to be late because I lost my pants'?"

"Uh huh."

"So, what's up?"

"I found some texts. I just wanted to run them by you, see what you thought."

"What kind of texts?" She sounded wary.

I read them to her. All of them. With each sentence, my stomach felt a little tighter, my lungs contracted, and panic buttons went off in my head. I knew what I thought. I just needed confirmation.

"Yeah. That's an emotional affair," Holly said slowly. "I mean, at least the start of one, if we're going to give him any leeway. Did you know he was going to some group?"

"No."

"Fuck. I'm sorry, babe. I suggested he do that while you were working on the case. Not have an affair, but find some sort of support group. I guess good thing you saw these now before it went..."

She didn't need to finish the sentence.

"Yeah. I know," I said. "We don't know, though, how far..."

Jonah walked back into our room.

"Fifteen minutes is up," he said. He stopped walking when he saw me holding his phone, and registered the anger on my face.

"I have to go, Holly," I said and hung up. "Rachel texted," I said calmly. "She wanted to know if—let me check the actual text—you 'wanna get coffee again after group this week.' Let me text her back for you."

"Casey, let me explain—" His face went pale. I'd known him almost half my life, and yet it was the face of a stranger.

"Just a sec. I'm going to text 'GET YOUR OWN FUCKING HUSBAND, BITCH.' And... send. And number blocked. Contact deleted. Texts deleted. And—oh, what were you saying? You were about to explain how you started some sort of affair almost a month ago? At least, according to your texts. Has it been longer?" I asked, somewhat sarcastically, somewhat seriously.

"I just met her through an epilepsy support group. She's nothing, there was nothing—"

"Fuck you, Jonah!" I screamed. "You thought you shouldn't tell me that you were going to a *support* group? You thought, what? I'd tell you *not* to go? That I wouldn't be supportive or that, unlike *fucking Rachel*, I wouldn't 'understand'?"

"We just went out to coffee a couple of times—"

"A *couple of times*?" I yelled. "She thought it was your 'regular place'! And you went out with another woman without telling me? And these texts? You think that these are texts between *friends*? Friends don't receive heart emojis, you piece of shit! *Friends* don't go 'grab coffee' behind their spouse's back! If she's 'just a friend,' why hide her?"

"I just—"

"Because you were *cheating on your wife*, asshole! And telling this bitch everything, it seems. Everything that—let's see, what was the text—telling her 'things I can't even tell Casey.'" I shoved the laptop to the side and jumped to my feet. "There shouldn't *be* things you don't tell me! I'm your *wife*! You don't get to keep secrets from me! That's part of the marriage deal!"

"I didn't want to stress you out more than you were! There was a lot of stuff of going at G&H last fall when you were in Cleveland, and I didn't want to burden you with it. You know, I was really frustrated at work, and then when Dwayne got the promotion I thought would be mine, and—"

"No, *no*, I don't know because you *never told me*! I'm not a fragile piece of glass that has to be protected at all times, Jonah. But I *am* a woman who doesn't want a husband who cheats on her!"

"I don't know what to say." He looked down at the floor. "I'm sorry, Casey."

I waited for more. For something to tell me that he was truly sorry. Maybe for him to get down on his knees, and beg for my forgiveness.

"Did you fuck her?"

He shook his head, still looking down. "No."

"Did you kiss her? Any sort of sexual touching?"

"No."

"But I know you wanted to."

He stared at me. "I couldn't ever do that. I would never—"

"Fuck you. If I hadn't seen these, you know how far it could have gone." All I wanted was for him to deny it, but he just shook his head. That meant nothing. "Here!" I yelled, throwing his phone at the wall.

I heard it crack before it landed at his feet, skittering onto the hardwood floor. "I don't even *know* you anymore! Your fucking secret life! You know what? I almost *wish* you'd fucked her because then on Friday, after the trial, I could go over to John Dorwitz's office and get him to represent me in our divorce. Now, I'm actually going to have to think about it, but guess what, Jonah Scott, you lying, cheating little excuse for a man—I'm leaning towards *yes*." The fury in my chest translated to my eyes, and I knew I was glaring at him with the look he despised—the dark look I could call up of disgust and hatred. "Get the fuck out of my room. You're not sleeping in this bed tonight."

"Casey—"

"Don't fucking 'Casey' me. Here's your fucking pillows!" I threw them at him. "Now get out! Go meet Rachel and whine to her about your *wife* doesn't *understand* you. Go ahead and fuck her. Have fun cheating on your wife, who you promised to *love and honor*. Who you promised to *forsake all others* for. Remember that? Our *wedding day*?"

He blinked his eyes rapidly, and his breath became deep and ragged as he tried to hold back the tears.

"Go on and cry," I snapped. "It's the least you can do."

He left abruptly, and I listened to the front door slam. Then, I heard the kids playing Lego in Sam's room, and suddenly wanted to be with what remained of my family. Still shaking with anger, I closed my laptop and walked downstairs.

I made my way to Sam's room. He and Sadie were sitting on the floor, creating what looked like some sort of rickety structure out of the colorful bricks.

"Hi guys," I said. "Can I play?"

Sammy's face lit up at the question. "Yes! Yes, Mommy! Come play!"

Sadie nodded in agreement and reached up to grab my hand. I sat crisscross on the carpet and began to build.

"I thought you had to work all day. Your trial's tomorrow, right?" Sam asked, focused on pushing two green bricks together.

"I'm taking a break," I said. "I'd rather spend time with you guys." As I rustled Sadie's hair, I realized that those words were true. *I'd rather spend time with you guys.* I would rather be with my family, more than with anyone else. And that was partly why I felt so heartbroken about the texts. I thought Jonah and I were best friends, that we told each other everything, especially after I told him my true, deepest, darkest feelings on the couch. But, best friends didn't hurt each other this deeply. Best friends stayed faithful.

The knot in my stomach came back with a vengeance. An emotional affair was almost worse than a physical one. Both broke trust, the backbone of a marriage, but the emotional meant that there was someone closer to your spouse than you were, and that thought ripped through my heart like a knife.

"Mommy, you okay?" Sadie asked, her eyebrows drawn together as she tried to interpret my expression.

"Oh, yes," I said. "I'm just having trouble putting these Legos together. Can you help me?" I pretended to be confused and put them together backwards. Sadie and Sam giggled.

"I help you," Sadie said, taking the Legos from my hands. She quickly pushed them together and handed them back. "See? It's easy!"

"It *is* easy, Sadie. You're so smart." I kissed her head, and she leaned into my body.

Wiggling her way onto my lap, she passed me two yellow bricks to work with. Sam considered the structure.

"I think it needs more on the bottom," he said, pulling out a red brick from the box.

There's always a reason for people's behavior, my mother had said again and again when I was growing up. *But what would make him do this?* I wasn't looking for an excuse. There was no excuse, but there was a *reason.* It could be anything, really. Maybe she was hot. But that didn't seem to be enough. She obviously filled some void that I'd ignored or not known was even there. *My seizures were part of the reason, at least in the beginning.* The stress he tried to withhold from me made him more stressed, and finally lonely. And then he found someone he thought he could confide in without her brain blowing up.

Not an excuse. But perhaps the reason.

But, the problem was, he could have come to me any time. How could he not know that? We would have dealt with the challenges. Together. Team Scott, as we had always been.

I stared at my children, working so hard to build a structure that — Sam was right — was too top-heavy, and would soon crash. Like our family. Maybe we were too top-heavy. Maybe we were two parents whose egos blinded us to what really mattered.

I stayed building and rebuilding Lego with Sam and Sadie, turning flat bricks into pathways, square bricks into walls, thin bricks into towers, until, finally satisfied, they announced that our building was done.

"Can I have a snack?" Sadie asked, predictably.

"Sure." Sliding her off my lap, I rose and walked to the kitchen. Jonah's phone lay on the kitchen counter; the screen was cracked like a spider web, useless at the moment, but a physical reminder of his infidelity. I picked it up and turned it around in my hand. Then I hurled it into the garbage can, filled a glass with water, poured it over the device, and started making a sandwich for Sam and Sadie.

•　　•　　•

I heard Jonah come home after the children fell asleep. He climbed the stairs towards our room, and, as he leaned against the frame, I could see he wasn't sober. *Oh, to have that luxury. Just drink it all away.*

"I'm sorry, Case."

"How's Rachel?"

"That's not where I've been. I don't even know where she lives."

"Then where have you been?"

"The Brick."

"The bar down the street? For seven hours? How many numbers did you get? Or do the girls you pick just skip the pleasantries and fuck in the bathroom now?" I was still furious, but quietly so. So, I gave little cuts. Little cuts that would all add up to — what? Something. Hopefully something that would hurt.

Jonah looked down and shook his head. "I'm sorry."

"For Rachel? Or because you got caught?" I didn't wait for an answer. "I can't deal with this right now. Get your shit and go sleep in the guest bedroom."

"What?" I could see he wasn't expecting this. He thought I would have calmed down, changed my mind about sleeping apart.

You know me better than that, Jonah. "Get your shit," I repeated slowly, "and go sleep in the guest bedroom. I have a trial tomorrow morning."

Turning my back on him, I clicked off my light and feigned sleep while he shuffled around the dark room, trying to gather what he thought he would need.

"I'm sorry, Casey," he said before he closed the door.

After he left, I buried my head in my pillow and screamed, finally crying myself to sleep.

·　　·　　·

As I sat next to Kathy Kellan in the large federal courtroom, there was nothing on my mind except the case. I closed my eyes and breathed deeply. Last night's fight with Jonah seemed a distant memory, and I shoved it out of my conscious for now: I couldn't fight successfully in the courtroom and at home, so I had to pick. And I picked the courtroom. At this moment, I prayed for just five days without a seizure. Aura after aura crashed through my brain over the past three weeks, but I'd kept my head down, my rescue meds near, and pushed through. Now, I just needed five more days. *Just five days. Is that too much to ask?* As I opened my eyes, I knew that only time would tell.

Wearing a light purple suit that I had picked out specifically for this occasion, with her hair combed back into the low ponytail of her video deposition, and her make-up lightly done, Kathy Kellan looked like a suburban PTA Board member, not a woman who had done time in prison. She wouldn't be the first plaintiff on the stand, but she would be the face of the trial. I had treated every woman to a similar outfit in varying colors: subtle sky blue, sea green, light yellow. Innocent colors. All their make-up resembled Kathy's, and their hair had been tamed. Georgia Leverene, the first woman to report a rape to no avail, was testifying today. She was terrified. I'd assured her that I would be there for her no matter what Doug Randall said. After the pep talk, she looked a little less terrified.

We rose for Judge Rosta and sat as he called the room to order, announcing the trial of Kellan versus the Oregon Department of Corrections. I hadn't heard from Doug since I rejected the settlement offer, a phone call where he sounded surprised, insisting that I would never get more from a jury. *You'll see, Doug. You'll see.*

Jury selection had gone well for us: I eliminated a cop and a woman who thought all prisoners deserved to be treated like shit. Portland was a relatively liberal area, and I felt confident about the rest of the jurors: they seemed, if not left-leaning, at least open-minded, which was good considering my clients' backgrounds.

"Mrs. Scott, your opening statement," Judge Rosta said.

I rose and strode across the floor in my gray skirt suit. A sense of calm came over me that I'd never experienced in court before, especially not in an opening statement, where my nerves were usually the highest. I knew at that moment that this was my courtroom. These were *my* people and nothing would get in the way of *my* verdict— nothing Doug did, nothing the judge did, nothing the press said throughout the week. Nothing. I smiled and nodded to the jurors before I spoke.

"May it please the Court, counsel, Jury," I said, standing evenly on my heels, shoulders back, fueled with passion for my case, "this week you will hear about four women who wanted protection from a predator, asked for protection from this predator, but were ignored by the only people who could help them, the only system that could help them. It's ugly, but true." The trial had officially begun.

• • •

On Tuesday, I stood in the hallway outside the courtroom, holding a sobbing Kathy around the shoulders next to the enormous windows.

"He's making me look like such a—a—slut," she cried. "Like I wanted to go in that shed. Like I asked for it." She took great hiccupping breaths, and I was glad that I asked for a quick recess.

"Kathy, listen to me," I said. "He's making himself look like an arrogant, close-minded, woman-hating asshole. This isn't 1992—it's 2017, the time of the #MeToo movement, where people *listen* to women. There's no 'she asked for it' anymore, and everyone on that jury knows it. We're trying our case: the D.O.C. supervisors knew about these rapes and did nothing. That's all we need. That's our theme. Do you understand?"

She looked up at me and nodded, her face puffy-eyed and runny-nosed. I handed her a small Kleenex from my traveling make-up purse, and she wiped her tears.

"Whatever he says, whatever he does, I will fix it, okay? Do you understand that? I can fix it." *There is at least one thing in my life I can fix,* I wanted to add. I glanced at my watch: three minutes until we had to start again.

"You stay strong," I said, wiping the mascara from under her eyes. I almost pulled out the lipstick for her to reapply, but as long as her eyes were clean, I wanted the jury to see her anguish, not to hide it by make-up. Turning back to enter the courtroom, I repeated the mantra to her that I would have to say to all the women in this case throughout the week as Doug abused them on the stand: *I can fix it.* And I knew I could.

CHAPTER 40

Jonah

Monday, Tuesday, and Wednesday came and went with Casey and I living the routines of our everyday lives in icy, tense silence. Every day Casey returned home from the courthouse exhausted, rubbing her temples on and off, and ignoring me; a freeze seemed to emanate from her body whenever I tried to approach.

With the children, she was warm, loving, everything-is-fine Casey, but she took her dinner at the dining table, so she could work on the following day's question and strategies. And avoid any contact with me, I supposed. I slept in the guest room again and again, waiting, hoping for footsteps to come down the hall and invite me back to our bed, but the footsteps never came. I watched through the crack at the bottom of the door as her light turned off at ten, then turned mine off, and rolled away from the door, trying not to cry.

Thursday morning, she kissed Sam and Sadie, ignored me, and slid into the Uber, her face ready for battle. With my new phone, I tried to gather as many contacts as I had before, but it was slow going. I did not have Rachel's number, and I felt cleaner with that knowledge. Since the day I zeroed in on Casey over a decade ago, there had been no doubt that we were meant to be together forever. Now, the question was, would she let us? After arriving at work, I again googled 'Couples therapists Portland', but this time, I wrote down the names and numbers. An hour later, after fifty phone calls, I had a handwritten shortlist of five therapists. I smiled as I slipped the paper in my back jeans pocket. Then, I turned to the other project that I hoped would help save my marriage.

I noticed Whitney walking by my office, her head down, frowning. She was usually the smiling one, the clown who kept everyone going; I had never seen her frown. I had seen her concentrate, but even then she just put a pen in the corner of her mouth and chewed on it while she thought. I gathered my laptop and walked over to the Morrison Room for our team meeting, watching Whitney, who seemed to slow her pace as she opened the door.

I let the door swing shut behind her before going in, observing from a far as she slumped into a seat at a corner of the large, rectangular table.

"Hello," I said cheerfully as I entered the room. "How's everyone today?"

"Good," they mumbled.

I narrowed my eyes as I sat, and studied my team. "Good?"

"Fine." Whitney said. She stared at her lap.

"Okay..." I opened my laptop and pulled up a file. "Alright, let's see what Creative has come up with for the Coors summer ads."

Everyone in the room opened their laptops. Usually beer ads brought out some sort of immature joke from this crew, but today the room was quiet. I stood up.

"What's going on here?" I asked. "Did someone die? Get sacked? Why are we all in a bad mood?"

The team looked over at Whitney. José nodded at her, which seemed to give her a nudge. She rolled her eyes and shook her head.

"It's Dwayne," José said. "He's just, I mean, we all know that he's acting like he's a little king and sending ridiculous emails that just sound so condescending. But this morning he sent Whitney one that threatened to put her on a P.I.P. I mean, *what?*"

Whitney remained silent, her lips now a thin line, as if drawn on by a red pen.

"You know, four months ago, he was on our level," José continued. "Annoying, yes, but at least part of the team. It's like now that he can do more things, he's just doing them. He doesn't even have any reason to say that to Whitney. Do you know how hard she works? And *she's* the one that came up with the 'Oregon Travel' tagline. He'd know that if he paid attention, but he's just up there — *on the third floor*, in case you didn't know — like he's Jesus looking down on his disciples. Except I think Jesus was nice. You'd have to ask my mother. She's the practicing Catholic."

The door opened behind me and Jonathan came in.

"Jonah," Jonathan said, "can I see you in the hall for a minute?"

"Sure." I turned to my team. "Alright, we'll talk more about this when I get back. Meanwhile review Creative's Coors' ideas." Closing the glass door, I faced Jonathan in the hallway, my eyebrows raised. "How can I help you?"

"Do you have time for a meeting today? Say, this evening?"

"Not this evening." I did not even have to look at my calendar to know that was true. "But how about from noon to one? Over lunch hour?"

Jonathan looked surprised: perhaps he expected me to agree to his first time slot suggestion, but I was not about to create more stress in my household for a short meeting that likely consisted of asking for my opinion on a pitch idea. "Sure," he said, putting on a smile. "Just come up to my office."

"Anything to be worried about?" I asked, suddenly wary.

"No," he said, clapping me on the back. "Nothing to worry about."

I re-entered the Morrison Room, where the mood had not improved, and continued to listen to my team complain about Dwayne's terrible leadership skills, half of them accompanied with empty threats to quit or revolt by just not doing what he asked.

"Look, I've got a meeting with Jonathan and probably Jacob at noon today," I said. "I'll bring all this up and see what I can do."

"It should have been you," Whitney said, looking at me dead-on. "You know it should have been you."

I swallowed and turned my attention to the first slide, refusing to revisit that feeling of anger that I had finally muted. "Well, it wasn't, it isn't, so we're just going to have to get used to it, aren't we? Now, what the hell is *this* bloody picture?" I said sharply, grimacing at the first drawing, which showed a bunch of thin, white, twenty-somethings, floating down a river, holding or drinking beers. "Is this a 1999 Abercrombie and Fitch ad? No. Absolutely not." I sighed and stretched my neck. This could be a long day. "Tara, can you go get the creatives working this ad and bring them in here? We need to explain the concept of diversity to whoever drew this. I can't pitch this rubbish." We had a lot of work to do.

●　　●　　●

Before the lunch meeting, I checked online to see if there were any updates to the Kellan case. On Monday, *The Oregonian* ran a front-page article about the case which basically said the facts, focused on the sexual abuse, and lacked a quote from either side. Almost every other news website did as well, from the *New York Times* to Fox News. It was just click-bait, but still publicity — the eyes of the nation now on Casey's performance. Most reporters updated every day on Twitter, and gave live updates of the trial each morning on their respective shows. Editorials were penned in various news outlets — *The Journal*, *The Times*, *The Oregonian*, *The San Francisco Chronicle* — some in favor of a win for Casey's clients, some planting doubt on the reliability of prisoner sexual assault reports. Every civil rights talking head on every evening news show called this the "prison trial of the decade," and had already assigned a verdict. *So, no pressure, Case. I'm sure your brain will be just fine.*

I glanced at the Twitter feed.

@TheOregonian: Defense continues. Trial expected to finish tomorrow. Might continue to Monday. #KellanCase

@nytimes: Stilton explaining rape investigation. "We did all we could." #KellanCase

So, Doug Randall was probably on the floor now. I wanted to talk to Casey about how things were going, how she felt about the case, but right now it was as if we did not even live in the same house.

I tried to push the thought of my crumbling marriage out of my mind while I walked up to the third floor towards Jonathan's office. Through the glass wall, I could see that he stood next to Jacob, staring out the window, his hands clasped in front of him, his back to the door. Jacob shook his head while Jonathan nodded his. Finally, Jacob shrugged and nodded. I knocked on the door, and they turned around, a smile lighting up Jonathan's face, a small grin on Jacob's. Jonathan gestured for me to come in.

"Jonah!" said Jonathan, as if my visit was a surprise. He gestured to the light gray sofa against the glass wall, and I sat, admiring the space. The long coffee table in front of the sofa was glass, and somehow spotless. Two large, leather seats, a deep indigo cover, faced the sofa: their iron curved arms and legs gave the section a retro feeling. Like me, Jonathan had a standing desk and two monitors, but, near the corner, his vast office included room for a large rug and another table, this one round and surrounded by the same style of retro-chair, but in white. It gave the impression that the room was really a loft—half for work, half for play—even though it was all for work.

"Coffee?" Jonathan asked, as Jacob sat across from me.

"No, thank you," I said.

"Jacob?"

Jacob shook his head.

"Just for me then." Jonathan took some time making an espresso for himself from the machine behind his desk. It was then that I noticed a clock on the wall. 12:05. The support group was yesterday at this time, but I had not even noticed the hour pass, and I knew that I would never go back. The knowledge did not touch me as much as I thought it would. It was not the right group for me on many levels. Hearing the stories in that room, I realized that I was not a caretaker as much as a necessary piece of the puzzle in the Scott family life. I felt for my fellow group members, but I currently had a wife in federal court trying the civil rights prison case of the decade with national attention on her every move. She did not need my caretaking. She just needed me. And I needed her.

"Finished," Jonathan said, bringing his steaming cup over and setting it on a G&H coaster. "So, Jonah, I bet you're wondering why I asked you here today."

"I *am* curious," I said.

Jonathan nodded at Jacob. *Oh, the old dance. One and then the other and back again.*

"We've been hearing some rumblings," Jacob said. "About Dwayne and his new role in the company. It seems he isn't quite the leader he presented in his interviews."

"Perhaps he just needs a bit of training," I said. "It's a big jump for him." I hoped that comment hit home. What it meant was *'You made a huge mistake and picked the wrong person for the wrong reasons.'*

Jonathan blew on his coffee and took a small sip. "He's not bad at his job," he said. "He's getting results. It's just the *way* he's getting them. It seems like he's, well, killing morale around here a bit. So, it's hard. Here we have a guy who can land clients, but may have been given too much too soon—do you know what I mean?"

I was not sure what I was supposed to say, so I stayed quiet.

"Do you know what I mean, Jonah?" Jonathan asked again.

"I understand the idea, yes." I said, feeling impatient. *You picked the wrong man.*

"How's your team doing?"

"I think they're struggling a bit," I said. "There were some hurt feelings today. Dwayne emailed Whitney and told her that the three of you were considering putting her on P.I.P. Why would you do that? She's an amazing asset to the team. She comes up with the most brilliant taglines—"

"We didn't make that decision," Jacob said. "That's an example of how Dwayne might be biting off more than he can chew here. He seems to be speaking without consulting us."

"Perhaps Dwayne's still settling in," Jonathan mused. "But he had Kevin's guidance until the end of January, and has been on his own since early February—now it's April. We'd hope that he would have the hang of the position by now, understand that threats aren't going to get what he wants."

"It's always better to use the carrot instead of the stick," I said.

Jacob and Jonathan nodded together.

"There's a position in our San Francisco office that just opened up—head of the marketing team over there," Jacob said. "He'll be reporting to the director in San Fran, but he's fine with that—he'll still be a leader. And we'll send him to the G&H spring leadership retreat before he starts."

"Wait? So Dwayne is moving?" I asked.

"Yes. We talked to him about it this morning," Jacob said. "Of course, we left out the rumblings and inappropriate P.I.P. threats because I think the leadership retreat will take care of that, but he's game. I mean, he's thirty-five, single—well, dating, but still single—just renting a place here. He'll still be working at G&H, and, hopefully, he'll grow to be a good leader. Realize that the carrot is better than the stick, right?" He grinned at me.

I smiled back, beginning to see the point of this meeting.

"Which leads us back to Kevin's spot," Jonathan said, taking over. "You know it was down to the two of you. And," he glanced at Jacob, who subtly nodded, "we apologize. We should have given the promotion to you. To be honest, Kevin has a terrible marriage and never saw his kids as they grew up, so, although he bragged about being a family man, he wasn't quite the family man he held himself out to be."

Jacob nodded in agreement. "We'd like to offer you Kevin's position," he said.

I sighed. Everything I wanted professionally was right in front of me, but I had to give an answer that I knew they would not like.

"I'd love to take it, of course, but I have to talk with Casey first. And, Jonathan, Jacob, my terms are still the same: I can stay late for emergencies or if really needed, and the same for weekends, but I have to put my family first. I can work from home in the evenings—with Wi-Fi and a work laptop, I can work anywhere, really—but, again, I need to put my family first. I'll show the team how to work faster and smarter, to get the results you want, but I'm the man who comes at eight and leaves at five to be with his wife and children. If you can accept that, I'll talk to Casey and let her know about the offer. With her support, I'm in."

"We understand," Jonathan said. "You're a role model, Jonah, of how tech can really work, of actual work/life balance. Of how to be a true family man while working hard. Talk to Casey tonight and let us know tomorrow."

I'm not a role model of how to be a husband, I wanted to say. *And I'll talk to Casey if she'll let me.*

I rose from the sofa, and shook hands with both men. Returning to the second floor, I went to my office and finished up the most important marketing pitch of my life.

•   •   •

On my way home, I wondered if things would ever thaw between Casey and I. When I entered the house with the kids, I smelled roasted chicken and vegetables: Casey was in the kitchen, making dinner, and greeted Sam and Sadie with a smile and a hug, ignoring me. She sat with us at the kitchen counter while we ate.

The children recounted their days, and she asked me to pass the salt. I pushed the glass salt shaker towards her, and she picked it up without speaking.

"How's your trial going, Mommy?" Sam asked.

"Very well, I think, Sammy. Tomorrow morning the other side will finish their case, I'll get to ask a few more questions, but I think that we should be done by the end of the day tomorrow." She smiled at him, and he grinned back. "I have some work to do tonight, so Daddy will put you to bed." Sam's face fell. "But, I'll come give you a kiss and hug. We'll do so many bedtime cuddles next week, you won't be able to stand it!"

"Me too!" Sadie interjected.

"You too, love," Casey said, rubbing Sadie's soft hand with her long fingers.

I sat silently, cutting up the chicken on my plate, waiting for someone to talk to me, to ask about my day. Both children focused on their mother as if it were a three-person meal, and I was a stranger who joined them.

"I'm going to work in my room now," Casey said, putting her plate in the dishwasher. "Don't give Daddy too hard a time!" She kissed Sam and Sadie and walked past me without a glance.

•   •   •

After putting the children down, I sat in the guestroom bed with the door open, killing time by scrolling through the New York Times website. I heard footsteps in the hallway and glanced up as Casey rapped at the door. She looked tired, and I was not sure if it was the strain of our marriage or the weight of the trial that was wearing on her. Probably both. She leaned against the doorframe and cocked her head while staring at me, like a psychic trying to read my mind.

"How was your support group?" she asked casually, as if my answer did not matter to her. Maybe it didn't.

I rubbed the back of my neck. "I didn't go. I'm not going again."

"I don't believe you."

"Well, it's true."

"And how's the ever-understanding Rachel?"

"Casey."

"What?"

"I didn't go to the support group."

"I'm sure you've been in touch."

"No."

A beat passed, and she moved her gaze to the green comforter on the bed, the one we picked out together, so long ago. She shook her head, sighed, and turned to leave. "More lies, Jonah."

"I'm not lying, Case." I felt my chance at redemption slipping away. "Wait."

She paused and turned back.

"Here." I passed her a sheet of paper that I had worked on fervently — almost manically — since Monday: reviewing it, redoing it over and over, waiting for the right time to pitch it. I brought it home today, hoping to give it to her before she went to sleep, but not finding the chance and too shy to try. Until now.

Her cheeks flushed as she looked at it. "When did you do this?"

The paper was a heavy, cream-colored, matte finish, with "The Law Office of Casey Scott" on the top, and a thick line underneath, finishing the look. The font took all week to choose, as well as the wording. I tried "Casey L. Scott, Esq.", "Casey Louise Scott, Attorney at Law", among other combinations. *Of course, it could all be changed,* I wanted to tell her. *Anything you like.*

"This week. I started Monday." I watched her face soften, and she ran her fingers over the letters. "They're raised," I said, quickly, "but we could take that out, if you don't fancy it."

She looked up at me.

"I mean, I. *I* could take that out if you like. It's just a start, you know. Case, you're such a brilliant attorney. You could keep going; I know you could. Start your own place. Imagine — you control your caseload, your stress. I just thought I'd show you, maybe, what could be — if you wanted. And I'd be behind you for that. Supportive, you know?"

She stared back at the paper. "No, I think it's nice, the raised font." She sat on the bed and put the paper in her lap. We stayed silent. I could not tell if she was waiting for me to speak, and finally took a breath to begin the conversation that I wanted to have all week.

"I'm sorry, Casey."

Casey traced the outline of the flowers on the comforter. She seemed to be considering my words. "Sorry for what?"

"For betraying your trust. I should have told you about the group. I should never have..." I could not finish the sentence. I felt disgusted with myself for everything I had done, dirty inside.

"Why'd you do it?"

"I don't know," I said.

"That's not an answer, Jonah. Look at me."

I met her eyes.

"Why'd you do it?"

"I guess I felt lonely," I said. "And then Holly suggested therapy, but you took the case, so she suggested a support group, and everything had been so much over the fall with G&H—I'd kept so much from you. I went to this support group, and it seemed like I could just tell everyone all my problems and everyone would understand. Tell her my problems." I did not say her name. I would never say it again. "And I didn't have to worry about anyone having a seizure or getting stressed—"

"Jonah, you can't walk on eggshells around me in our everyday life. That's not how our marriage works. You do that, and this is where it gets us." Her voice rose and trembled. "Secrets, in *our* marriage? When have we ever kept secrets?"

"But with your seizures getting worse, and then you being gone while all the interviews were going on—"

"When did you find out about Kevin retiring?"

"September," I admitted. "The same day you got the Kellan case and Harold mentioned the partner position."

"You should have told me about it that day, Jonah. I—you should have *told* me!"

I felt that I was losing her again. "I know, I know. I'm sorry. I thought—I just thought it was the best thing to not. I thought I was going to get this promotion, and then I was saying you couldn't get yours and... I just thought it was the best not to say anything."

She turned away and shook her head. "No. You should have let me weigh in."

"I didn't get the promotion because I told Jonathan and Jacob that I wanted to put my family first," I said. "Dwayne didn't have those restrictions, so, okay, maybe I was resentful. Not about you—about the whole picture. And then with you depressed, not driving, not working, I didn't want to bring home how bad things were at work, that I was disappointed and angry about not getting the promotion. That Dwayne was acting like such a bastard. By that time, the secrets were so many, I didn't know how to start. And I didn't want to argue."

She stared at the door. "I never thought we would be here. That my seizures would get so bad you would think that not telling me about your life would make me better. That you would confide in some *other woman*. What kind of marriage is that? What if I hadn't seen those texts? I mean, how long were you going to let this go on?"

"Casey," I said, grabbing her hand so hard that she had to look at me. "I'm sorry about... her. I'm sorry about all the secrets. It was all a huge mistake on my part. I promise, no more secrets."

She stared at me as if I was a foreign object that she'd never seen before, something unimaginable to her that suddenly appeared. "No," she said slowly. "No. How can I trust you anymore? Do I check your phone every day? You're not a child. That's not a marriage. That's—that's not what I want." Her shoulders lifted and fell as she took a deep breath. "I don't think I can do this."

No. No. No. My voice broke. "Casey, please, I can't be without you. Please. Please believe me."

"Even with my seizures? With how bad they've become? Would you have married me if you'd know this was where we would end up—seizure-wise?"

"I'd have married you even if we knew."

Casey lay back onto the big green pillows next to me without touching my body, and exhaled. A ball of hope appeared in my chest.

"I used to think that there was nothing we couldn't figure out together," she said.

"That's still true."

"Is it?" She turned her face to look at me. "I'm not sure."

"Here." I handed her another piece of paper: this one had been folded and kept in my back pocket all day. "I did this today. This morning. I called about fifty offices, and these looked like the best ones that were taking new patients. Couples, I mean." I watched her study the names on the page. "I thought you'd like a female therapist for us."

"I don't know, Jonah," she said, staring at the list. "I don't know that anything can fix this."

"Please," I said again. "Please give us a chance. I'll support you if you want to open your own place, if you want to litigate somewhere else —"

"I don't want to work for someone else again. And I can't." She held up the stationary; the paper looked rich and professional. "But this…" She exhaled a deep rush of air. "I would do this."

"I would be there for you."

She switched her attention from the thick paper to the thin sheet with the list of names. "I'll do this, Jonah, but not for you – for Sam and Sadie. They shouldn't be punished for your decisions. And, yeah, I think that a female would be good. Make me feel more understood and comfortable."

"And someone probably a little older, right?"

She passed the list back to me. "You pick. I'm sure they're all fine."

"All right."

She ran her finger over the raised font on the stationary, and I found that encouraging. She also did not make a move to leave: a start.

"So, what was all the G&H drama that you kept from me?" she asked, stroking the edge of the heavy matte paper. "I'm tired of talking, thinking. I've been doing it all day. You talk now."

I told her all about the fall. The interviews, the promotion that had been given to my underling, the P.I.P. threat afterwards. "Today, though, I had an interesting meeting with Jonathan and Jacob."

"What'd they want?"

"Dwayne is moving to the San Francisco office. They want me to take Kevin's old position." I gave her the details of the conversation— Dwayne's unfortunate leadership skills, his ability to switch offices without too much upheaval in the company. "I told them I'd have to talk to you first before I gave them an answer."

She studied the ceiling before she spoke. "Would this mean longer hours?"

"No. I've made it clear again and again that I'm not working longer hours. Family first. They didn't like that last fall, but now they do."

"Pay raise, though, right?"

"Oh, yes. Massive pay raise." I smiled, thinking of the extra money.

"Well, as long as it doesn't take you away from the family, I can get behind it." Her voice still sounded lackluster, tired, but she had agreed. That was not the most important part, though. Not by a long shot.

"See?" I said.

"See what?"

"Looks like there's still nothing we can't figure out when we work together." I kissed her on the cheek and she pulled away, shaking her head. *Too soon.* "Sorry."

She shrugged. "Whatever."

"Do you feel alright about the trial, then?"

"Yeah." She smiled. Finally. "Really good. Will you come see my closing tomorrow? I think it'll be late morning. It might be the last time I do a closing in a courtroom. At least for a long time." When she finished talking, I could feel the weight of that sentence sinking in.

"I'll be there, Case."

"Good." She stood up and looked at the stationery again. Finally, she nodded, a hint of a smile on her face. "Well, I'm exhausted. Come to bed."

Together, we walked down the hall to our bedroom.

•   •   •

Gossip spread quickly around the office, and I arrived early Friday morning to a cheery team. Until the official email from HR, I could neither confirm nor deny any of the rumors about Dwayne's departure and my promotion, but somehow people knew, giving me fist bumps and saying "Congratulations, you deserve it" in the hallways.

"I don't know what you're talking about," I replied. Hurrying to the courthouse, I ran up the marble steps of the gigantic building, sped through the lobby, and pushed the elevator button impatiently again and again. *I cannot be late.* Finally, I arrived at the courtroom door, and checked my phone one last time before entering the room. There it was: the announcement.

Dear G&H employees,

We are pleased to announce that Dwayne Richards will take over as head of the marketing team in our San Francisco office. Jonah Scott will be our new Director of Marketing at the Portland office. We are confident Dwayne will be successful in his new role, and Jonah will continue to be the strong, inspiring leader we know him to be.

Sincerely,
Jonathan Howe & Jacob Grossman

And with those words, it was done.

I turned off my phone and walked into the packed courtroom, finding the last seat against the wall. Scanning the crowd, I saw video cameras set up in corners with camera men stuffed behind them; reporters and lawyers lined the back walls, and crammed next to each other on the benches, like a game of sardines; various family members of Casey's clients were scattered throughout the front rows on Casey's side; insurance adjusters in dark suits sat behind Doug Randall, mumbling to each other in low tones. And there was Harold, sitting in the second row behind her table. *Come to watch the student become the master.*

And she had become a master of the craft of litigation; it really was in her blood. She rose for her closing argument and walked slowly towards the jury box, her long hair styled so that the side growing in was barely noticeable. Moving comfortably around the area between the counsel table, jury box, and judge's bench, in her white collared shirt and navy skirt suit, she began by giving off a vibe to the jury that invited them to join her: her body language, her proximity — always staying within six feet of the jurors — turned them into a community with Casey as their leader. She did not use the tall wooden podium, nor did she rely on notes. Occasionally, she would pause in her speech, put a hand on the side of the podium, and let the previous point sink into the jurors' minds, but she was never silent for long.

Her tone rose and fell with the points she made, and the pacing of her words varied: her genuine indignation at a system that she believed failed her clients reverberated throughout the courtroom.

"The supervisors *knew* that Officer Hawkins raped these women," she said emphatically. "And what did they do? Swept the reports aside and continued to employ the rapist."

Casey told me that women litigators, unlike men, had to walk a fine line between emotion and aggression. Even in 2017, juries liked their female lawyers to remain a little "feminine," and that meant that Casey had to show just enough passion to capture the jury and keep them on her side, but not too much acrimony. Otherwise, she risked being labeled as that "bitch attorney" by a juror, and even just one juror, if that juror held enough sway, could lose her the case. That was why she wore a skirt suit, why she wore her hair down, why when she gave descriptions of what could have happened, what should have happened versus what did happen, her voice filled the courtroom with a practiced amount of frustration.

By the end of her closing, she held the jury in her hand, leading them down her road like the Pied Piper. To finish, she stepped towards the jury box, her voice soft and gentle. She looked at each juror, showing no preference for any one person, but empowering each to show the Department of Corrections that inmates had rights in the only way that the D.O.C would listen: making them pay money. Her performance was nuanced, effective, and perfect. When she finished, I wanted to applaud.

Doug Randall never had a chance. He stood behind the podium and lectured. His closing argument sounded trite and condescending compared to the impassioned speech we had all just witnessed from Casey. His reasoning for his clients' inaction fell flat in his snide voice. He questioned the integrity of Casey's clients. *These felons*, he called them, insinuating that they were lesser people with lesser rights than those not serving time. When he finished, he seemed to be just another heartless attorney defending a corrupt government.

Casey's rebuttal was short, subtle, and left goosebumps with her last lines.

"It's in your hands now. Work together, and together you can change the system."

She strolled back to her seat, and our eyes quickly met as she sat. Then, I slipped out of the courtroom, knowing I had just witnessed my wife convince a jury to return a historic verdict.

CHAPTER 41

Casey

The courtroom was packed on the last day of the trial — lawyers, law students, clerks, family members from both sides, D.O.C executives, insurance adjusters, reporters from all over the country — all there to witness our closing arguments.

I had done it: made it through the week without a seizure. Some auras, but nothing to note. I asked Jonah to come, and, as I scanned the crowd for his face while I walked back to my seat after my closing, I found him against the back wall. Slowly sliding into the large leather chair, I felt a twinge of grief, as if I had given away a part of myself forever, left a piece of my identity on the courtroom floor next to the jury box. I barely heard the judge excuse the jury for deliberations. After they left, I walked to the elevators with Kathy, shielding her from the onlookers, and suggested that we grab a coffee close to the courthouse in case the jury came back quickly.

There were so many theories about the amount of time juries spent in deliberations: a quick deliberation meant a defense verdict in a civil case, a longer one a plaintiff's, as it must have included discussing an appropriate amount of money, but *too* long and they might be arguing about liability, so maybe a defense verdict again. But, these were all just theories with no science behind them or studies: old wives' tales passed down from trial lawyer to trial lawyer as a way of making conversation while the jury was out.

An hour passed. Two hours. Kathy began to get nervous.

"What does this mean?" she asked anxiously.

"I don't know," I answered. "And anyone who says he knows is a fool." My phone rang and my heart sped up.

"They're ready," the court clerk said. "They've reached a verdict."

We rushed out of the coffee shop to the courthouse, speeding up to the courtroom where Doug and his cronies crowded around his counsel table, laughing.

"Welcome back, Casey," he said, smirking, as if he knew an important secret. "Looks like they're ready. Should've taken that settlement offer." He swung his chair to face the table.

I escorted a trembling Kathy to her seat. "Kathy, whatever the verdict, you've put up a good fight. We've done all we can."

"I know we have," she said and reached for my hand. "Thank you."

Thank you. The words echoed through my mind, words I might never hear in this setting again: in a courtroom after a trial, just before the jury returned.

"Thank *you*," I said.

Hearing footsteps behind me, the noise increased as the courtroom filled up. News traveled quickly in the legal community — the lawyers who sat through the morning, or perhaps the whole week, the families of the women, and the reporters waiting for any sort of comment to bring back to their news outlets would not want to miss the culmination of the trial. Although tempted, I didn't turn around.

We stood as the judge and jury entered the room. Staring at the twelve faces who had just decided the fate of my clients, I had a modicum of doubt. None of them looked at me; then again, none of them looked at Doug, either. They stared at the judge as he asked if they had reached a verdict.

"We have, Your Honor," said the forewoman, handing the verdict sheet to the clerk who passed it to Judge Rosta.

I held my breath as Judge Rosta unfolded the paper and looked at the verdict. Time seemed to stand still, even though it could only have been seconds until he read the jury's decision.

"On Count Number 1, Violation of Due Process, the jury finds for the plaintiffs."

At these words, Kathy broke down completely.

"On Count Number 2, Supervisory Officials Failure to Intervene, the jury finds for the plaintiffs."

As each allegation came in favor of my clients, I saw Doug sitting straighter than I'd ever seen him do, absorbing his defeat.

At the amount of punitive damages, I stared at the forewoman, and our eyes met in understanding. She gave me a slight nod, which I returned.

Eight million dollars in punitive damages. The total verdict was $10.2 million dollars.

By the time Judge Rosta excused the jury and left the bench, the courtroom had erupted in various sounds: joyful crying from the plaintiffs' relatives, discussions from suits on the defense side, disbelief from attorneys at the never-before seen amount of the award in a prisoners' civil rights' case, reporters scurrying towards the doors to position themselves on the steps of the courthouse for interviews. Supporting a sobbing Kathy by the arm, I escorted her to the bathroom, briefcase in one hand, client on the other.

"You did it, Kathy," I said, as she sniffled into a paper towel, then blew her nose on the thin, gray material. "You and all the other women, you all did it. You were great." I handed her some lipstick from my traveling make-up purse, and watched her apply it, missing some edges, but good enough for the last few minutes of this show. "Let's go talk to some reporters. You don't have to say anything, but you can look happy now."

Kathy smiled through her tears. "I can't believe it," she said, her voice shaky. She stood straighter and put her shoulders back. I could see a glimpse of the woman that she would be now that we had won: stronger in the knowledge that sometimes, *sometimes*, life evens out and the scales of justice tip the right way. With a deep breath, she took my arm. "I'm ready."

Walking through the calming federal courthouse lobby, past the silent waterfall, and into the waiting throng of reporters, I was ready to talk about the change that would be made by this huge verdict. And then I would walk away from the courtroom and return to my family.

CHAPTER 42

Jonah

"You did it!" I shouted as I ran inside our house with Sam and Sadie on my heels. I scooped Casey up and spun her around. "Brilliant! Amazing! Well done, Case! I can't believe—I just—you did it!"

She was beaming, her smile so natural and genuine, I wanted to bottle it up and save it. The tension was gone from her body, as if she could finally release the breath she had been holding for weeks. Throughout the afternoon, I kept checking Twitter and refreshing the Oregon Live website for an update, until finally the jury returned with an unheard-of amount of money for Casey's clients. The entire city was buzzing about the amount of damages awarded—over $10 million dollars in total. Most of the press were calling it a landslide victory, a message to prisons around the country to shape up, a huge step forward for the civil rights movement.

Sadie and Sam crowded around us, wanting to make it into a group hug.

"It couldn't have gone any better," she said to me, eyes aglow with excitement.

"I'll say. What did Harold think?"

She shrugged. "Oh, you know. He's thrilled. Obviously. Asked me back." She giggled. "I gave him a hard 'no.'"

Of course, he asked her to come back. But right now, I did not care about that. I had the old Casey back. Everything was going to be all right; I could feel it.

"This calls for a celebration," I said, looking at Sam and Sadie. "Who wants to go out to eat?"

"Yay!" Sam shouted, and Sadie clapped her hands, bouncing up and down on her little toes.

"Sounds good," Casey said. "I don't feel like cooking. Let me just change out of this suit."

She squeezed my arm affectionately and headed upstairs. The excitement was palpable, and a relaxing weekend stretched out in front of us. The trial was over; Casey could rest and reset. She would be fully present and engaged with the three of us. I would be fully present and engaged as well.

I heard a thump on the ceiling. Sam stiffened and met my eyes, alert and on guard.

Racing out of the room, I sprinted up the stairs and thrust open the door to the main bedroom. Casey lay jerking on the red wool rug next to our bed. Blood rushed down the left side of her face, her eyes still open, but her cheeks had turned a grayish-blue. Running to my wife, I rolled her onto her side and grabbed a pillow to put under her head.

The familiar sense of panic gripped my stomach, but it was because of something much worse. This was a new type of seizure. She was awake, it seemed, but otherwise it was the same as before the ablation. I had not seen one of these yet.

"You're okay, Case," I whispered, stroking her hair. "Breathe, please, breathe."

Casey's rigid body paid no attention to my pleas; her brain was some place unreachable until it decided to return. Stuttering, guttural noises shot out from her throat. I knew we had no midazolam in the house. I had no power except to wait. Wait and see.

I began to time the seizure on my watch. A minute passed. Two minutes. Her body relaxed, muscles releasing as she softened into the rug and stopped moving. Her eyes came into focus and found mine. She gasped for air and the color returned to her face.

I rose to get a hand towel. After running the soft, white fabric under warm water and returning to wipe the blood gently from her cheek, I explored the right side of her head for the cut while she lay limp. A deep slice ran from the top of her scalp, front to back. I scanned the room for the culprit, and saw a dark stain on a corner of our night table. Turning back to Casey, I continued the examination and clean-up. Some of the blood sank into my clothes.

"Jonah," she whispered. "Jonah. . ."

I pulled her hair back from the wound to get a better look, pressing the hand towel gently on the gash. Our daughter's wails floated up the stairway and through the open door. Sam's small voice spoke to her softly: I knew he was trying to comfort his sister in her despair over my abrupt departure. Lifting the towel, I surveyed the wound again. It did not look too deep, and the blood had already started clotting in her hair. This would not be a hospital-visit seizure, just a sleep-it-off one.

"Casey," I whispered, pulling her slight body into a sitting position. "Let's get you in bed, shall we?"

But another seizure had started. This one I recognized as she lost consciousness. One seizure right after another made the situation dangerous.

I slipped the pillow back under her head, and reached for my phone.

"9-1-1. What's your emergency?" said the deep voice that answered the call.

CHAPTER 43

Casey

I awoke to a pain in my arm, and a rush of cold in my veins.

"Some Ativan. This should stop any further seizure clusters," a man's voice said.

"She's just had a stressful week," said another voice. *Jonah.*

"Well, it's up to you, but we should probably take her to the hospital for monitoring."

"Can you just leave some liquid Ativan or a midazolam vial or something here, and we can handle it? She has a seizure disorder, so the only really new thing is one seizure after another. But, as I said, she's had quite a week."

"Yeah, can't do that, buddy. I'd probably get fired for that."

"Right." Jonah sounded tired.

"Jonah..." I could feel another seizure coming on, and wasn't sure why. Then I realized: my evening seizure meds. I hadn't taken them yet, and the interviews had kept me from getting home until after I usually took my nightly dose. "My meds, J—" The seizure hit, but stopped quickly. I couldn't finish the sentence as another seizure tried to break through, but, again, stopped quickly. Jonah understood what I was trying to communicate. I felt another pinch in my arm, and an icy sting of more Ativan.

"Oh—see, she hasn't taken her evening meds yet," he said to the paramedic. "That's what's going on. I mean, at least partly."

I could see Jonah's shadow as he stood up and crossed the room to my bedside table, and heard the click as he opened my medication container. He knelt down and placed two pills in my mouth.

"Here's some water," he said, holding my head up enough for me to drink and swallow. "She'll be better now, I bet."

Through my haze, I could see the paramedic shrug. "So, no to the hospital?"

"No for right now, thank you," Jonah said. He lifted me into our bed. "I'll just stay with her while she sleeps. We'll call again if we need to go to the ER."

The soft mattress felt amazing, like sinking into a puffy cloud. Drugged down with the Ativan, the last thing I saw before my eyes closed was Jonah, pulling up a chair next to the bed.

"I'll be right here," he said.

I knew, without a doubt, that he would be.

• • •

Starting the following Monday, Jonah took two weeks' vacation time for us to be together while the kids were at daycare, which was an interesting way to start a new job, but he appointed Whitney as head of his team, and checked in daily. Things at G&H ran fine without him in the office.

With the time that we had, we relearned each other. Without distractions, we talked about life, parents, careers, the change that children had brought to our lives. Our relationship began to heal just through being together, uninterrupted.

"Casey, do you forgive me?" he asked a week into our time together, while I curled up next to him on the couch, my hands wrapped around a ceramic mug of tea.

"For what?"

"For forgetting you," he said. "For lying to you. For her." He plucked at the gray, woolen blanket that covered my legs and feet, and I knew he was unsure of my response. I knew that he needed to hear that for all his faults, for any misjudgments over the past year, I officially forgave him or at least could forgive him.

"The honest answer, or the answer you want to hear?" I asked.

"The honest answer."

"For some things, yes. For something things, not yet. I sort of get why you would want to shield me from stress, but I can't forgive you yet for going to another woman with the information you should have told me. For basically an emotional affair that could have gone..." I didn't even want to say it. Imagining what could have been made my stomach twist and my lungs feel as if all the air in the room had vanished. "That part is too, too... raw." The gash on my heart had started to heal, but when I thought of the two of them at coffee, sharing secrets about their lives, it opened again. I wasn't ready to move on from that. "But, couples' therapy could get me there. I want it to get me there. One day, I want to be able to say yes, and let go of it all." I squeezed his hand. "One day."

I knew it wasn't the answer he wanted, but we don't always get the answers that we want right when we want them.

"Do you forgive *me*?" I asked.

"For what?"

"For being stubborn about work. Making my career more important than my health, my family. More important than us. I was so angry that you were right about the stress of my job. I felt like if I wasn't a litigator I wasn't anything, and I didn't know what to do with that."

"Case, I was short-sighted. After you stopped working, when you were home alone, I didn't ask questions because I didn't *want* to know. I just wanted life to go on as normal, as before you quit, for you to be fulfilled—like when you were working—but without the stress. I know that I didn't support you like you should have been supported. When your life got too dark, I turned away."

"It was dark," I whispered.

"Case, you're so brave, you don't need forgiveness. For anything. But, just to soothe your mind, I forgive you, alright?"

I scooted my body over to give me room to stretch out on the couch and rest my head on his lap. "Brave." I breathed the word. "I am brave."

"We'll find a way to keep you in the game." Jonah stroked the short side of my hair, now baby-soft and half an inch long. "Do you like the stationary?"

"Yeah. I like it. You know, I could start by doing contract work — charge by the hour for projects. It wouldn't be trials, depositions, hearings or anything, but I could do research for other attorneys, write briefs, that sort of thing. And then maybe I'd be able to start my own firm — total control over my caseload, my hours. Just a one-woman shop, you know?" I rolled over to look up at his face. "Did I tell you that I've had three attorneys call me this past week and leave messages offering me a job?" I grinned at the look on his face: a mixture of shock and fear, his eyes wary. "Don't worry — I haven't returned their calls. But, it'll be a no."

He relaxed and kissed my nose. "Contract work sounds like a good way to keep going right now. And I like the idea of hanging up your own shingle."

"Maybe there'll be something new for my epilepsy soon — or not soon, but sometime." I shrugged. "Have to keep that hope, right?"

"Hope is everything," Jonah said.

"We should tell that to Dr. Duncan," I said, and he laughed. As we laughed together on the couch, time seemed to pause, and it became one of those moments where, just for a second, everything was perfect.

AUGUST 2017

CHAPTER 44

Casey

Nineteen days since my last seizure, almost three weeks, and the seizure hadn't even been a bad one. Three weeks was not something to get too excited about, but it was something, and this past week felt different: aura-free. The *absence* of the auras threw me. They had become a part of my daily life over the last few years. Now, for an entire week, my brain had been completely quiet. The quiet in my brain felt unfamiliar, almost uninvited. I didn't want to get my hopes up — not yet. *But,* a little voice within me said, *This is what you wanted, isn't it?* It seemed as if someone had hit a mute button, as Dr. Alem described: as if music was turned off that I hadn't even known was there. Sometimes I shook my head, trying to bring the noise back so I could concentrate on life again, instead of the silence. *This must be how normal people's brains feel. Just quiet all the time.* It was unnerving, and, at the same time, amazing.

With five months of couples' therapy under our belt, Jonah and I were in a good place. I had more requests for contract work than I could handle, was being called by television shows around the nation to give input on different civil rights issues, but had learned my limits. I'd learned how to say no if I didn't feel that I could fit the project or the interview into my schedule. Jonah settled into his new role as Director of Marketing, and was also setting limits at his job — working set hours unless something came up that needed extra time or attention. There was a peace in the house, a lack of tension that all four of us embraced. Our family became closer, as Jonah and I managed our new professional roles with our marriage in mind first.

The money came in from the Kellan case: all the D.O.C.'s appeals were overruled by the higher courts. The Ninth Circuit declined to even hear any argument, and the government finally had no choice but to cut the check. To celebrate, Jonah took a day off. The four of us loaded into his Subaru, and sped towards Tamanawas Falls, a family-favorite hike.

We arrived at the gravel parking lot next to the trailhead mid-morning. The trail wound through a forest with a high canopy, up and down small hills and ended at the broad curtain of the waterfall, which fell over a 110-foot lava cliff. Boulders fallen long ago allowed hikers to rest and enjoy the mist floating in the air. Bright blue skies stretched from Portland through the Columbia Gorge, making today the perfect day for this hike. As Jonah put the car in park, Sam and Sadie began wiggling in their seats, begging to be let out to explore the trailhead.

"Alright today?" Jonah asked me, unbuckling the kids and watching as they raced from the car to the edge of the forest. I stood up and pulled on my backpack, which was filled with snacks and a first aid kit.

"Strangely so," I said. I'd told him about the absence of auras the past seven days. "It's the *lack* of feeling that seems to set me off balance. You know, you get used to your brain, your body, working a certain way, to walking around with anxiety all the time, worrying, never sure of how things are going to go. And if that feeling has been there for years, it almost seems to be a part of your being. So, when it's gone, it's..." I tried to find the right word. "Noticeable. Not bad," I said quickly. "Just different."

Jonah passed me a water bottle. "Different is good, isn't it?" he said. He opened the hatchback to fill his backpack with sweaters, bars, and more water.

The wind caressed my arms: a gentle seventy-degree warm breeze with a cool edge. Watching the children run around in the woods, the dappled light creating sunny circles on their t-shirts and shorts, I wondered what the future would bring. Then, knowing that wondering was an exercise in futility, I turned back to the present, patted the midazolam in my short's pocket, and followed Jonah, Sam and Sadie down the trail.

ACKNOWLEDGEMENTS

I am indebted to the following people for their contributions to this book:

To Sybil and my fellow Yale Writer's Workshop group. You provide me with inspiration, invaluable feedback, and I love meeting up to keep the momentum of our projects going. To my first readers, Alisa, David, and Jennifer. This book would not be what it is without your feedback. To all the medical providers I worked with over the years to manage my epilepsy, who have made this book as accurate as possible, and helped me get to where I am today. To everyone at Black Rose Writing, for seeing potential in my manuscript. To Max and Miriam, for asking me regularly, "How is the book, Mommy?" and keeping me going through dark times. You have inspired me more than you know. To my whole family, for their love, support, and encouragement. Kyra, you were right when you predicted that I would one day become an author.

And to Tyler, for all your love, and for being my best friend and my greatest champion. You and me forever.

ABOUT THE AUTHOR

Sara Staggs grew up in Dallas, Texas, and practiced civil rights litigation for several years. She now lives in Portland, Oregon, with her husband and children. She has been published in several literary journals, The Huffington Post, the BrainAblaze blog, and attended the Yale Writers' Workshop. *Uncontrollable* is her first novel.

You can visit her website at www.sarastaggswrites.com.

NOTE FROM THE AUTHOR

Word-of-mouth is crucial for any author to succeed. If you enjoyed *Uncontrollable*, please leave a review online—anywhere you are able. Even if it's just a sentence or two. It would make all the difference and would be very much appreciated.

Thanks!
Sara Staggs

We hope you enjoyed reading this title from:

BLACK ROSE
writing™

www.blackrosewriting.com

Subscribe to our mailing list – *The Rosevine* – and receive **FREE** books, daily deals, and stay current with news about upcoming releases and our hottest authors.
Scan the QR code below to sign up.

Already a subscriber? Please accept a sincere thank you for being a fan of Black Rose Writing authors.

View other Black Rose Writing titles at
www.blackrosewriting.com/books and use promo code
PRINT to receive a **20% discount** when purchasing.

CPSIA information can be obtained
at www.ICGtesting.com
Printed in the USA
LVHW070732270623
750860LV00003B/363